A Horseman on The Horizon—

Silhouetted against the sunlight he was a sinister figure. Then he turned and galloped over the desert towards us. His loose coat flew in the wind while his voluminous hood seemed to float from his shoulders. As he drew nearer, I saw that he had the face of a brigand—deeply tanned skin, strong, harsh features and unruly raven locks spilling over his forehead. His lips were full, curling sardonically. His eyes glowed. They were the eyes of a hunter.

Suddenly he swooped down, and in an instant I was swept astride his stormy stallion as he sped me silently over the barren land.

DANGER at DAHLKARI

Edwina Marlow

A BERKLEY MEDALLION BOOK
published by
BERKLEY PUBLISHING CORPORATION

Lenninger Literary Agency, Inc.
437 Fifth Avenue
New York, N. Y. 10016

Library of Congress Catalog Card Number: 75-24850

SBN 425-03448-8

*BERKLEY MEDALLION BOOKS are published by
Berkley Publishing Corporation
200 Madison Avenue
New York, N. Y. 10016*

BERKLEY MEDALLION BOOK ® TM 757,375

Printed in the United States of America

Berkley Medallion Edition, JULY, 1977

In memory of my beloved sister,
PATSY RUTH HUFF

One

The desert sand was a tannish gray, the sky the color of
steel. Heat waves shimmered in the air like semitrans-
parent yellow veils, and as the camels and horses
trudged along with that infuriating slowness, small
puffs of dust rose and hung suspended over the
caravan. Bells tinkled. Harness clattered. Heavy
wooden wheels creaked and groaned. In the distance I
could see yet another jungle, a black-green line on the
horizon, and a dense stretch of jungle ran along the
desert on our left. Occasionally, over the jostle and
jangle, I could hear the monkeys chatter, hear the
brightly hued birds cry out in shrill discord.

Weary of the silk-hung palanquin carried by four
strapping bearers, I walked along in the sand, trying to
ignore the heat, trying to hold back the sense of
apprehension I had felt for the past two days. Joining
Yasmin Singh's caravan had seemed a wonderful idea
back in Delhi, the perfect solution to my problem. A
Lieutenant Parks and his men were to have escorted
Sally and me to the garrison at Dahlkari, but two days
before the scheduled departure the unfortunate
lieutenant had come down with a severe attack of the
measles. It had been the cause of much merriment in
the English settlement, Lieutenant Parks the butt of
many a joke, but I had felt sheer frustration. It had

taken us so long to come this far, so many endless weeks. Another delay had seemed impossible to endure. Learning that the caravan was about to depart, I immediately made arrangements to join them, quite scandalizing all the English ladies who deemed it unthinkable for two English girls to travel upcountry alone with a band of natives. Adamant and defiant to the end, I went ahead with my plans, leaving the ladies of Delhi both shocked and dismayed and causing considerable consternation among the military personnel who had tried their best to dissuade me from such an impulsive course.

Red-cheeked and blustering, Colonel Hendricks had tugged at his bushy white mustache and informed me that it simply wasn't done, implying that he would have me tossed into the stockade if I didn't give up the idea posthaste. Calm, composed, icily polite, I informed him that I was a civilian and could do as I bloody well pleased. The colonel seemed on the verge of apoplexy when I left his office, but there really had been nothing he or anyone else could do. Sally and I had been traveling with the caravan for four days now, and I was beginning to wish I had listened to reason back in Delhi.

The first two days had been pleasant enough. We had passed a number of villages with their drab brown huts and water holes, sleek black buffalo lolling in the mud, and we had passed beautiful temples festooned with garlands of flowers, moving across rich, verdant green countryside sparkling with brooks and streams, cascades of water splashing down rocky inclines. I responded to this country of my youth, loving anew the flame trees abloom with scarlet, the tamarind, the peepul, the wild plum. Seeing the long-horned white cattle grazing placidly in the flat, watery jade green fields brought back so many memories of my youth, as did the cry of the myna bird and the sight of an elephant moving ponderously along the misty blue horizon. I had been twelve years old when I left India, an orphan, both my parents victims of the cholera, and seven long years had passed, years endured in an ever-so-respectable academy for young ladies in Bath. It was glorious to be back, to know that I would soon be joining my beloved Dollie and her Reggie, now commander of the garrison at Dahlkari.

Dollie McAllister had been my mother's best friend. She had been like a second mother to me. Her husband, now Lieutenant Colonel McAllister, had been the executor of my parents' estate, and it was he who had arranged to have me sent to the academy in England. Dollie had kept in touch all these years, her letters as fussy, witty and vivacious as the lady herself. When, upon my graduation, she wrote to suggest that I join her and Reggie in Dahlkari and select myself a husband from among the many potentials abounding there, I wasted no time in accepting the invitation. I wasn't interested in finding a husband, but I *was* eager to see the McAllisters again, eager to return to the land I had loved so well.

I was delighted when Sally decided to accompany me. An orphan like myself, though not nearly so fortunate in background, she had been taken on as a parlor maid at the academy, a bright, saucy and alert young minx who longed for adventure, particularly the kind involving members of the opposite sex. Our friendship had quite alarmed the staff at the academy, but I had found Sally far more engaging than any of the prim, sedate young ladies of my own class. When she learned I was to go to India, Sally promptly informed me that I couldn't possibly go alone, that I would need a personal maid, that she was taking the job. Her liveliness and insatiable curiosity had turned a long, dreary journey into something of a lark. Though her behavior left much to be desired so far as the proprieties were concerned, I couldn't have done without her.

So we had come to India, landing at Bombay with its beautiful temples and shrines and gold and ivory palaces, its palm trees, crowded and exotic bazaars, its sedate and exclusive English settlement that had as little as possible to do with the natives. Sally had been enchanted by the elephants and snake charmers and the sacred cows that ambled leisurely down the crowded streets and among the stalls. She had been enchanted by the tall bronzed Sepoys in their red jackets and white turbans and even more so by the profusion of English bachelors on hand. A natural and uninhibited flirt, she had captivated a score of them during the two weeks before we departed for Delhi. In Delhi she divided her time between a ginger-haired sergeant and a strapping young corporal, both of whom lavished attention on her and took her to dimly lit native establishments that respectable English girls shouldn't even have known existed. Sally had become an expert on native dishes, on the use of the hookah, on exotic nautch dancers with spangled veils and vermilion-stained feet. Curious about everything, the girl already knew far more about India than I did.

Both the sergeant and the corporal had been desolate when we left Delhi four days ago. Both had tried to persuade her not to leave with the native caravan, saying it was unsafe, unseemly, unheard of for two English girls to travel in such a manner. Sally retorted that Miss Lauren didn't care a fig for convention, that Yasmin Singh was utterly respectable, spoke English quite well and would protect us with his life, as would his servants. Truth to tell, Sally had already met Ahmed by that time, and she had lost interest in her two English suitors. The son of a silk merchant, Ahmed was a handsome Indian youth who was transporting some merchandise for his father, traveling with Yasmin Singh's caravan for security's sake, and Sally declared that she had never seen such a beautiful creature in all her born days.

Tall and lean, Ahmed had a dark, creamy tan complexion, a wide pink mouth curling in a boyish grin and large, luminous black eyes that flashed with mischievous delight as he tried to frighten Sally with tales of cobras and tigers and bands of brutal Thugs, at the same time assuring her that he would keep her safe from all danger. Ahmed wore kidskin boots, formfitting white trousers and a jade green silk tunic that splendidly displayed his muscular physique. His white silk turban was fastened in front with an ornate jade clasp. No more than nineteen, he was an amiable lad, as flirtatious as Sally herself, but even Ahmed's jaunty high spirits had begun to dampen after the first two days.

Leaving the rich and lovely agricultural area behind, we began to move over rough, rocky terrain that eventually turned into stretches of burning sand broken by vast clumps of jungle that had sprung up around the streams. It was an oppressive landscape, one that seemed laden with some heavy, invisible menace. The bearers grew tense and nervous, moving through the deep jungle with obvious apprehension, keeping an eye on the horizon as the caravan made its way over the stretches of sand. A pleasant and voluble fellow who had spent the first two days boasting about his immense wealth, his numerous wives, his high standing in his home community, Yasmin Singh fell silent, too, his plump face tight with fear, his heavily beringed fingers tugging worriedly at the folds of his robe. Everyone seemed relieved when five heavily armed men joined the caravan on the afternoon of the third day. Their white trousers baggy, their loose white tunics tied at the waist with colored sashes, they had dark, impassive faces and were decidedly unfriendly. There being safety in numbers, Yasmin welcomed them with enthusiasm nevertheless, and the men themselves seemed only too happy to have found a large caravan traveling in their direction.

"They're on their way back to their village," Sally informed me that night. "It's a long ways off, way beyond Dahlkari. Ahmed talked to them. They're a fierce-looking lot, all right, but they're as nervous as everyone else."

"I don't understand why—"

"Thugs," Sally said meaningfully.

"Nonsense."

"They swoop down on travelers out of the blue and strangle the lot of 'em with scarves, bury 'em in the ground and make off with all their money and jewels. Many a caravan has simply disappeared, just like that, leaving a town one day and never heard of again. These Thugs belong to a cult that worships the goddess Kali, and—"

"I've heard all about the Thugs, Sally," I said impatiently, "and I'm sure it's all been highly exaggerated. Captain William Sleeman uncovered

6

their foul practices several years ago, and he's been working all this time to rid the country of them. Thousands of Thugs have been arrested over the years, and the danger has been thoroughly eliminated."

"Not in this area," Sally retorted. "Oh, that Captain Sleeman has done a lot, true, but the Thugs still exist. This area is the last great stronghold of their cult. Ahmed said so. He knows all about it. Sleeman hasn't a clue about their activities here."

"Ahmed's just trying to frighten you."

"He's worried, too. Hasn't been himself all day. He keeps watching, expecting them to attack at any moment."

There was an excited tremor in her voice, and she seemed quite taken with the idea. I smiled, putting the whole thing down to her inordinate love for drama. She scurried off to seek Ahmed, and as I stood there in front of our tent I thought about what she had said. Nonsense. Of course it was nonsense. Even if the Thugs *were* still active in this area, they weren't likely to attack a caravan so large, with so many men. I looked at the five strangers huddled around their fire a short distance from the rest of the camp. It was nice to know they were with us, nice to know they had pistols and daggers. With these new arrivals there were a good twenty men. It was foolish to feel so apprehensive.

Yet I did, and so did the others. Fires burned low, glowing orange blossoms in the darkness, and tents flapped and billowed in the wind. The horses and camels stirred restlessly. A huge moon hung in the sky, gilding the sand with milky white light, intensifying shadows. Monkeys chattered in the nearby jungle. There was a rustling noise in the brush, a gentle cough. I knew the sound well from my youth. A leopard was watching us, and as I peered into the dense black jungle just yards away, it seemed I could see a pair of gleaming yellow eyes. I felt suddenly vulnerable, suddenly afraid, and not because of the leopard. He was merely curious and would go away eventually. I felt vulnerable because I was English, and female, because Sally and I were alone with strangers in the middle of a land that now seemed hostile and threatening.

Men spoke in low, subdued voices, all in their native dialects, and I wished they were English, wished they were hearty, jovial soldiers with polished boots and clattering spurs. I hadn't the typical English suspicion of "the natives"—I had been raised with them, had been devoted to my native ayah—but I was acutely aware that Sally and I were the "foreigners" in this camp, tolerated because we were white and therefore important, mistrusted for the same reasons. Though he had been exceedingly voluble, Yasmin Singh had maintained a certain reserve from the first. His men had been silent and withdrawn, pretending not to speak English. Only Ahmed had been friendly. As I watched the camp fires flickering red-orange in the dark and heard the soft flap of tents billowing, I wished I had listened to reason back in Delhi. We should have waited for Lieutenant Parks to recover. I had known that at the time, but my eagerness to see Dollie had blinded me to all reason.

As the turbaned guard moved nervously around the perimeter of the camp with rifle held against his shoulder, I thought about the Thugs and their dreadful cult. It had existed for centuries, like a great cobweb of horror spreading all over India, but it was only in recent years that it had come to the attention of the British. The Thugs believed that Kali had given the roads to them, that any traveler was their natural prey. Their victims were strangled with the rumal, a handkerchief or scarf they had been trained to use with great skill, the corpses broken and mutilated and buried, never a trace to be found. I had read about the Thugs and shuddered, as had all God-fearing Christians, for it was the horror story of the century. One Thug alone had calmly admitted to killing over eight hundred innocent people, showing no guilt, no remorse, for he had done it in the name of Kali, the sacred goddess of death and destruction. Men like Captain Sleeman and Captain Meadows Taylor had devoted years to suppressing the cult and breaking up their hideous bands. Captain Taylor's book, *Confessions of a Thug*, had appeared only last year. I wished now I hadn't read it.

Surely the roads were safe, I told myself. Surely Ahmed had merely been teasing Sally. I tried to put the horror out of my mind, but it was a futile endeavor. I slept little that night, and now, as the caravan moved slowly across the sand toward the black-green line of jungle on the horizon, I scolded myself severely and resolved to think of other things. The yellow heat waves shimmered. The puffs of dust rose and swelled and hung suspended in the air. I thought about Dollie and Dahlkari and the joys of reunion awaiting me there.

"You get the sunstroke, maybe," Ahmed said.

I turned, startled to find him moving along beside me.

"Parasol not enough," he said, "You get back in palanquin, yes?"

"I'm perfectly all right, Ahmed," I informed him.

"English Missy stubborn," he replied, grinning that

charmingly boyish grin. "Our women, they wear the burka. It keeps out the sun and keeps the men from seeing what they should not see."

"English customs are different, Ahmed," I told him. "It—it isn't improper for a man to see a woman's face and—and shape in English communities."

Ahmed nodded with mock severity. There was a mischievous gleam in his dark brown eyes, and I was very aware that my white muslin frock sprigged with tiny violet flowers was rather low cut, the waist formfitting, full skirt flaring over half a dozen ruffled petticoats. Hardly a suitable garment for traipsing in the desert, I thought, but at least the muslin was cool, and most of my other things had been shipped on ahead to Dahlkari two weeks ago. The matching parasol I carried warded off the fiercest rays of the sunlight.

"I shan't stay out too long," I promised, "and besides, the sun has already started going down."

Ahmed nodded. "Soon we camp. We camp at the edge of the jungle. They must like what they see, Miss Gray, the sahibs, I mean. You have a very pretty face."

"Why—thank you, Ahmed," I replied, a bit startled.

"Your complexion so creamy, soft pink at the cheeks like rose petals, yes? Your mouth is the color of coral, and your hair—it is, yes, I have it, it is the color of moonlight on teak."

My hair was a rich chestnut brown, and in a certain light it did indeed have a silvery sheen. Moonlight on teak. Ahmed was most poetic, and rather too forward, I thought. While Sally might relish his flowery compliments, I found them a trifle irritating. I knew that I was exceptionally pretty with my high, sculptured cheekbones and classic features, but it was

10

not at all important, not nearly as important as my intelligence. While I had no vanity about my looks, I was inordinately proud of my mind.

"You find husband in Dahlkari?" Ahmed continued.

"I—I'm not interested in finding a husband," I retorted. "That's not why I've come to India."

"No? All the other English missys, that's why they come—the ones not so pretty. They don't find a husband in England, they take the ship to India to marry one of the soldiers. English missys very smart, know the English men in India don't see many English girls, so even the not-so-pretty missys always get a husband. Is very smart."

"You—you're very observant, Ahmed."

"Me, I *like* the English. They my friends. I learn to speak the English well, no?"

"You speak quite nicely," I replied.

"Is good for business," he confided. "my father, he doesn't speak the English at all. Is bad. The English sahibs buy much silk for their women. Me, I do all the business with them."

"Your father must be proud of you."

"Is very proud, says Ahmed a shrewd fellow."

Ahmed grinned, pleased with himself. I detected a touch of arrogance, a purposeful determination that wasn't at all in keeping with his affable facade. He was an exceedingly handsome youth, strong and virile, and if he swaggered a bit it was only natural. He walked beside me for a few minutes more, describing the ruined temple in the jungle ahead, then sauntered off to speak to one of the grim-looking natives who had joined the caravan. The two of them spoke in quiet voices, and once Ahmed laughed. He kicked at a pile of pebbles in the sand and paused to pick one up,

11

scattering the rest in patterned disarray, then moved toward the back of the caravan and out of sight.

As we drew closer to the jungle, I could see huge gray boulders near the edge that looked for all the world like herds of gigantic elephants. As the caravan moved slowly on, the steel-gray sky gradually turned to yellow as the sun began to set. When we finally struck camp, the sky was a darkening yellow-orange, deep golden streamers on the horizon. The tents were pitched. Fires were started. Horses and camels were herded together in a makeshift rope corral. We were camped in a large clearing, the enormous gray boulders looming up on three sides, the jungle forming a fourth. The protective boulders afforded a sense of security missing on the open sands, and everyone seemed far more relaxed than they had been the night before. I was more relaxed, too, my fears quite forgotten.

"More curry," Sally said, strolling over to join me in front of our tent. "What wouldn't I give for a nice slab of beef and some Yorkshire pudding."

"I thought you adored the native dishes," I teased.

"I do," she retorted, "I do indeed. They're quite interesting, but seven days a week? I'm beginning to hate curry, Miss Lauren. I might as well confess it."

There was a mournful note in her voice, and I had to smile. Sally was a delightful creature, not quite as tall as I and exceedingly well endowed, a fact her gold and brown sprigged yellow cotton dress did nothing to hide. Her full, rounded bosom strained against the low-cut bodice, and the snug fit emphasized her slender waistline. The full skirt cascaded over flaring cotton petticoats. With her saucy brown eyes and long tarnished gold curls, Sally was indeed a fetching sight, a bit too bold, a bit too earthy to be a suitable

12

companion for Miss Lauren Gray of the Hampton Academy for Select Young Ladies.

"I suppose we'll get proper English food at Dahlkari?" she said.

"I should think so."

"No more of those dreadful chapati, I hope, and I must admit I've had enough rice to last me a lifetime. Have you seen Ahmed around?" she inquired abruptly.

"Not recently. Not since we stopped, in fact."

"I've been looking for him. Can't find him anywhere."

"I wonder where he could have gone?"

"I don't know," she replied wearily. "I wandered a bit behind the boulders, and—Miss Lauren, I saw the strangest thing. There was a gigantic hole, way over there, behind the largest group of rocks."

"A hole?"

"It—it looked freshly dug. I thought it most unusual."

"Why would anyone want to dig a large hole?"

"I don't know. It wasn't all that deep, really, not more than four or five feet, but it was very wide. An elephant could easily curl up in it. Strange—"

Sally shook her head, a slight frown creasing her brow. All around us there were sounds of camp. Small fires crackled. Pots jangled as the evening meal was prepared, exotic odors wafting through the air. Two bearers were feeding the animals, and in front of his tent Yasmin Singh was giving orders to his servants. The five strangers wandered around the camp separately, more friendly than they had been before. I saw one of them chatting with the men who carried my palanquin, another talking to a servant cooking rice in a bubbling pot. The sky was an ashy gray now, and on

13

the horizon streaks of dark crimson-orange glowed fiercely, gradually fading. Twilight was beginning to fall, a slight blue haze thickening in the air, and the intense heat was, thankfully, over.

"Why were you looking for Ahmed?" I asked.

"I wanted him to show me those ruins in the jungle. There's a crumbling old temple, he said, all covered with vines and adorned with the most unusual carvings. There used to be a city there, hundreds of years ago, but the temple's all that's left now."

"Ahmed told me about it. It sounds fascinating."

"I had my heart set on seein' it," she said, peeved. "Now why would he disappear like that, the rascal? Truth to tell, Miss Lauren, Ahmed's been acting a bit— well, cheeky of late. Like he can take liberties just because I'm *friendly*."

"I expect you'd best watch yourself," I told her. "Ahmed isn't like the others. He—he's not English. The natives have very definite ideas about women, about—"

"Don't I know it," Sally interrupted. "He'd like to ravish me and toss me into a harem or seraglio or whatever they call 'em in India. It's quite exciting, of course, but, all the same, there's something a bit frightening about it. He does look a dream with those glorious dark eyes and that enchanting grin, but—" She paused, searching for words.

"Ahmed isn't quite the uncomplicated youth he appears to be," I supplied.

"You got that impression, too, then?"

I nodded. "He makes me a bit uncomfortable."

"That's it. That's it exactly. Oh, he's a marvel with words, a regular poet, said my hair was like liquid gold, my eyes like dark topaz, my body like—well, uh, he *is*

14

poetic, but I have the feeling something savage is lurking just beneath the surface, ready to spring. It's most disconcerting."

Sally reached up to brush a lock of gold hair from her temple, a troubled look in her eyes. The horizon was a blaze of crimson now, the ashy gray sky turning darker. The blue haze of twilight grew thicker. A camel squealed. Horses neighed. Tents flapped as a slight breeze swept through the camp. One of the bearers had begun to play a flute. For some reason I was restless, and I could sense that Sally was, too. She sighed and looked at the green wall of jungle, trees festooned with garlands of vines and exotic plants. The birds and monkeys had grown silent.

"I did so want to see that temple," she said. "Ahmed said it was used for human sacrifice—Miss Lauren, let's go find it! It's just a short distance from camp, Ahmed said so. We could get there and back before it gets really dark."

"I—I'm not sure we should, Sally."

"Why not? You're not *afraid*, are you?"

"Well, I thought I heard a leopard last night, and—"

"I'll take my pistol," Sally informed me.

"Pistol?"

She nodded and scurried away, her yellow skirt fluttering over rustling petticoats. I wasn't really alarmed at the prospect of taking off into the jungle. None of the wild creatures would bother us, I knew, unless we bothered them first, but I wasn't greatly taken with the idea of encountering a cobra or some other poisonous viper. Still, Sally and I were both wearing high kid boots, mine white, hers brown, and she would have her pistol. I wondered where on earth she had gotten it.

"Corporal Hendricks gave it to me," she said, returning a moment later. "He said if I was fool enough to go traipsing off with a band of heathens I'd best have some protection. Isn't it lovely?" she inquired, brandishing it in front of me. It was long and black and looked perfectly villainous.

"Do—do you know how to use it?" I asked.

"I haven't the foggiest notion, but I'm sure it's simple enough. This is the safety catch. You just push it back and aim the barrel and pull the trigger. It can't be difficult."

"You've had it ever since we left Delhi?"

"I kept it hidden under the cushions of my palanquin," she said, "just in case we ran into some of those dreadful Thugs or something. Do let's go while there's still enough light, Miss Lauren. I'm quite eager to find that temple."

Our tent was nearest the jungle, pitched rather apart from the rest of the camp for propriety's sake, and no one seemed to notice as Sally and I moved across the narrow stretch of clearing and on into the natural tunnels formed by tree trunks and vines. The jungle wasn't really all that dense here, not nearly as dense as some of the stretches the whole caravan had passed through earlier on. There was a pathway of sorts between trees, and Sally moved ahead with great confidence, looking a bit ridiculous with petticoats billowing and the pistol clutched in her hand.

"I'm not at all sure we should be doing this," I told her.

"Where's your sense of adventure?" Sally asked. "Just think, Miss Lauren, you could be sitting in some prim parlor, doing embroidery. This is more *like* it!

16

Here we are, in the middle of the jungle. Who'd of thought it three months ago?"

"Certainly not I. I had no idea what I was going to do after graduation. I rather imagined I'd be a governess."

"I can just see *that*," Sally replied, most disrespectfully. "You've far too much spirit to be in charge of a passel of snooty brats. You never *did* fit in with those other la de dah girls, you know."

"I know. I feel rather guilty about it."

"Always arguing with the teachers, always breaking rules, sneaking up to the attic to visit with *me*, telling me all the things you'd been reading and thinking about."

"I—don't think I could have endured it without you, Sally," I confessed.

"And vice versa. They would have loved to have sacked me, but I was a treasure and they knew it. Besides, the orphanage placed me, and their board of directors were very important people who would have been most displeased. The academy knew which side their bread was buttered on."

"That's for sure. That's the only reason I wasn't expelled. Letters of complaint to my guardian were all they dared. Sally, are—are you sure we're going in the right direction? I—I'd hate to get lost. We really should have told someone what we were going to do."

"Ahmed said it was just a short ways from the campsite, due north. We're moving north, aren't we?"

"I've no idea."

"You're supposed to be able to tell by looking at lichen and things," she said chattily, "but I don't see any lichen. If we keep walking we're bound to run into it."

17

Deeper and deeper into the jungle we moved, tree arching overhead and trailing thick vines studded with pink and white blossoms. For a while we had been able to hear sounds of camp, but now there was no sound but that of kid boots moving over damp, spongy earth No other sound. It was puzzling. Why weren't the monkeys, scolding us from branches? Why weren't the birds calling? It... it was almost as though they'd been frightened away, I thought, apprehension beginning to mount inside. Thin rays of pale yellow light streamed down through the treetops like wavering, mote-filled columns. How long would the light last? This was indeed foolish. I should never have let Sally talk me into it, I knew, but I was too stubborn to let her see my apprehension. She despised vapid, nervous females almost as much as I did.

"—tiger," she said.

"What's that?" She had been chattering all the while, and I hadn't heard a word she was saying.

"I said I hope we don't run into a tiger."

"This isn't tiger country," I told her.

"That's a relief. Is—is that a *co*bra, Miss Lauren?"

"It's only a vine, Sally."

"Goodness, it gave me quite a start. I—I would have thought we'd have run into the ruins by now," she said. "I'd say we've come at least half a mile."

"At least," I agreed.

"I—I wonder what's happened to the monkeys?"

Sally was beginning to feel it, too, then. A curious atmosphere hung over the jungle, something I couldn't place. Ordinarily it would have been noisy and almost friendly with the green parakeets and white cockatoos flitting through sunlight and shadow, the small, boisterous gray monkeys swinging and jabbering overhead, but now there was a strange, expectant hush that was most unnerving. Shadows deepened all around us as the wavering columns of yellow light grew thinner, paler, everything green and black and ominous. I had the feeling that someone else had been here just recently, had passed this way only moments before.

"Maybe we'd better go back," I suggested.

"Not till we've seen the ruins," Sally said stubbornly. "They can't be far now. Come on, Miss Lauren. I—I've got my gun. There's no need to be *ner*vous—"

She seemed to be trying to convince herself of that as well. Squaring her shoulders, she moved on down the twisting pathway, ducking to avoid the overhanging branches, pushing flowering vines aside, and I followed close on her heels, trying to convince myself that there was no reason for my apprehension. Still, it was patently absurd for two English girls in summer frocks and kid boots to be trouping through the jungle like intrepid explorers, pistol or no. Most improbable. What on earth had possessed me to be so foolhardy? I had always been impetuous, yes, but this was carrying it altogether too far.

"Sally, this is insane. We're turning back right now, and I want no argument—"

"Look," she said quietly.

She stopped, holding back a vine, and I hurried up to stand beside her. Ahead there was a small clearing in the jungle, completely surrounded by trees and not much larger than an average sized room. It was flooded with sunlight, yellow-orange now, the light deepening, streaming over the ruins. I was stunned, horrified by what I saw, and Sally was, too. She stepped into the clearing and I followed her, but neither of us had any desire to move closer to the hideous thing on the other side. Sally reached for my hand and held it tightly, both of us staring at the crumbling ruins of the temple and the grotesque goddess that perched there.

There were two broken columns on either side of a flat platform, rock pink-gray and weathered, streaked with rusty stains, and Kali perched obscenely on the platform on one foot, the other leg raised, four arms waving, hands clutching vile objects, tongue thrust out and hair like coiling serpents. The idol was black, some kind of marble, I thought. It was the most frightening thing I had ever seen. The deep orange rays of light wavered, and the idol cast long black shadows over the ground of the clearing, shadows that seemed to move and dance. I noticed the dark, ancient stains on the platform in front of the centuries-old idol and remembered what Sally had said about human sacrifice. I wouldn't have been at all surprised to have seen a pile of skulls and shattered bones.

"Kali," I whispered.

"It—it fairly gives me the shivers," Sally said. "It seems—almost alive, like it was looking at us, daring us to come closer. She's the one the Thugs worship, the one who tells 'em to do their foul deeds."

"It's—only a statue," I told her.

A sudden wind swept through the jungle. Leaves rustled violently and tree limbs groaned, vines swinging. Sally gripped my hand tighter as the shadows seemed to dance like dark demons. Kali seemed to dance, too, arms waving viciously, the raised foot ready to stamp and crush, the long tongue thrust out lewdly as rays of dark orange light spilled over her like liquid fire. My blood seemed to run cold. There was a moment of sheer, stark horror, and then the wind ceased and the shadows grew still. The silence returned, even more ominous now.

It was then that I felt it. Someone had been here.

"Miss Lauren—"

"You—you feel it, too?"

Sally nodded. "There was someone here—just recently."

The air in the clearing was filled with vibrations, as though retaining the impressions of those who had just left. It was like a room that had been vacated only moments before. At first I had thought I was imagining it, but Sally had the same feeling. She was still gripping my hand, so tightly that my fingers felt crushed. Her cheeks were pale, her soft pink lips parted, and her eyes were dark and troubled, a deep crease between her brows. Sally was the most levelheaded person I had ever known, absolutely fearless, but she was deeply shaken now.

"Th—there," she said. "On the ground. Look—"

I followed her gaze and saw the pick axe half-hidden in the grass only a few feet in front of us. The blade glistened brightly, razor-sharp, recently polished, and the long handle was carved with bizarre, intricate designs. I knew what it was immediately, for I had read about their axes. The Thugs used them to break up the bodies of their victims to make burial simpler, used them to puncture stomachs so that gases wouldn't cause the corpses to swell in the ground and give away the secret burial places. I shuddered, and for a moment I thought I was going to faint. Sally gripped my hand even tighter, staring at the axe with sheer horror.

"They were here," she said. "One—one of them must have dropped it. It—it must have slipped out of his sash while he was leaving."

"You know what it is?"

"I know," she said grimly.

"Sally, we—we must get back at once. We must warn—"

"I imagine it's too late," she told me. "That hole I saw—I know what it was for. They—they select the site in advance, and they have men in their bands whose duty is to prepare the—the grave so that it will be ready. They—they generally infiltrate the caravans they plan to attack. Miss Lauren, and—"

"Those five men who joined us—"

Sally nodded again, and both of us looked at the obscene black idol of the goddess of death and destruction. It seemed to mock us. I remembered all the things I had read about the Thuggee, almost overcome with horror now as I thought about the caravan and what might be happening to it at this very moment. Yasmin Singh, Ahmed, the bearers...all of them brutally murdered, yellow scarfs slung around their throats, mercilessly tightened. Dark waves seemed to rise and swell inside my head, and I could feel my knees grow weak.

"It may not be too late," Sally said, suddenly calm, her voice hard and determined. "Perhaps we can get back in time, warn them—it's the element of surprise that enables the Thugs to move so effectively. The men are armed, and if they're prepared, expecting an attack—"

"You're right," I said. "We—we must hurry."

We left the clearing without a moment's hesitation, rushing back toward the caravan over the twisting, turning pathway, limbs and vines pushed out of the way, thorns tearing at our skirts. It was darker now, the last rays of sunlight almost gone, the jungle a mass of

22

black and green-black shadow, rustling leaves, slithery noises, ominous, frightening. A bird called out in shrill alarm, a nerve-shattering sound that caused my heart to leap. I stumbled over a root, almost falling. Sally seized my arm. We had to hurry. We had to warn them. There were tears in my eyes as we raced through the jungle, panting now, both of us, and then Sally stopped abruptly.

Her cheeks were chalk white. Her mouth was set in a hard line. Her dark brown eyes filled with anger and sadness and fear. I stood beside her, panting, one hand held tightly against my heart. Why had she stopped like this? There was no time to lose! I started to protest, but she made a violent gesture, silencing me.

It was then that I heard the first terrible screams.

Two

I was numb, totally numb, and I had no will of my own. Sally took hold of my arm and pulled me into a large clump of shrubbery beside the path as the screaming continued, shrill, anguished screams followed by terrible gurgling sounds that were even more terrifying. We had come a long way from the clearing and were, I realized, only yards from the edge of the jungle and the campsite. If Sally hadn't stopped we would have rushed directly into the midst of the terrible slaughter. Huddled in the shrubbery, concealed by large, rubbery-green leaves and garlands of vines hanging from the tree overhead, Sally and I listened, our arms wrapped tightly around each other as those nightmare noises filled the air.

One of the native bearers came rushing into the jungle, hotly pursued by two Thugs. We could see it all clearly through the network of leaves, the three of them almost close enough to touch. The bearer stumbled, falling to his knees, and the Thugs were upon him. He let out a bloodcurdling scream, throwing his arms up, and the scream died as a long yellow scarf was slung around his throat. The strangler wrenched mightily, twisting with savage strength, his eyes narrow slits, teeth bared, while his colleague seized the bearer's arms and pulled in the opposite direction. There was a gasping, choking sound as the bearer thrashed and struggled, his face reddening, eyes bulging out in their sockets, and then there was a crisp snap and the body fell limp. The Thugs let it drop to the ground, grinning at each other.

I buried my face against Sally's shoulder. She held me tightly, arms like bands of steel, and I could hear her heart pounding, pounding. Both of us trembled violently, and when I finally looked up the Thugs were wandering back toward the caravan, dragging the corpse behind them as though it were a limp sack of potatoes. There were no more screams now, just the excited merry babble of voices as the Thugs discussed their success. They began to move about the campsite, taking down tents, gathering various articles, dousing the fires, and there were heavy, scraping noises as the corpses were dragged behind the boulders toward the huge hole Sally had discovered earlier.

We could see part of the campsite through the dense congestion of leaf and branch and vine, see without being seen, and both of us grew still, arms still entwined, staring through the thick greenery at the scene of horror unfolding. There were at least thirty Thugs moving about, some of them folding up tents, some of them digging holes, burying the remains of camp fires, others kneeling on the ground, bundling up goods. They chattered away with jolly good humor, frequently laughing. Some were old, some very young, in their early teens, all wearing loose white trousers and long-sleeved white tops tied with sashes at the waist, heads turbaned. One of them held his long yellow rumal stretched between his hands, demonstrating to a companion how he had twisted it about a throat. His companion nodded with approval and pounded him on the back.

We saw them dragging the bodies away, so very casual about it, holding onto a foot or a hand and letting the body bump and bang over the rough ground, disappearing behind the boulders with their terrible load. I saw the fat, rotund body of Yasmin Singh, still wearing the elaborate apricot silk robe and maroon trousers, saw it bounce and bump as two men pulled it across the ground, each holding onto a foot. The head joggled up and down like a rubber ball. It was a scene of unimaginable horror from a nightmare world, not real at all. It can't be real, I told myself. This can't actually be happening.

"Are you all right?" Sally whispered.

"I—I think so. Sally, it's—"

"I know. We—we have to be strong, Miss Lauren. We have to survive. That's all that matters now—survival."

"Those men who joined the caravan—they know we were there, know we weren't murdered. They'll come looking for us—"

"Maybe not," she said. "It all happened so quickly. Perhaps they'll think we were murdered, after all, our bodies—buried under the others. They—they seem to be in charge of the goods. See. They're the ones giving orders. The grave will probably be half-full before they finish. Perhaps they won't find out we escaped—at least for a while. We'll just have to hope so."

"What—what are we going to do?"

"Wait," she said. "They generally leave the area as soon as possible, make their getaway promptly. If—if all goes well, they'll be gone in a little while. We might as well make ourselves comfortable."

Sally sat down, making an inordinately loud noise in the leaves, and I sat down beside her. There was a large tree trunk behind us, and we rested our backs against it, skirts spread out. Sally was still gripping the pistol, and she let it rest on her knee, looking completely calm and composed. Grass and vines and thorny shrubs concealed us, the limbs of the tree dipping down to form a tentlike shelter, but we could still see sections of the campsite through rifts. The last rays of sunlight had vanished and pale, milky moonlight bathed the scene. The figures moving about cast long black shadows over the sand. There were fewer men about now. All the corpses had been carried away. Most of the goods had been bundled. Men were leading the horses and camels away. In what seemed a matter of moments the campsite was deserted, the sand smooth, not a single sign of the caravan remaining.

"That—that noise," I whispered.

"Try to ignore it, Miss Lauren."

Because of the curious acoustics formed by the walls of the boulders, the noise was magnified, echoing into the night loud and clear. It was a crunching, splintering sound, followed by dull thuds, the sound of bodies being broken and hurled into the ground. With bones broken, corpses could be folded up, wouldn't take up so much room in the grave, and when there were so very many corpses... I tried not to think about it. I tried to ignore it, as Sally had suggested, but it was impossible. When the noises finally ceased, there was the sound of shoveling, then stamping, and then voices talking quietly in the night. Long moments passed and then one voice seemed to chant, with others joining in, and I could make out "Kali," repeated over and over again, "Kali," then a sing-song chant. I knew they were

27

performing their ceremony now, celebrating their victory and offering a blessing to the goddess. Coarse brown sugar would be passed around, and each Thug would partake of it, eyes exalted, faces glowing with religious ecstasy.

"It—it's hideous," I said.

"It's almost over," Sally replied. "At the moment I'm far more worried about cobras than Thugs. I do hope one doesn't decide to venture our way."

"I—I wish you hadn't mentioned it."

"I wish I hadn't *thought* about it."

There was something almost like humor in her voice, and I admired her for it. Sally was every bit as terrified as I was, but she knew we couldn't give way to our fear, couldn't afford to let hysteria overcome us. She was putting on a brave front, and I took courage from her, feeling the terrible panic subsiding a little. For some reason we had been spared, and now we both had to call upon every ounce of courage we possessed. We had to use our intelligence, keep calm, hold back the hysteria that lurked just beneath the surface.

"I longed for adventure," Sally said, "but I didn't have anything like this in mind. Right now I'd give anything to be back in that dull, wretched academy, snug in my own attic room, listening to the rain pattering on the roof. Even if I *did* have to get up at five o'clock in the morning."

"I know. I feel the same way. I hated that place, but it seems like a paradise now."

"They—they've stopped chanting. With any luck, they'll be leaving shortly."

"They might leave someone behind," I said. "We'd best stay here—at least for the rest of the night."

"My sentiments exactly. Thank goodness our trunks

were sent on ahead. All your beautiful dresses—mine, too. At least they weren't taken."

"That hardly concerns me now."

"My red dotted swiss—the one I bought just before we left. Remember? I'd be crushed if it were lost. I paid a fortune for that dress, almost all my savings, but I must say it was worth it. Does wonders for me."

"How can you talk about clothes at a time like—"

"I'm trying, Miss Lauren. I—I'm trying—"

And then I saw the tears in her eyes, and I hated myself for not realizing what she was doing. Her chatter about clothes didn't mean she was insensitive. Quite the contrary. She was chattering to keep from thinking, trying to distract me at the same time, and I loved her for it. I put my arms around her, and we comforted each other as best we could, silent now as night noises surrounded us, birds calling quietly, leaves rustling, a single ray of moonlight slanting through the limbs overhead and dusting us with softly diffused silver. Time passed, and I grew drowsy, but I knew it would be impossible to sleep, knew it would be foolish even to hope for sleep, and hours seemed to pass and insects buzzed with a monotonous rhythm and the birds called out and somehow, somehow I slept.

The monkey jabbered loudly, mocking me, and I awoke with a start, staring up at that tiny, wizened gray face framed with black fur. The monkey gave a loud, shrill cry and swung to another limb, disappearing from sight. I was stiff and sore, my hair tangled, my white muslin dress streaked with dirt and stains. Gleaming yellow-gold rays of sunlight spilled through the canopy of leaves overhead to make shadow-flecked pools all around. It took me a moment to realize where I was, and then I gasped, realizing that I was alone. Where was Sally? What had happened to her? I stood up, my heart palpitating, and then I heard her voice.

"Not for you, you little scoundrel. Get away now. Go on. My, you *are* persistent!"

I stepped through the shrubbery and onto the narrow pathway just in time to see a rosy-cheeked and radiant Sally holding up a piece of fruit to a nimble gray monkey who, hanging from a branch by one hand, seized the treasure with the other, chattering excitedly and scurrying on up the tree with his bounty. Sally held several pieces of fruit gathered up and caught in the fold of her skirt.

"Oh, you're up. I don't rightly know what they *are*," she said, "but I saw a monkey eating them and figured they couldn't be poisonous. There're two kinds, one bright red, one brownish orange. I imagine they're something like pomegranates."

"Thank God," I whispered. "I woke up, and when you weren't there—"

"I've been up for hours," Sally admitted. "Thought I'd best go scouting for food and water. I didn't have any luck with water, but I did find these—I was rather hoping for bananas. Do bananas grow in India? Anyway, they're delicious. I've already eaten two."

"You shouldn't have gone off like that," I scolded.

"Oh, I carried my gun. Gives me *such* a feeling of security. I didn't see any cobras, just those adorable monkeys and the *prett*iest birds! Lovely flowers, too, blue and purple and white and pink. Here, Miss Lauren, eat some of these. They'll help quench your thirst, too."

I was ravenously hungry, thirsty as well, and the fruit helped considerably. Sally continued to talk about her explorations, determinedly cheerful, as though this were one grand lark we had planned ourselves, and I admired her attitude. Panic wouldn't help. We were stranded in the middle of the wilderness, without proper food or water, and only sheer fortitude would see us through. We were still alive, and that was something of a miracle. I finished the fruit, wiping my hands on the tattered hem of my skirt, feeling much better.

"It seems we're in a bit of a mess," I remarked.

"Yes, indeed," Sally replied, "but we'll muster through. We English are celebrated for it. Stiff upper lip and all that. It isn't going to be *easy*, but we'll make it."

"Of course we will."

"The—the Thugs are gone. They never came looking for us, so—so perhaps we're safe on that score. Then again, those men who knew we were with the caravan might start comparing notes with the others. . . ." She hesitated just a moment, frowning. "They might realize we weren't killed after all. They—they might send some men back to finish the job. We've got to take that into consideration, Miss Lauren. Might as well face the facts. The Thugs never leave witnesses—"

"And that's what we are," I said.

"If one of those five men happens to mention the two English girls, if they. . . ." Again she hesitated, her eyes dark and troubled. "They'd probably only send two or three men back to finish the job," she continued, "and this pistol is fully loaded."

"It's something we'll just have to face if—if the time

31

comes," I replied. "They probably traveled all night. They're bound to be dozens and dozens of miles away by now."

"We'll just have to persevere," Sally said. "It won't be so bad. We have a lot of *walk*ing ahead of us—"

"That won't hurt us. The caravan was just two days from Dahlkari. If we just keep moving—"

"It *will* be a bit warm, that sun's already fierce, but— I know what we'll do, we'll make parasols from those big green leaves I saw back there, and that'll help. We'll carry lots of this fruit."

"And maybe we'll find some water. I—I think there are wells along the way. I'm not nearly so thirsty now, not after eating that fruit. We'll skirt the edge of this jungle and head due east. Thank goodness both of us are wearing kid boots."

"It'll be *fun!*" Sally exclaimed.

And then, realizing how ridiculous her exclamation was under the circumstances, we both burst into gales of laughter, for all the world like two schoolgirls. There was a slight edge of hysteria to the laughter, but I felt much, much better for it. Each of us was being resolute and optimistic for the sake of the other, realizing that any show of weakness would be fatal. It wasn't a lark, far from it, but we had to keep up our spirits somehow. It would be all too easy to panic, and panic could only lead to defeat.

"You go gather more fruit, Miss Lauren, lots of it, and I'll get those leaves and make our parasols. The fruit trees are just down the pathway, on the right. You can't miss 'em. Watch out for the monkeys, though. They're greedy little demons, will try to snatch it out of your hands."

She smiled, tossing her head, long tarnished gold

32

locks spilling about her shoulders, brown eyes sparkling. If I had to be stranded in the middle of nowhere, I was glad it was with Sally. I hated to think of how one of the girls from the academy would have reacted under the same circumstances. Sally bounced down the path, gold and brown sprigged yellow skirt fluttering over her petticoats, a merry creature, full of verve and vitality and not about to admit defeat. She disappeared, and I could hear her scolding back at a monkey. I took heart, telling myself that things weren't nearly as bad as they might seem.

Spirits rising, I brushed a smudge of dirt from my skirt, and then I saw the ground and realized that I was standing in almost exactly the spot where the bearer had been murdered last night. I could feel the color leaving my cheeks, feel my pulses leap, and a wave of weakness swept over me. Remembering the horror, I had to brace one palm against a tree to keep from falling. I closed my eyes, and for a moment the hideous nightmare replayed itself in my mind. I bit my lower lip, praying for strength, and after a moment it came. It had been a nightmare, yes, and . . . and that was how I had to classify it, a shimmering illusion of horror, dreamlike, unreal, something that had never really happened at all. If I let myself dwell on it I wouldn't be able to go on.

Poor, boastful Yasmin Singh, plump and pleasant, bragging about his wealth and prestige. Ahmed, young and swaggering and full of life, such a beautiful youth. All the servants and bearers, men who probably had large families. Yesterday so alive, and now. . . . I took a deep breath and stood up straight and deliberately forced the images out of my mind. I couldn't allow myself to think about it. I thought about Dollie and

Reggie and the warm welcome awaiting us at Dahlkari. They... they wouldn't miss us because they didn't know when we were due to arrive. They expected us to arrive with Lieutenant Parks and a full military escort. We could expect no one to come looking for us, not for days and days, no one except the Thugs who might return to finish the job.

Stop it! I admonished myself sharply, and this time I was successful. The nightmare was over, over, and the sunlight was radiant this morning, slanting through the dark green treetops in dazzling yellow-gold rays, creating soft blue-gray shadows, and white flowers blossomed on vines like tiny showers spilling down. Bright green parakeets flitted overhead, singing and scolding, while the ever-present monkeys swung from limb to limb, making a friendly, noisy clatter. The jungle was anything but ominous now as I moved purposefully down the path to the tall grayish-tan trees so heavy with fruit that the boughs nearly touched the ground, fruit like Christmas tree ornaments, dark-orange, bright red.

As we would have to carry the fruit, I unceremoniously lifted my skirt and ripped off one of my petticoats, folding it into a makeshift carry bag which I slowly began to fill. A swarm of white and yellow butterflies suddenly materialized, hovering over me like scraps of fluttering silk, hanging there for a moment, trembling on air, then passing on. Sally was right about the monkeys. One brazen little creature perched on a limb nearby and watched me with head cocked to one side, finally swooping down and snatching a piece of fruit from my hand. I laughed, a lovely, spontaneous laugh, and I knew then that it was going to be all right.

Sally had already fashioned our parasols when I returned with the heavily laden bag. The leaves were thick and heavy, a very dark green, almost two feet in circumference, and she had fastened the stems of five together for each parasol, attaching the stems to the top of long sticks with strips of white cotton that had previously been ruffles on one of her petticoats. I had often grumbled about the necessity of wearing so many undergarments, anything less than five considered shockingly lax by the ladies at the academy, but they were certainly proving useful now. By the time we finally reached Dahlkari we would probably both be down to our bloomers, I thought, smiling.

"That bag looks familiar," Sally said. "Oh, dear, one of your very best, too. At least mine are just *cotton*. Here's your parasol, Miss Lauren. Quite the thing, isn't it? It'd set a new style in Bath. Let me take that bag. I see you brought plenty."

"At least two dozen. I wasn't sure we'd be able to find anything else to eat. Are—are we ready?"

"Ready as rain," she said brightly. "We—we'll have to pass through the campsite and around those boulders. I hope it won't—"

"It won't upset me at all," I lied.

Sally jammed the pistol in the waistband of her dress, slung the bag of fruit over one shoulder, propped the parasol over the other and gave a twirl. We left the jungle and passed across the large clearing surrounded by the enormous gray boulders. When we had left it, it had been filled with tents and campfires with bubbling pots and men who talked in quiet, relaxed voices, and then . . . I thrust the threatening images from my mind, peering up at the sky, a pale, pale blue that looked as hard as baked enamel, hot, like the rays of sunlight that suddenly seemed fierce without the protective leaves to diffuse their strength.

"I explored a bit earlier this morning," Sally told me, leading the way around one of the immense boulders. "I—well, I crept about with the gun clutched in front of me, just in case they'd left someone behind. Took a lot of nerve, I don't mind telling you. Miss Lauren—"

"Yes?"

"I couldn't find it. The—the place where the hole had been. There was no hole, nothing that looked like there *had* been. They left no signs whatsoever. As fas as the world is concerned, the caravan just—vanished, just like hundreds of others before it."

"It's incredible to think this has been happening for centuries and no one has been able to do anything about it until Captain Sleeman came along. It—staggers the imagination."

"I know," Sally agreed. "I read that book by Captain Taylor, and it fair gave me the shudders. I read all those dreadful accounts in the penny press, too, each more lurid than the next, some of 'em with drawings. The Indians seem to have just ac*cept*ed it, traveling at their own risk, and if someone failed to return from a journey, their folks just took it as fate, rarely making inquiries."

"Of course, there're no proper roads, no trains—at least not yet. That has a lot to do with it. The Indians have a different way of looking at things. Because of their religious beliefs, life here and now doesn't have as much value as it does to us. Something like—like what happened last night could never take place in England. The criminals would be hunted down until every last one of them had been caught and hung. Here in

India...." I paused, noting the expression on Sally's face.

"That smell," she remarked, wrinkling her nose. "So sharp, almost like pepper. Those little seeds scattered over the ground...."

"Fleawort," I said. My cheeks grew pale.

"Miss Lauren, what's wrong? You look—"

"That's what they use—the Thugs. Kali—Kali commands them to scatter fleawort seeds over—over the graves, supposedly as a token to her. It has a very useful purpose, too. It keeps the jackals away, keeps them from digging up the ground to get at the—"

I couldn't go on. Sally looked as horrified as I, and we quickly made a wide circle around the stretch of ground scattered with seeds. Neither of us said anything else for at least a quarter of an hour. By that time we had passed through the area of boulders, had skirted the tip of the jungle and were moving east, the jungle to our left, to our right a seemingly endless expanse of desert sand broken only by occasional clusters of rock. Although it was still morning, the heat was already intense, the sun a fierce yellow ball. Heat waves filled the air like barely visible gas. Our large leafy parasols kept off the direct rays of sunlight, protecting faces and arms, but they did nothing to alleviate the extreme discomfort. Nice English girls weren't supposed to perspire, but Sally and I were already perspiring freely, hair damp, bodices clinging wetly.

"I'm beginning to dislike this country," Sally confessed as we trudged along. "I mean—well, those handsome Sepoys were adorable, and I dearly loved all those gorgeous marble palaces and things. The nautch dancers were interesting, too, and those cows running loose all over the place, but I can't say that I care for the *cli*mate."

"It's not this bad everywhere. This is desert, after all."

"What wouldn't I give for a nice cool drink of water."

"Maybe—maybe we'll find a well. Best not think about it."

"Best not," she agreed.

"You'll like Dahlkari," I told her, hoping to divert both our minds from the thirst that was already such torment. "Dollie told me all about it in her letters. There's a large native village, quite colorful, with fascinating shops, and then up above the village is the military garrison. A little bit of home, she calls it, nice English houses, English gardens, even a polo field. The local rajah has his palace less than a mile away. It's something to see, Dollie wrote. He frequently entertains the English there, gives lavish garden parties."

"I've never been to a garden party."

"You'll go to one in Dahlkari," I promised. "I—I'm sure you'll have all the enlisted men vying for the privilege of taking you. You're going to set them on their heels."

"I imagine I will," Sally said frankly. "I imagine you'll find a beau, too. You may pretend not to be interested, but you are. You're not quite the cool bluestocking you pretend to be."

I made no reply, knowing all too well the truth in Sally's statement. Try though I might to suppress it, there was an infuriatingly romantic streak in my nature. Proud as I was of my mind, my scholarship, my

38

ability to read Latin and Greek and discuss philosophy and ancient cultures, I nevertheless consumed florid, flamboyant romantic novels featuring adventuresome heroines and dark, dashing heroes who were usually rogues of the first water. How many such books had I read? How many times had I imagined myself in the arms of a man such as those I read about? Cool and prim in the classroom, translating the *Aeneid* of Vergil, writing dissertations about Socrates, I had burned the midnight oil night after night, consuming the sensational novels I took from the lending library by the score, keeping them carefully hidden from the other girls. Who would have imagined that the oh so poised, ever so erudite Lauren Gray had a fantasy life featuring swash-buckling pirates, highwaymen with gypsy blood, noblemen as reckless as they were handsome? The novels were my secret addiction, and no matter how many times I tried to cure myself of them, I always returned to the lending library for yet another batch. I wondered if Sally had discovered some of the books in the bottom of my wardrobe back in Bath.

"You're very beautiful, you know," she continued. "Those marvelous patrician features, cheekbones ever so high and elegant, hair such a glossy silver brown. I wish *I* looked like that."

"Nonsense. You're very fetching."

"I have something men like," Sally admitted, "but I'll always be a hoyden at heart. No one'll ever take me for a lady. Guess I wouldn't want to be taken for one, come to think of it. I have ever so much more fun the way I am. I'm not having much fun at the moment, though."

"Do you want to stop for a while, Sally?"

"I—I reckon we'd better keep walking as long as we

can," she replied grimly. "We can't afford to pamper ourselves. We've got to endure."

Endure we did, no longer talking, no longer making any attempts to cheer each other up with inconsequential chatter. The heat grew worse, and we grew tired, yet still we walked, both of us wrapped up in our thoughts and trying to ignore parched throats and aching bones and sore feet, trying not to think about the man or men who might come riding back with a yellow rumal to finish us off. We finally stopped for lunch, moving into the jungle and sitting under a tree to devour the fruit. It didn't taste so good this time, nor did it do as much to alleviate our thirst. I wondered what we were going to do if we didn't find a well soon.

We rested for an hour under the shade of a tall banyan tree, and then we resumed our journey, trudging over the sand, silent, skirts dusty and ragged at the hems, hair damp and tangled, bodies covered with perspiration. This evening, when we stopped, we would have to search for a stream in the jungle. Heaven only knew how contaminated it might be, what tropical diseases we might be courting, but we simply couldn't go on without any water. The thirst was like torture now, and I was beginning to feel weak and dizzy. I knew Sally must feel the same way, but both of us knew we had to keep moving.

An hour passed, another, and it must have been around four o'clock in the afternoon when Sally gave a little cry and grabbed my arm. Her face was pale, her eyes wide with alarm, and I wondered what in the world could be the matter with her. Then she pointed, and I saw the horseman on the horizon. He stopped, much too far away for us to make out any details. Silhouetted against the sunlight, he was a sinister figure, a figure of great menace. After a moment he turned the horse around and began to gallop over the desert toward us. As he drew nearer I saw that he was a native with the face of a brigand. We both knew what he was and why he had come.

Three

For a moment both of us were too terrified to do anything but stare in horror as the rider approached on the magnificent stallion that kicked up clouds of dust, and then Sally dropped the bag of fruit and dropped the parasol and took the pistol out, holding it in front of her with both hands as he swooped down upon us. I felt faint, and my heart was pounding, but I didn't scream, nor did Sally. Neither of us had the strength. The rider jerked on the reins and the horse reared up on its hind legs a few yards from us, front hooves waving in the air, silky black coat gleaming in the sunlight, and then it grew still. The rider sat there in the saddle, staring at us with dark eyes, his face inscrutable.

"Hold it, you brigand!" Sally cried. "Don't get off that horse! If you do, I—I'll blow your head off!"

His face remained inscrutable, Sally's words having no effect whatsoever. He wore sturdy brown knee boots, tight white breeches and a loose, flowing tan and white burnoose, hood thrown back, long sleeves full at the wrist. The garment was shabby and dusty, the sort of thing an Arab might have worn, and, indeed, he looked much more like an Arab than an Indian. He had deeply tanned skin, strong, harsh features and unruly raven locks, several of them spilling across his forehead. His lips were full, curling sardonically at one corner, and his nose was hawklike, but it was his eyes that dominated, dark, glowing eyes, brown-black, the eyes of a hunter observing his prey. His lids were heavy, half-concealing those incredibly hypnotic eyes, his dark brows highly arched, flaring out at the corners. His was a cruel, ruthless face, the face of a killer.

"Stay right where you are!" Sally ordered.

There was a tremor in her voice, and she held the gun rigidly out in front of her as though afraid it might go off at any moment. The man merely stared at us, not the least bit perturbed by the pistol or the frightened young woman who pointed it at him. The sleek, magnificent horse pawed the ground restlessly. The rider touched the side of its neck with a strong brown hand, murmuring something unintelligible, and the horse grew still. The man sat casually in the saddle, as though born to it. There was a certain rugged grandeur about him, a curious magnetism I couldn't help but notice, even under the circumstances. He was no humble native peasant, that much was certain.

"Back off!" Sally cried, waving the pistol.

"Be—be careful with that thing," I cautioned her. My voice sounded hoarse, barely audible. "You've never fired it. It might go off. I don't believe he understands English, Sally."

"He understands this pistol well enough. Back off, you fiend!"

"He doesn't—he doesn't look like any of the others. None of them wore a robe like that. He might not be a Thug after all. He might just be a—someone who happened to come along."

"Thug or no, look at that face! I know a killer when I see one. He's a cold-blooded, merciless heathen. Look at that twisting mouth and that beaklike nose. Look at

43

those *eyes*! Hold it, you brigand! Don't make a move!"

"He does look—rather savage," I agreed, "but we mustn't make snap judgments. He might well be our salvation. He might be able to take us to Dahlkari."

"Dahlkari," he said in a harsh, guttural voice.

"See, he—he understood that word. Dahlkari," I repeated. "We want to—to go to Dahlkari. Do—do you understand? Dahl-ka-ri. Mc—McAllister."

A deep crease formed above the bridge of his nose as he frowned. "McAllister," he said, nodding slowly. "Eng-lish. So-jour." He spoke with great effort, obviously finding the words difficult to pronounce.

"He knows who Reggie is, Sally. He knows he's an English soldier. I don't think he's a Thug. Let me talk to him. I—perhaps I can make him understand what we want."

"I don't trust him, Miss Lauren."

"I—I don't either, but we—we haven't much choice."

Most of my fear was gone now, and my voice was steady. I pushed a damp brown wave from my brow and stepped a bit closer, standing beside Sally. I saw the large leather canteen hanging from his saddle horn, and the rider noticed me looking at it. He grimaced and reached for the canteen, tossing it toward us. It landed at my feet. Sally's arms had begun to droop a little, as though the pistol were too heavy for her to hold. She watched me pick up the canteen and unfasten the top.

"You drink first," I told her. "Take—just a few little sips. I don't think you're supposed to drink too much at first."

"You go ahead," she said, "I'll keep him covered while you drink. I don't like the sly look in his eye. He—he looks like some bloodthirsty pirate on

44

horseback, probably has a dagger concealed under that robe. You finished?"

With one hand Sally held the pistol pointed shakily at the rider, taking the canteen with the other. She drank cautiously, her eyes never leaving the man, then returned the canteen to me. I took one more tiny sip before fastening the top back on. Nothing, I knew, would ever taste better than those few sips of cool, lovely water. Already I could feel the dizzy weakness leaving, some of my strength returning.

"I—I think he's friendly, Sally. If he planned to murder us, he'd hardly have given us the water. Let me try to make him understand. Just because he has a—a treacherous face doesn't necessarily mean he *is*."

"Talk to him then," Sally said, "but I'm keeping him covered. If he tries anything, I'll blow him to kingdom come—" Sally was beginning to enjoy herself, the pistol giving her considerable confidence.

"Dahl-kari," I said carefully. "We want to go to Dahlkari, to Lieutenant Colonel McAllister. Do you understand? Dahl-kari, Mc-Al-lis-ter. Look, Sally, he's nodding. I think he understands. Will you take us to Dahlkari?" I used appropriate gestures, pointing first to him, then to us, then to the east as I said "Dahlkari," speaking as I might speak to a particularly dense child.

"Mc-Allister," he growled. "English soldier. Dahl-kari."

"Let him try something," Sally muttered, "just let him try."

"McAllister will—will give you much money. Money? Rupees. Many, many rupees. You—take—us to—Dahlkari. McAllister—pay—many—rupees."

He nodded again, a terse, abrupt nod, and I felt

45

certain that he understood. He slung one leg over the saddle and slid to the ground in one quick movement. He was extremely tall, well over six feet, with a powerful build. He resembled no Indian I had ever seen. Though deeply tan, his complexion was not the smooth, creamy tan of the Indians, and his features had none of the softness of the race. Could he possibly be an Arab? That's what he looked like, a savage, virile Arab sheikh with scowling mouth and glowering black-brown eyes.

"Don't come any closer!" Sally cried.

"I don't think he means any harm, Sally. I think he wants to help us get to Dahlkari."

"Stand back, ruffian!"

The man paid no attention to her. He moved toward us in long, brisk strides, seized Sally's wrist and took the gun out of her hand, slipping it into the waistband of his trousers. Sally was dumbfounded, and her bluster vanished completely, leaving her much too terrified to protest. He stood there in front of us with his legs spread wide apart, his hands resting lightly on his thighs, a towering, intimidating figure in his striped robe and boots. Sally swallowed and seized my hand, gripping it tightly. Some of my own confidence vanished, but I tried to maintain some semblance of composure, knowing it would be an error to show fear. Those dark black-brown eyes glared at us with a fixed intensity, and he seemed to be contemplating exactly what he should do with us.

"Miss Lauren—" Sally began shakily.

"He's not a Thug, Sally. I'm convinced of it." My own voice wasn't nearly as steady as it had been earlier.

"He'll murder us both! Look, he's *leer*ing—maybe he intends to rape us first. I've never *been* raped."

"Be quiet," I said sharply.

"We go Dahlkari," the man said, pronouncing each word slowly and with considerable difficulty. "McAllister soldier pay many rupees."

"Yes, that—that's right," I encouraged him. "He *does* understand, Sally. He's going to take us to Dahlkari."

"He's not taking *me* anywhere, thank you. If you think I'm going to go traipsing off with a cold-blooded fiend like this one, you're out of your mind, Miss Lauren. I know something about men, and this one—why, he'd as soon slit our throats as—"

"Be quiet!" the man growled, parroting my earlier admonishment.

Sally cut herself short, her lips parted, her eyes wide with fright and bewilderment. With her damp, tangled gold curls and the stained and dusty yellow dress she looked like some wretched waif. I knew I must have looked just as bad. I had put the parasol down earlier when I picked up the canteen, and the sun was merciless on my exposed face.

"We go," the man said.

He pointed toward the horse, and then fastened strong brown fingers around my wrist. Still nervous, I tried to pull back. He gave my wrist a savage tug, causing me to stumble forward, and it was then that Sally flew at him with balled fists, pounding viciously at his chest. The man sighed heavily and gave her a shove, brushing her away as he might have a bothersome gnat. Sally stumbled and fell to the sand on her backside, giving an outraged yell. Ignoring her, he pulled me across the sand to the horse and then lifted me up, swinging me into the saddle with no effort whatsoever, as though I were weightless. Returning to

Sally, he pulled her to her feet, and when she tried to hit him again he swung her up over his shoulder like a sack of feed. She kicked and struggled and pounded at his back with her fists, but his face remained utterly impassive as he sauntered back over to the horse.

"Unhand me, you brute!" Sally yelled. I began to suspect that she had not only discovered my cache of novels but had read them as well.

The man deposited Sally up on the horse behind me, showing no emotion when she seized a handful of raven hair and began to pull it violently. He reached up, caught hold of her wrist and freed himself, giving her a look that caused her to be still instantly. Emitting a little sob, she placed her arms around my waist and held on for dear life. The man sauntered back to the place where we had been standing and kicked at the bag of fruit with the toe of his boot, frowning when the red and brownish-orange balls rolled out. He picked up one of the leaf parasols and brought it over to me, indicating that it should serve for both of us, and then, taking the reins in his hand, he began to lead the horse over the sand, heading east.

The parasol was large enough to shield both of us from the sun. I held it over my shoulder, holding on to the saddle horn with my free hand. I had clung to the precious canteen throughout all this, and I slung it back over the saddle horn now, feeling it would be wiser to wait awhile before we drank more. I could feel Sally relaxing, her grip not as tense as it had been before.

"I just know he's got something dreadful in store for us," she remarked after a while.

"Nonsense."

"Rape," she said chattily. "One of the girls at the

48

orphanage—this was years ago—*she* was raped, and she said the best thing to do is just relax and *enjoy* it." I could tell the minx was beginning to warm to the idea. "Of course, he might be a white slaver," she continued. "We might end up in some dreadful *house!*"

"I do wish you'd hush, Sally."

"It *is* rather exciting," she admitted, "and I must say riding on the back of this splendid horse beats trudging over the sand. My poor feet! Do you really think he'll take us to Dahlkari, Miss Lauren?"

"I feel sure he will. He knows Reggie will give him a large amount of money for rescuing us."

"You're probably right," Sally agreed, sounding almost disappointed. "This has been quite a day. At least I'll have something to tell my grandchildren. Not that they'll be*lieve* it. Who would? It's like something out of one of those books you were always reading on the sly."

"So you did find them?"

"'Course I did. Read a couple of 'em, too. They were a lot more interesting than those dreary foreign things you read the rest of the time. I couldn't make head nor tails of *those*."

Sally was her old cheerful self again, and I felt my own spirits rising. It had indeed been an incredible day, but things were definitely looking up now. Our guide was fierce and sullen, but at least he hadn't whipped out a yellow scarf and strangled us. He knew that the English soldier McAllister would give him many rupees, and I felt confident that his desire for the reward would make him think twice about doing anything uncivilized. He *did* look quite capable of rape, but, after all, Sally and I were English.

The hood of his burnoose pulled up over his head,

the native moved at a steady pace, leading horse and riders over the burning sand and showing no sign of weariness. An hour passed, then another, the sun beginning to move gradually west, the rays not quite so intense now, the hard blue sky softening to blue-gray. Sally and I drank more water, almost emptying the canteen. Both of us were ravenously hungry, and I wished our guide hadn't been so disdainful of the fruit. Hot, hungry, weary and worn, both of us grew silent, although Sally made an occasional comment about her backside. She was certain it had been bruised when that vicious brute had knocked her down, and bouncing up and down on the back of the horse didn't help a bit. The sky had taken on a pale violet hue and deep crimson banners were beginning to smear the horizon when our native guide turned the horse toward the jungle and, reaching its edge, stopped and indicated that we should dismount.

Sally slipped off the horse with considerable alacrity, rubbing her posterior with both hands as soon as she was on the ground. I thought I saw a smile play on the native's lips, although it might have been a grimace. He reached up and took my hand, helping me dismount, and, bone-weary, I was grateful for the assistance. I noticed again how very tall he was, how strong and powerful that lean, muscular body was. He made me feel exceedingly vulnerable, exceedingly feminine, and I was horrified by the realization. The man was a native, a brutal rogue if not an out-and-out villain, and I suddenly realized that he looked exactly like one of those wildly unprincipled gypsy-vagabond-highwaymen who swaggered through the pages of the romantic novels I had consumed so avidly. Certainly not handsome, the man had a ruthless virility and a raw, primitive magnetism that was much more powerful than good looks could possibly have been. I was shocked at myself for even noticing it.

"What now?" Sally said grumpily, still rubbing briskly.

"I suppose we'll make camp for the night," I told her.

"In the jungle? With all those cobras and jackals?"

"I—I imagine it'll be safer. The Thugs might return, Sally. We mustn't forget that."

"I haven't," she said, serious now. "All the time we were bouncing along I kept my eyes peeled. Truth to tell, I feel a bit safer with Laughing Boy here at our side. I fancy he could take on any number of Thugs with his bare hands. They wouldn't send back more than two or three to—to tidy things up, and, if worse came to worse, I'd put my money on Chuckles. He *is* grim, isn't he?"

"Rather," I agreed.

"Regular barrel of laughs. I'm *still* not convinced he isn't planning something perfectly foul—he certainly looks the type. Sure, he wants the gold he'll get for rescuing us, but his unbridled lust might be stronger than his greed." There was a wistful note in her voice.

"You're outrageous, Sally."

"I know *men*," she retorted.

Taking the reins again, the tall native motioned for us to follow him and led the horse into the jungle. It was denser here than it had been near the campsite last night, and there was no visible pathway, but our guide moved briskly and with great confidence, obviously very familiar with this particular area. Sally and I trudged along behind him, frequently stumbling, thorny shrubs and low-hanging branches making it an obstacle course. Although it was rapidly fading, there was still plenty of light. Monkeys chattered noisily overhead, swinging from tree to tree, and the birds were shrill. Complaining vociferously, Sally freed a lock of hair from a branch, kicked a rock out of her way and made highly unflattering remarks about our leader.

"Slow down, you rogue! What is this, a five-mile sprint? Watch that branch, Miss Lauren. I'm a game girl, but enough is enough! I might as well save my breath," she groaned. "He's a thoroughly heartless brute any way you look at it."

We finally stumbled into a tiny clearing in the middle of the jungle, not even as large as the one with the idol had been. Limbs stretching overhead formed a rustling ceiling, tree trunks and flowering vines closing in on every side. I could hear a pleasant gurgling noise in the distance, the sound of running water, and realized there must be a stream. The native motioned for us to remain here and then, pushing back a curtain of vines covered with scarlet flowers, led the horse out of the clearing and toward the sound of water. Sally and I crumpled to the ground. It was surprisingly soft and spongy, covered with a mossy grass. It was sheer paradise to be off our feet.

Both of us were too weary to talk. Sally looked like a battered doll with brassy hair and nervous, exhausted features, a smudge of dirt on her cheek. Her once bright yellow dress was in deplorable condition, covered with dirt and stains, the bodice ripped. My own white muslin was in an even worse state, the skirt torn in several places, one sleeve hanging down sadly. A few fading rays of sunlight streamed through the rustling leaves to make flickering pools on the grass, and to the monkeys peering at us from the trees we must have

52

oked like two ragged nymphs. It seemed an eternity
go since we had left Delhi, I thought. I leaned back on
he grass, closing my eyes, and when I opened them the
learing was brushed with hazy silver, shadows
preading over the ground.

Sally was still fast asleep. I had no idea how much
ime had passed. It was cool now, much cooler than it
ad been the night before. I shivered, wondering where
ur guide was. The jungle was silent, the monkeys
sleep, the birds still, faint rustles and crackles only
ntensifying the silence. Sally groaned in her sleep and
urned over on her side, her head cradled on her arms.
tiff and sore, my bones aching, I stood up and
tretched, beginning to grow alarmed. Where was the
ative? What had happened to him? Surely... surely
e wouldn't abandon us?

It was then that the curtain of flowering vines parted
nd the native stepped into the clearing, the carcass of
ome small animal slung over his shoulder. I gave a
ittle cry, startled, and he shook his head to indicate I
houldn't be afraid. I wondered where the horse was.
He had probably left it tethered nearby after feeding
and watering it, I reasoned. He slung the animal to the
ground, squatted and took out a long, sharp knife that
gleamed in the moonlight. Ignoring me completely, he
began to skin the animal, and I turned away, repulsed
by the grisly sight. I had no idea what kind of animal he
had killed, and it was probably best that I didn't. At
least we were going to eat tonight, and at the moment I
would welcome anything.

Animal skinned and spread out on some leaves, the
man used his knife to dig a small hole in the ground. He
circled it with stones, filled it with wood and then thrust
two Y-shaped sticks in the ground, one on either side of

the hole. Reaching inside his robe, he withdrew a flin
and in a moment the fire was burning pleasantly, brigh
orange flames driving the moonlight away and fillin
the clearing with dancing shadows. Spearing th
remains of the animal on a long stick, he placed
across the fire, letting the homemade spit rest on th
two upright sticks. Flames licked at the meat, and soo
grease was dripping and popping and the mea
crackled as he squatted beside the fire and turned th
spit. He had not looked at me once. I might not eve
have been there.

Sally awoke with a start, sitting up abruptly.

"Is that *meat*?" she exclaimed.

"Of sorts," I said.

"I was having this glorious dream—I was dreamin
of a fat roast pig, all pink and juicy, stretched out on
platter with an apple in its mouth. It was so real I coul
smell it. What's he cooking?"

"I don't know, but I doubt that it's pig."

Whatever it was, it was absolutely delicious. Whe
the meat was done the native cut it into sections, placec
the sections on leaves and handed Sally and I each
serving. Then, squatting on the other side of the fire, h
took a meaty joint between his two hands and began to
eat with considerable relish. Sally and I exchangec
glances, and then, shrugging, she took up her sectior
and imitated the native, as did I. Sitting with our leg:
folded under us, skirts spread out, we ate in a mos
undignified manner. We each had a second helping anc
finally, tossing the last bone into the jungle, wiped ou
hands on our skirts and drank from the canteen the
native tossed over to us.

"It was probably jackal or something," Sally said
thoughtfully, "but I've never enjoyed a meal more."

"Nor have I."

"We—we've been very lucky, Miss Lauren."

"I know that."

"I keep thinking of—what happened, can't help myself. I keep thinking of Ahmed, that poor, beautiful boy." She paused for a long moment, peering into the low-burning flames. "We—we just missed them, Miss Lauren. They'd been in that clearing with that horrible idol, perhaps just moments before we arrived. They slipped through the jungle another way, moving toward the campsite as we entered the clearing. If—if they'd gone by way of the path we took they'd have run right into us."

I nodded, trying not to shudder.

"It's a wonder they didn't hear us crashing through the jungle," Sally continued. "Some special providence was looking out for us. We had a very close call. I'll be so glad when this night's over." She glanced around at the dark, encroaching jungle. "The way I figure, I figure if they don't come back by tonight, they won't come back at all."

Our guide stood up abruptly and stepped toward the curtain of vines, lifting them and disappearing. I could hear the horse neighing nearby, hear his voice low and melodic as he soothed the animal. He returned a moment later with two rather mothy looking blankets he'd taken out of the saddle bags. Dropping them in front of us, he moved to the other side of the clearing and stretched out on the ground to sleep. Sally and I examined the blankets with dubious expressions.

"Probably full of fleas," she remarked, "but they're better than nothing, I suppose. It's already chilly, and the fire's almost burned down. I don't fancy I'll be able to *sleep* much."

"We might as well try," I told her.

The night air was indeed chilly, and the blankets were snug and warm, smelling of horseflesh and leather and perspiration. The jungle was still, so still I could hear the soft buzz of the insects and the sound of the stream. The fire was a heap of glowing dark orange coals, gradually dimming, dark shadows spreading over the clearing like heavy black veils. The moonlight was thin, only a few pale rays sifting through the treetops, emphasizing the darkness. I could barely make out the form of the native stretched out across the way, his burnoose a faint blur in the dense darkness. I tried to sleep, but it was a futile endeavor. I kept listening for the sound of stealthy footsteps. At least an hour passed, perhaps two, and still I was wide awake.

"You can't sleep either," Sally whispered.

I gave a little jerk, so startled that I almost cried out.

"You're a bundle of nerves, just like me," she said. "I've been tossing and turning for hours—this mothy old blanket doesn't help, nor does this lumpy ground."

There was more moonlight now, or perhaps my eyes had just grown accustomed to the dark. The fire had completely burned out, and there were shifting pools of pale silver on the ground, shadows moving as a very faint breeze caused leaf and limb to sway gently. It must be well after midnight by now, I thought, wishing the night were over. Faced with stark, shattering reality Sally and I had both acted with admirable calm, but now, in the dead of night, in the middle of a silent, menacing jungle, our nerves were taut, both of us on edge.

"It's the not knowing," she said. "I keep—waiting, not knowing if they'll come or not."

"Perhaps those five men never mentioned us."

"Perhaps not, but if they *did*, those fiends will know for sure the bodies of two English girls weren't thrown into that grave. They couldn't afford to let us live."

"There was no sign of them all day long. Perhaps—"

"The men might not have mentioned us until say, lunchtime. They would have sent someone back for us immediately, and it would take them at least half a day to come back and find us. That—that's why I'm so nervous tonight. This would be about the right time."

"Let's don't talk about it, Sally. Let's—try to forget it."

"I only wish I could."

"The native looks very capable. He—"

I cut myself short. Sally gripped my arm. Both of us heard the noise at the same time. A twig had snapped in the jungle, snapped loudly. In the silence the noise was almost like a gunshot. There was a rustling sound now, as though someone were pushing aside a branch. Sally and I both stood up, tense and alert. The native sprang to his feet. He stood very still, listening, peering into the jungle, and then he turned to look at us. The clearing was bathed with a faint, pale silver now as the moon came out from behind a bank of clouds, thin, luminous beams streaming through the leafy canopy above. I could see him clearly, see his grim expression, his tight, resolute mouth.

"He—he heard it, too," Sally said.

The native put his finger to his lips, warning us to be silent, and then he moved across the clearing and disappeared into the jungle, seemed to melt into it as if by magic, making not a sound.

"It's them," Sally said. Her voice was flat.

"Perhaps it was just—just some animal."

"It wasn't. It's them. I can feel it in my bones."

57

Several long minutes passed. I wondered why I was so calm. I should have been trembling with fear, my pulses leaping, my knees weak, yet I felt none of the things I should have felt. It was as though I had no feeling whatsoever. I stood motionless, hardly breathing, cold, so very cold, and I was as calm and clear-headed as I had ever been in my life. Sally was motionless, too, a hard, determined expression on her face. The jungle was still, silent but for the faint rustle of stiff leaves and the pleasant gurgle of the stream. Perhaps we had been mistaken. Perhaps it had merely been some animal after all.

Then we heard the cry and the sound of scuffling.

It was difficult to tell where it came from, near or far, in front or behind. There was a violent thrashing of leaves, the loud, popping crackle of branches snapping, footsteps shuffling, a dull thud as something heavy hit the ground. Two men were in mortal combat, each fighting for his life, a loud groan now, another crash. After a long, tense moment of silence there was a shrill, piercing scream that ended in a hideous gurgling sound, then another, louder thud. Was it the tall native? Had he been strangled to death by one of those deadly yellow rumals? Was the Thug even now on his way to the clearing?

"Someone's coming," Sally said in that flat, expressionless voice.

She took hold of my hand. That curious, inexplicable calm still possessed me, as though this were a dream and I knew it was a dream and therefore couldn't really be frightened. Stealthy footsteps approached. Someone moved slowly, cautiously toward the clearing. I stood stiff and rigid, frozen it seemed, unable to do anything but watch calmly as the curtain of flowering vines slowly parted. Sally was gripping my hand so tightly that it seemed she would crush my fingers into pulp. Neither of us made a sound as the tall Thug in white stepped into the clearing and stood there no more than five yards from us.

He stared at us. He wore a white turban, and his face, clearly visible in the moonlight, was dark like polished mahogany, a mask of evil, the thin lips slowly curling in a smile of anticipation as he pulled the yellow scarf from his waistband, catching each end and stretching it taut between his hands. Legs spread wide apart, sandaled feet firm on the ground, he popped the rumal once or twice, testing its strength, and then that horrible smile vanished and he glared at us with savage resolution.

"Kali," he said, and then he screamed, "Kali!"

A muscular arm shot out from behind him, swinging around his throat in one rapid, brutal curl that crushed the scream abruptly. The robed native reared back, squeezing with all his strength, and the Thug dropped the rumal and thrashed about in frenzied panic, on his tiptoes now, clutching at that merciless arm as the native leaned back, applying even more pressure. Gasping, gurgling, fighting for his life, the Thug jerked about like a puppet gone berserk, his feet no longer touching the ground. Arm wrapped murderously around his victim's throat, the native reached under his robe with his free hand. I saw the knife blade flash in the moonlight as he raised it, saw it swing in the air for a split second before plunging into the Thug's chest. His body jerked convulsively as the native drove the blade in deeper, twisting the handle with a savage precision, and then the Thug fell limp, the native's arm still curled about his throat.

It was a grotesque tableau, not real at all, something from a nightmare, and I was far, far away, seeing it through the haze of moonlight and shadow, everything gray and black and soft silver, without color, without substance. The native let the body drop to the ground in a heap of tangled limbs, a puppet with its strings cut, broken, lifeless. The native casually wiped the blade of his knife on the puppet's white sleeve and then he caught both limp wrists in one hand and pulled the thing out of the clearing and into the jungle.

"It's over," I said. I might have been telling her the hour. "There must have been just two of them. They wouldn't have felt it necessary to send more."

"He was one of the ones who joined the caravan," Sally remarked. "I recognized him. He was one of the ones talking to Ahmed night before last. I—I feel so strange."

"It's over, Sally."

"I wanted to scream, and I couldn't. I couldn't move."

Neither of us said anything else for a while. I could feel that curious numbness disappearing. My skin felt prickly, stinging slightly, and I could feel the blood circulating in my veins. I felt light-headed now, almost dizzy, and I wanted to laugh. For some reason I wanted to burst into gales of laughter, but I didn't. I sobbed, just once, a dry, painful sound that seemed to hurt my throat. Hysteria was so close, but I held it off, steadying myself, forcing back the waves of sensation threatening to sweep over me.

Sally let go of my hand. She had been clutching it all this while. I flexed my sore fingers, watching as she stepped across the clearing to the spot where the Thug had been standing. She reached down and picked the

60

yellow rumal off the ground, casually examining it.

"How—how can you bear to touch it?"

"It's evidence," she said calmly. "When we get to Dahlkari, they're going to want to know everything that happened, every last detail, and this yellow scarf is evidence."

She folded the hideous cloth and thrust it into her skirt pocket. Then she sighed and pushed a wave of tarnished gold hair from her cheek.

"I suppose we might as well try to get some sleep now," she told me. "Our friend probably won't be back for some time. It'll take him a while to dispose of the bodies. Tomorrow's going to be a long day. We'll need all our strength."

I would never have thought it possible, but sleep I did, sinking into unconsciousness almost as soon as I stretched out on the ground with the blanket wrapped around me. I awoke once, startled, and I saw the native step into the clearing and move over to where he had been sleeping earlier. I shivered, cold, pulling the blanket closer about me, and when I awoke again the rays of brilliant sunlight streamed through the trees and the magnificent black stallion stood in the clearing and Sally was helping the native pack the saddlebags.

"You're awake," she called brightly. "It's a perfectly gorgeous day, Miss Lauren. Look at that sunlight!"

I sat up, groggy, shielding my eyes. "What time is it?"

"Late," she retorted. "Do get up, sleepyhead. We must get an early start, you know. If we move right along and don't poke, we should reach Dahlkari late this afternoon. I can hardly wait. If you want to know the truth, I've had about *enough* of this. I'm ready for a change of scene!"

61

Four

The native stopped and motioned for us to dismount. I was vastly relieved, for we hadn't stopped to rest all afternoon, had, in fact, stopped only one time all day long, to eat some stringy dried beef he had pulled out of the saddlebags. Although the sun hadn't begun to go down yet, it must have been very late in the afternoon, I reasoned, stretching my limbs, glad to be off the horse at last. We had left the desert behind some time ago, burning sand giving way to rocky soil sparsely covered with grass, rocky soil eventually turning into a greener, richer area with trees and small hills scattered with wildflowers.

"My bottom will *never* be the same," Sally complained. "I don't care if I never see a horse again as long as I live."

"I wonder where we are?" I said.

"I don't know, but at least we're out of that dreadful area of desert and jungle. Dahlkari can't be far."

"Dahlkari," the native said, pointing toward a wide pathway directly in front of us. It wound over a gradually sloping hill wooded with frangipani trees abloom with waxy rose-pink flowers. "You go," he added in that deep, guttural voice.

"Dahlkari must be somewhere on the other side of the hill," I remarked to Sally. "He seems to want us to go on ahead."

"Dahlkari," he repeated. "You go."

Then, abruptly, he swung himself up into the saddle, his loose robe billowing.

"But," I protested, "your reward—English soldier McAllister, many rupees. You must come with us. You can't just—"

The native shook his head, his harsh face expressionless. Brushing a spray of raven locks from his forehead, he clicked the reins and rode away toward the north, leaving Sally and I both dumbfounded. We watched the sleek, powerful black horse galloping away, and then horse and rider disappeared in the distance, and we looked at each other in dismay.

"I—I don't understand it," I said. "Reggie would have given him a very generous reward. He must have known that. Why would he just—ride away like that?"

"I have a good idea," Sally replied.

"There's no logical explanation. He brought us this far, then just—"

"He probably wouldn't dare show his face at the English garrison, Miss Lauren. The man's undoubtedly a rogue, if not an out and out criminal. He's probably *wanted*. The way he killed that man last night—he did it so coldly, so professionally, as though he'd had plenty of practice. The English would probably clap him in irons the minute they saw him."

"Then why did he rescue us? Why did he protect us? He didn't have to bring us here. He could have just—"

"Who knows?" Sally said philosophically. "Let's just thank our lucky stars he *did*. We'll never see the man again, and it's just as well. He was *spoo*ky, downright spooky."

I shook my head, bewildered. Sally patted her hair.

"We'd best start walking, Miss Lauren. Dahlkari

might be further off than we think. There's not too much daylight left."

We followed the pathway over the hill, trees close on either side, and an hour later we were still walking. Flat expanses covered with light jade grass alternated with lightly wooded areas, the sky a pale blue-gray overhead. There was no sign of the village. I was thirsty again and incredibly weary, my whole body sore and aching, but still I walked, wondering if this ordeal was ever going to end. Sally was just as exhausted as I, her vivacity sadly dampened. Another half hour or so passed, the light beginning to fade, and then Sally suddenly grabbed my arm, her brown eyes wide with excitement.

"Soldiers!" she exclaimed.

"Wh-what? Where?"

"Over there, riding across that slope. Look at the uniforms! They're British, Miss Lauren. Glory be, they're British!"

Sally began to shout and wave her arms like someone demented, and the band of riders changed their course and came riding toward us, pulling up a few feet away. There were six of them, the blond lieutenant on his large white horse obviously in charge. He was excessively handsome, extraordinarily impressive, undeniably British with those deep blue eyes.

Sally and I began talking at once, almost hysterically, and the lieutenant raised his arm, silencing us, then, stern, severe, a professional soldier, ordered two of his men to dismount. He dismounted himself, and I saw that he must have been at least six feet two, a radiant creature in his dark, polished boots, clinging white doeskin breeches and the tailored scarlet jacket with swinging gold epaulettes. He introduced himself as

Lieutenant Michael Stephens and said he was at our service.

"We're on our way to Dahlkari," I told him. "We were with a caravan. It was attacked by Thugs. We—we were the only survivors. I'm Lauren Gray, and Lieutenant Colonel McAllister is my guardian and—"

"You can explain later. I'm sure you want to see your guardian as soon as possible."

"You—you're with the garrison, then?"

"Indeed I am. I'm your guardian's aide."

"Thank God," I said. "You have no idea what we've—"

"Later," he said gently.

Then he took my hand and helped me mount one of the horses, his sergeant performing a similar service for Sally. Lieutenant Stephens swung back into the saddle with graceful ease and, turning to the two men whose horses we had taken, told them they could walk back to the garrison. In a matter of moments we were riding east at a comfortable gallop, the lieutenant and his sergeant in the lead, Sally and I directly behind them, the other two men bringing up the rear. I was dazed now, and I felt weaker and more vulnerable than I had felt since the ordeal began, perhaps because it had come to an end and I could at last let down my guard.

The sun had started to go down now, and a faint haze had settled over everything as though the air itself had been stained with a soft violet-blue, long purple-black shadows spreading ahead of us as we rode, passing more fields, more wooded sections. The haze had thickened considerably by the time we reached the village, and it was clothed in shadow, lamps making warm golden squares. It was larger than I had imagined it to be, more small town than village and, because of the proximity of the British, far more prosperous than most. A river ran sluggishly alongside the village, and as we reached the outskirts I saw women with pitchers moving langourously toward it. There were water buffalo as well.

Beyond the village, the ground began to rise in a gradual slope, and there, dominating the hillside, stood the English garrison, larger even than the village with tall, shady trees and large white houses washed with pale blue shadows, their windows ablaze with dark orange reflections as the last sun rays faded in the west. The barracks and military buildings were white, too, and as we drew nearer I could see the parade ground and the polo field. I heard hearty male laughter and the sound of children playing and, as we reached the top of the slope, India seemed to recede. We were in England again with English sights, English sounds. When I saw the Union Jack waving proudly atop a tall silver pole in the center of the main green, I thought it was the most beautiful thing I had ever seen.

Lieutenant Stephens helped us dismount. Men came to lead our horses away, and the lieutenant led us on foot past barracks, past club house and mess hall toward the green. I was amazed at the flowers. They seemed to bloom everywhere—daisies and peonies and chrysanthemums and every variety of rose growing alongside more exotic, less familiar blooms. The green had plush, beautifully manicured grass, impressive houses facing it on all four sides. Each house had its own private gardens, flagstone paths leading up to the front doors, and the immense trees with their spreading boughs created an atmosphere of snug intimacy. There were powerful oaks and enormous gray banyan trees with thick, twisted roots exposed, teaks and tamarind and mangroves, too. The commanding officer's house was, naturally, the most impressive of the lot, large and rambling, two stories high, surrounded by long, cool-looking verandas. The grounds were spacious, shaded by over a dozen trees, rather untidy gardens on either side and in back. It was all so homey and comfortable and English that I could hardly hold back my tears as Lieutenant Stephens ushered us up the front steps.

An Indian houseboy led us into a foyer with dark varnished paneling and shabby Oriental carpets. Lamps shed warm golden blossoms of light, and a staircase with faded rose carpeting curled up to the second storey. I caught a glimpse of myself in the large mirror with an ornate frame, but I was too exhausted to care how I looked. The lieutenant spoke to the houseboy in a quiet voice. The houseboy nodded several times and peered at Sally and me with alarmed curiosity and then led the three of us down a hall to a huge, airy office with enormous windows facing the back and side gardens. There was far too much furniture, the furniture too heavy, and the place was literally awash with books and papers, military maps and prints covering all available wall space. The room smelled of leather and dust and tobacco, and there were several lamps with green glass shades, one of them on the gigantic desk with a littered top at which Lieutenant Colonel Reginald McAllister sat, poring over a heavy ledger and looking highly disgruntled as we entered the room.

He didn't bother to look up, didn't look up, in fact, until Lieutenant Stephens stepped over in front of the desk, stamped his boots in military fashion and presented a brisk salute.

"Stephens? What's this? What is it now? More

drunken behavior in the barracks? Another brawl? I'm busy, man, busy! Be quick about it! Can't you see I have things to do? Are the natives starting to uprise? Just give me the essential details. I've—" He cut himself short, seeing Sally and me standing behind the lieutenant. "I say, it can't be. Lauren? *Lauren?* But we're not expecting you for several days, girl! Dollie will have conniptions, that's what she'll do. She's been making such preparations, has talked of nothing else—"

He stood, tall and lean and incredibly well preserved for a man of his years. His short-clipped brown hair was beginning to gray, as was his neatly trimmed mustache, and with his piercing gray eyes, sharp nose and tan, weathered complexion he did indeed look formidable, particularly when he took up his monocle and screwed it into his left eye. Fierce and rugged, he had a stare that would make subalterns tremble in their boots, and he had the deep, thundering voice to go with it. Few suspected that beneath that querulous, snappish façade hid a kindhearted soul as tender and sentimental as they came. Reggie loved to bluster, but it didn't fool anyone who knew him well.

Hands on hips, Sally stared at him, not certain yet just how to take him.

"What's the *mean*ing of this!" he bellowed. "Explain yourself, girl! Explain yourself at once! And what on earth happened to your clothes? You always were a rowdy tomboy, running around, getting in the way, getting into scrapes, but you're a grown woman now! You look like you've been climbing *trees* again. How old are you? Eighteen? Nineteen? And who's this cheeky hoyden you've got with you?"

Sally bristled. She shot him a venomous look. Reggie leaned over the desk to get a closer look at her.

"What's your name, girl!"

"Sally," she spat, "and I'm not afraid of you!"

"You're not, eh?"

"Not at all, you—you bully! How dare you talk to Miss Lauren like that! You're a thick-skulled, insensitive oaf, and—"

Reggie grinned, taking to her immediately. "Spirit!" he cried. "I do love a lass with spirit. Can't stand these mealymouthed maidens always jumping at their own shadows and havin' the vapors."

"There's been a spot of trouble, sir," Lieutenant Stephens said quietly. "It seems the young ladies were traveling with a native caravan and it was attacked by Thugs. Everyone else was slaughtered."

"What? What's this? You were supposed to travel with Lieutenant Parks. It was all arranged. I sent him and his men to Delhi especially to meet you, and you were traveling with a band of *natives*?"

"Lieutenant Parks got the measles," I said calmly. "It would have been several days before we could leave and I wanted to get here as soon as possible. Yasmin Singh was leaving with his caravan, so—"

"Measles? Measles did you say? He's almost *thirty*! And he let you leave like that? He didn't try to stop you? I'll have his hide, that's what I'll do!"

"Everyone in Delhi tried to stop us," I replied, and my voice had begun to tremble now. "I—I was so impatient and Yasmin Singh agreed to let us accompany him and—and—"

I couldn't go on. The tears came in spite of all my efforts to hold them back. Reggie looked horrified, then embarrassed, and then he hurried around the desk and folded me into his arms.

"There now," he crooned, "there. Don't you cry,

darlin'. You've been through a terrible ordeal, but it's over now. Everything's all right. Buck up now, you hear? Do. Here, take this handkerchief."

"Bully!" Sally hissed.

I dabbed at my eyes, humiliated to have given way like that, particularly in front of a stranger. The tall, handsome lieutenant looked awkward and embarrassed, clearly at a loss. Reggie released me and gave Sally a thunderous look and told her she'd better show some respect. Sally gazed at him haughtily, not deigning to reply.

"Well now," Reggie said, moving back behind his desk.

"I suspect we'd better get all the details, sir," Lieutenant Stephens said. "We'll want to send some men—"

"Think I don't know my job, Stephens! I was putting down rebellious natives while you were still spitting out your baby food! These Thugs are a bothersome lot, but we'll soon see the last of 'em! Damn that Gordon! I wonder where *he* was? Uppity young ruffian! Imagine them sending him to Dahlkari, putting *him* in charge of rounding up the Thugs. Lot of good he's done, I must say. Fellow's never even *around!*"

"I believe he's on another of his secret missions, sir," Lieutenant Stephens said. "He left a week or so ago."

"I don't like it. I don't like it at all! Fellow's sent here with a set of official papers giving him complete authority—he doesn't have to take orders from anyone, but he can give 'em to *every*one. The papers don't even give the bounder's *rank*."

I wondered who this mysterious Gordon might be. Just thinking about him was plainly causing Reggie to work himself into another rage. Lieutenant Stephen

70

cleared his throat and drew himself up, looking very official and grave.

"The young ladies are exhausted, sir. Perhaps if you intend to question them—"

Reggie glared at his aide with flashing eyes, his leathery cheeks beginning to flush. Lieutenant Stephens was utterly unperturbed in the face of his superior's obvious wrath. Stephens, I suspected, knew exactly how to handle him. After a moment Reggie gave a deep sigh and shook his head, a martyr, terribly misused and put-upon.

"Perhaps you'd better tell me all about it, Lauren," he said quietly. "We'll want to get after those villains as soon as possible. Just relax and start at the beginning."

I tried to give him a calm, detailed account of all that had happened, but Sally kept interrupting with highly dramatic, colorful embellishments. Both Reggie and the lieutenant looked alarmed when we told them about the native who had come to our rescue, asking for a full description, asking why he hadn't brought us on in to Dahlkari. It was clear they both considered him almost as menacing as the Thugs. Lieutenant Stephens took careful notes on everything we told them, and when we were finished he asked me to draw a map of the campsite where the attack had taken place. I had hardly begun when the door burst open and Dollie flew into the room, plump cheeks flushed, black ringlets bobbing.

"Reggie McAllister!" she cried. "How *dare* you not inform me that the girls had arrived! I don't believe it! I happened to pass Kulloo in the hall upstairs and happened, just happened to ask him if someone had *come*. I said I thought I'd heard someone come in and he said, yes, Missy, the tall lieutenant and two English girls. Two *English* girls! And you've kept them in this office all this time and—"

"Steady, luv," he said patiently. "No need to get in an uproar."

"Don't you try to humor me! It's inexcusable. Inex*cus*able! Lauren, oh, you dear child, at last—and this is Sally, isn't it? We weren't expecting you for—" Noticing our tattered condition for the first time, she gasped, taking a step backward, hand clutched dramatically to her breast. "My word! What's happened? You both look like you've been in a brawl!"

"We were attacked by Thugs," Sally said calmly.

"Thugs!"

"They wiped out the whole caravan. Miss Lauren and I were the only two survivors, and we probably would have died of thirst if this fierce-looking native hadn't come along and—"

Dollie listened with horrified fascination as Sally gave her a rousing account of our ordeal, and when she had finished Dollie patted her girlish black ringlets and frowned and said it was horrible, just horrible, much too horrible to dwell on. She gave both of us a hug and said we were wonderfully brave, genuine heroines, and it must have been dreadful, dreadful, but we were here now and now we must forget it all and have larks and laughter and captivate every man in sight.

"You will, too," she promised. "I have such *plans*. Do you realize there are over two hundred bachelors at the garrison? And not a single unmarried girl around— oh dear, I forgot Prunella Dobson. I'm *al*ways forgetting Prunella. She's Captain Dobson's girl—thin as a maypole and just as stiff. Prays a lot, poor thing. Wears spectacles. You two girls are going to start a *riot*."

Dollie was just as I remembered her, small, plump, fussy, wearing an outlandish pink taffeta dress festooned with ruffles and much too young for her. With her preposterous black ringlets, her bright brown eyes and pouting cherry-red lips, she looked like a rotund, animated doll, a flighty creature no one would dream of taking seriously. Aflutter with gaiety and gossip, she seemed to breeze through life on wings of frivolity, but I knew full well that her frivolity concealed a deep reservoir of strength and wisdom. It was Dollie who was responsible for her husband's success, Dollie who kept her head during any kind of crisis and calmly took over while others panicked. A veteran of over thirty years of rugged military life under primitive and frequently dangerous conditions, she had seen her share of crises and had come through them all with merriment undiminished.

"You're both about to drop, poor dears. Interrogating them like that! Have you no sense of decency? Sometimes I wonder about you, Reggie, and you, too, Michael Stephens! Food, that's what you need. Hot food, and hot *baths*, too, as soon as possible. You men go ahead and file your reports and round up your suspects or do whatever you *do*. We're going upstairs now. High time, too!"

"There are—uh—one or two more questions—" Reggie began, but his wife rounded on him like a hen whose chicks have been threatened.

"Not another word from you, Reggie McAllister! The very idea of treating these poor girls this way. I'll have something more to say about that later on, Sir, you can count on it! Come, girls. Your trunks arrived days ago. Everything's all unpacked, your rooms prepared. Thank goodness for *that*. I must say, Lauren, you brought enough books! I do hope, dear, you don't plan to *read* them. A girl your age? All those deep, dreary things? It can't be healthy. I never *was* happy about sending you off to that wretched school...."

It was after one o'clock in the afternoon when the timid young Indian girl tapped on my door and came in with a tray. The comfortable, undeniably English room was a nest of blue-gray shadows, heavy furniture barely visible, large mirror a murky silver blur, and then the girl opened the shutters and dazzling silvery-yellow rays streamed in, gleaming on dark mahogany, making pools on the worn gray carpet with its pink and blue patterns. I sat up and rubbed my eyes. Dark, lovely, extremely shy, the girl smiled and indicated the tray she had placed on the bedside table, and then she slipped quietly out of the room, her apricot silk sari rustling softly.

I could hear a bird warbling throatily in the back garden and, in the distance, the sound of soldiers drilling. I yawned and stretched, feeling gloriously young and healthy and strong. It was like awakening after a bad dream, everything that had happened receding into a dream haze, barely recalled. I ate the breakfast, and it was delicious, and I performed my ablutions and sat at the dressing table brushing my long chestnut hair until it gleamed. What luxury to linger before the mirror, studying my reflection, noting the faint pink flush on my cheekbones, the lazy contentment in my blue eyes, and what luxury to open the door of the enormous mahogany wardrobe and find all the dresses I had purchased in Bath, to select one at leisure, a beige muslin with narrow bronze stripes, soft cloth clinging snugly to bosom and waist, full skirt billowing over ruffled petticoats. The square-cut neckline was modestly low, the puffed sleeves just off the shoulder.

In the mirror I saw a very attractive young girl in a very becoming frock, her long hair gleaming, a pensive smile on her soft pink lips, utterly unlike the tattered, begrimed creature who had arrived at the garrison the night before. I thought about the handsome blond lieutenant, and I was glad I was attractive, pleased that the frock was so becoming. Would I see him today? I felt a curious glow, a mild elation, and I realized it was anticipation.

Anticipation? What could it possibly matter whether I saw him or not? I had hardly noticed him last night. Well, yes, I had, too. I had noticed that cleft chin, that full, mobile mouth, the Roman nose and wide cheekbones and those deep blue eyes, dark brown brows arching above them. I had noticed the heavy wave of dark blond hair that kept spilling over his forehead. Tall, terribly tall, with the lean, muscular physique of an athlete, he was almost indecently good-looking and so very stern and impressive in his uniform. The girls back at school would have carried on like a flock of silly geese, tittering and pretending to swoon, but I was much too sensible. I wasn't at all interested, I told myself, and I promptly and forcibly put Lieutenant Michael Stephens out of my mind, irritated at myself for having thought about him in the first place.

The large rambling house was silent as I went downstairs. I wondered where Sally was. Her room had been empty when I had looked in. Reggie would be at his office at regimental headquarters, of course, but surely Dollie hadn't left the house. I heard no merry chatter, no tinkling laughter. I wandered through the friendly, cluttered rooms downstairs: heavy plush sofas and marble-topped tables, brass andirons and lace doilies and potted ferns. Cool, shadowy, mote-filled rays of sunlight stealing through the louvers of the closed shutters, it might have been a comfortable middle-class dwelling in the English suburbs, only an occasional Oriental ornament to indicate we were in India.

I met Kulloo, the houseboy-butler, in the front hall. Wearing a turban, a tailored yellow jacket and loose white trousers, he nodded gravely and, when I inquired about Dollie, informed me that she was in the back garden. He pointed to the door at the far end of the hall and then slipped quietly into the drawing room. As I reached the back of the house I could hear a noisy clatter from the kitchen and smell delicious, spicy smells as something cooked. A large, overweight Indian woman with steel gray hair and a belligerent expression opened the door to peer out at me, her blue cotton smock dusted with flour, a butcher knife clutched in her hand. For a moment I thought she was going to attack me with the knife, so fierce was her expression, but she merely jabbered something in her native dialect and then slammed the door with vicious force. All native servants obviously weren't calm and inscrutable, I reflected, smiling to myself as I stepped out onto the rear veranda.

The back lawn was spread with moving patterns of sunlight and shadow as the sun streamed through the leafy shade trees. The flower beds were decidedly untidy, tall purple hollyhocks vying with pink daisies and blue larkspurs. Several gigantic gray banyan trees grew at the foot of the property, their exposed roots like arthritic fingers. In wide-brimmed yellow straw hat, soiled white gloves and a lilac-colored dress adorned with purple frills, Dollie was on her knees, clipping at the grass edging one of the flowerbeds. Spying a seed, she gave a little cry, uprooted it violently and tossed it over her shoulder. I moved down the steps and, seeing me, she waved gaily and climbed to her feet.

"There you are!" she called, brushing at her skirt. "I was afraid you'd sleep all day, so I sent Blossom in with a tray. Sleep well? I must say you *look* it—you're a picture of blooming health, dear, and so well dev*el*oped! Oh, for a figure like that again, not that I ever *had* one." Dollie's conversation was invariably scattered with excursions, scraps of light chatter sprinkled with apparently unrelated observations, "Of course it didn't really matter," she continued. "I had *flair*, and that's so much more important."

"You still have it, Dollie," I assured her.

"Oh, dear, do you really think so? I worry, you see. Being the wife of the commanding officer is *such* a responsibility, and I'm afraid I'm not *serious* enough. I should be haughty and imperious and make everyone kowtow to me—that's the way it's *done*, you see—but I'd much rather gossip and have a good time."

"I'm sure everyone adores you."

"They think I'm a foolish, flighty creature without an ounce of sense, but I must say I keep things *or*ganized. Social life is always in danger of deterioration out here—it's not easy being so far away from home, even in a comfortable garrison like this. A number of the army wives tend to lose their perspective—it's hard on their nerves, you see,

77

particularly the younger ones. Some of them fall apart, have to be shipped home. Some of them take to drink, and some—well, some amuse themselves with men who are not their husbands. I could tell you *tales*, dear. Such a responsibility," she repeated. "I try to keep things jolly, keep the petty feuds and rivalries at a minimum. One must try to be a credit to Queen and Country."

Dollie peeled off the soiled gloves and removed her straw hat, reaching up to pat the foolish ringlets that framed either side of her face. She led me over to a white table under the shade of one of the trees, matching chairs around it. "Let's sit and chat for a while, dear. I told Blossom to bring out some iced lemonade—oh, here she comes!"

Dollie plopped down in one of the chairs, and I sat facing her. The timid Indian girl in the apricot sari moved gracefully across the grass bearing a silver tray with two glasses and a frosted pitcher of lemonade, ice tinkling. She set the tray down, made a lovely half bow and moved back toward the veranda with the poise of a young fawn.

"She's a treasure," Dollie confided. "Just fourteen years old, a local girl. Her brothers and sisters come to help out when we have parties. Charming children, efficient, too."

"Speaking of servants, I think I somehow upset your cook. She glared at me as I came out."

"Olana? That woman! She's a gem, a real gem, but so temperamental! You'd think she ran the entire household. She's put out because there are two more people to cook for. She'll calm down. Been with us for years, ever since Bombay. So has Kulloo. He's not temperamental, but I fear he's a dreadful snot, *very* conscious of Reggie's position. Here, let me pour this lemonade. You have no idea how difficult it is to get *ice*."

"I wonder where Sally is," I remarked. "I looked into her room before I came down, but she wasn't there."

"*That* one!" Dollie exclaimed. "She was up bright and early, bustling about like a young colt! Chattered all through breakfast—ate enough for three people. I've never seen Reggie take to anyone so quickly. Teased her dreadfully, and she came right back—such cheek! She said she was interested in meeting some of the *men*, and I'll be bound if Reggie didn't take her off to headquarters with him."

"That's Sally," I said.

"I'm sure I don't know what to *make* of her, Lauren. I've rarely encountered a lass more engaging, but this interest in *men*." Dollie shook her head, her large brown eyes bewildered. "Of course, there are plenty of them *about*."

"Sally came along as my maid, Dollie, but—actually she's more friend than maid. I—I couldn't have done without her."

"I understand perfectly, dear, and she'll be treated as an equal in *this* household, never you fear. I rather imagine, though, we'll have to find her a husband rather *quickly*."

"I don't fancy she'll need much help. If I know Sally she already has half a dozen swains trailing after her, eating out of her hand."

Dollie looked rather alarmed, and then she smiled, obviously delighted by the girl but feeling she must show at least a token disapproval. Taking a sip of lemonade, she set her glass down and sighed. "If you only knew how lovely it is to have you girls here. It's going to be such fun! Things have been dull, dull, dull of late what with all these futile expeditions against the Thugs."

Dollie looked up at me, alarmed, afraid she'd said something wrong. I gave her a reassuring smile and reached across to squeeze her hand.

"It happened," I said. "There's no use trying to pretend it didn't. We—we survived, and it's over now. I—I'll never be able to forget the things I saw, but—I'm made of pretty strong stuff, Dollie. I'm not one of your wilting Victorian maidens. You needn't be afraid to mention Thugs around me. I imagine I shall be hearing quite a lot about them."

"You're a brave, brave girl."

"I'm sensible," I said quietly. "Swooning and having hysterics aren't going to erase anything that happened. I—I'm not unfeeling, please don't think that. I just know I have to—to go on in spite of it."

"Of course you do, dear. These dreadful Thugs—" Dollie stared across the garden, not really seeing it, her bright red mouth a tight line. She finally turned back to me with serious brown eyes.

"This is their last stronghold, you see. The secret society of Thuggee was thriving all over India. It's been pretty well broken up everywhere else—Captain Sleeman and his men have done such a tremendous job of bringing those awful assassins to justice—but it's still thriving in this area. No one's been able to break their cover. Someone very powerful is behind them— some say it might even be a white man who's in league with them and helping to provide cover for a share of the spoils. Poor Reggie has done all he could, but he's had no luck. That's why they sent that terrible Robert Gordon out here."

"Gordon? I think Reggie mentioned him last night."

Dollie puffed up like an angry robin, eyes snapping.

"That man's a thorn in all our sides!" she exclaimed. "So arrogant and aloof, so independent! He's on Sleeman's staff, and he's sent out here with special papers giving him full authority to handle the Thuggee situation. He doesn't have to take orders from anyone, is free to do exactly as he pleases! He disappears for long periods of time, Gordon does, and heaven only knows what he's up to while he's away. Secret missions, 'undercover work,' he calls it. He doesn't confide in anyone, not even *Reggie*. It's scandalous!"

"It does seem a bit unusual," I agreed.

"He has rooms here at the barracks, naturally, rooms filled with books and papers and outrageous native statues and a whole jumble of bizarre objects. When he's not skulking around the countryside in disguise he's making secret reports to Sleeman and telling him God knows what about us all!" Dolly paused, visibly fuming. "I never could abide spies!"

"Sleeman must have a great deal of confidence in him."

"Oh, Gordon's *brilliant*, I'll have to hand him that. He speaks over ten languages and any number of dialects. The man's not yet thirty, and he's already had a number of books published—quite shocking anthropological studies about native tribes and some of their—well, more un*civ*ilized practices. He's done translations, too." Dollie lowered her voice. "Ancient marriage manuals," she said, "and even worse—the kind of books no Godfearing Englishman would allow in his home."

"How very unusual," I remarked.

"He simply doesn't Fit In," she continued, verbally

81

capitalizing the last two words. "I suppose you'd have to say the man is fascinating—I've never encountered anyone quite like him—but, all the same, he gives me the shivers. That savage face, those *eyes*. Some women find that sort of thing attractive, of course. A number of the younger wives tried to shine up to him when he first arrived. Gordon wouldn't give them the time of day and didn't even try to hide how boring he found them. He doesn't have time for *women*, I can tell you that much!"

Despite Dollie's vehement tirade against him, I thought Robert Gordon sounded like a rather romantic figure—unconventional, independent, going his own way against established patterns. A bit bizarre, perhaps, but his own man. Dollie was obviously rankled because Gordon had supplanted some of Reggie's authority, and it was only natural she should resent him. I finished my lemonade and tinkled the ice idly against the side of the glass, wondering about the enigmatic Mr. Gordon. What sort of man would translate erotic Oriental classics and write studies of native tribes, disdain the attention of English ladies and disappear for long periods at a time on secret military missions? Certainly not the sort who would fit into the stuffy, ultraconventional English military establishment.

A myna bird cried out suddenly, and a flock of tiny green parakeets scattered in the air and settled in the boughs of one of the banyan trees. It was so serene here, so peaceful with the untidy flowerbeds filled with carefully nourished English flowers, the large, sprawling house with its cool, shadowy verandah so very reassuring. Time seemed to melt away, and I saw another garden as cozy as this, another large house, this one with a screened-in porch, and I saw a little girl in black pumps and white silk stockings and a starched pink dress, her long brown curls bouncing as she played on the lawn under the supervision of her ayah, a serene native woman in blue and silver sari. A beautiful, vivacious woman in lilac stepped outside, followed by a tall, stalwart man in full uniform. The little girl raced over to them, laughing merrily, her arms raised, and the man scooped her up into his arms and held her tightly and the woman put her arms around them both, and for a moment the three of them were entwined, the child safe and secure between two beloved bodies. The image seemed to melt away, the colors blurring, and I saw the same little girl at twelve, wide-eyed, face pale and tearstained, both those beautiful, vital loved ones gone, taken from her by the dreaded cholera.

"I know, dear," Dollie said.

"I—I'm sorry. I was..."

"I know. You were thinking about your parents. I could tell. It still hurts, doesn't it, dear? After all these years...."

"I think of them often. Being back here like this—" I paused. "It seems to bring them closer."

"It's what your parents would have wanted," Dollie said quietly. "They would have wanted you to be with your Own Kind in the country they loved so well. You'll meet some fine upstanding English officer here in India and do your part for the empire, just as they expected."

"I don't know about that part. I'm really not interested in—"

"But of course you are!" Dollie protested. "You're young and you're female and you've come to a veritable treasure trove of eligible men. It's going to be ever so exciting! All those dreary years at school surrounded by books and chalk dust and ink-stained desks are behind you, and now it's time to enjoy yourself. How I envy you! I'm ever so eager to get *started*. We're going to have a dance at the mess hall, I've already arranged it, and the rajah is going to have a party in your honor and—"

Dollie chattered merrily, telling me about all the plans she had made to launch me, and I listened with a half smile, trying to feel some of her enthusiasm. I know myself, and I knew I could never be the bright, carefree social butterfly playing one man against the other as I searched for just the right husband, but, for Dollie's sake, I would try to enjoy all the parties and fêtes she had been anticipating ever since I had agreed to come to Dahlkari. She and the other army wives needed them far more than I did. I fully realized that.

"And speaking of *men*," she continued brightly, "Michael came by to inquire about you this morning. You were asleep, of course, but I told him you were eager to thank him for all he had done."

"Michael? You mean Lieutenant Stephens?"

"He was disappointed at not being able to see you. He was getting ready to leave, you see, taking a group of men to try and track down those horrible Thugs who attacked your caravan. Reggie wanted to send another officer, but Michael made a special request to go himself."

"He seems—very efficient."

"Oh, he's *that*, all right. A superb officer, one of the best. He's quite the prize catch of the garrison, you know. Michael's a bit formal, a bit too reserved, but don't let that fool you. Some of the discontented wives ave literally *thrown* themselves at him, shamelessly, nd Michael—well, he's a man, and when women...." he hesitated.

"I think I know what you're trying to say," I said ryly.

"Take Valerie Simpson, for example—she and her usband came to Dahlkari three months ago, and she's een making a spectacle of herself over Michael since hey arrived. Strikingly attractive woman, exceedingly eurotic—her husband's a sergeant-major, dull as itch water. Valerie took an overdose of laudanum nly two weeks ago. She claimed it was an *ac*cident, of ourse, but rumor has it Michael turned her out."

"I—I'm really not interested in Lieutenant Stephens, Dollie."

"No?" She arched a brow in disbelief. "Well, dear, e's certainly interested in *you*. I could tell by his nanner when he came by this morning. Quite :oncerned, he was, and quite disappointed you weren't ıp, even though he tried to hide it. Michael Stephens is he most handsome male I've ever seen, no doubt about t. And you're not interested? Well, dear, we'll just have :o wait and *see*...."

Five

The dress was undeniably becoming, but I wondered if it might not be just a bit too sophisticated for the occasion. Pale, creamy white satin, it had off-the-shoulder sleeves, a rather low-cut neckline and formfitting bodice, the full skirt cascading in gleaming folds over bouffant petticoats. It was the kind of gown a rather worldly countess might wear, I thought, admiring myself in the mirror, but was it suitable for a dance in the mess hall of a military outpost in India? I really didn't care, pleased that it made me look older. My hair was worn pulled severely back from my face with three long ringlets dangling in back, the cluster of tiny pink velvet roses fastened over my left temple my only ornament.

Dollie had gone on ahead to supervise things at the mess hall. Reggie was waiting for us downstairs, no doubt already highly impatient. I took a final look at myself: a bare suggestion of rouge on my high cheekbones, a hint of coral on my lips, lids faintly brushed with blue-gray shadow. I needed no mascara to heighten my long lashes and dark brows. I knew that I had never looked better in my life, and I knew that it couldn't have mattered less. The dance would be a tedious affair, overexuberant, everyone working doubly hard to convince themselves they could have a good time even if they were stuck out here in a remote outpost. The women would be overly vivacious, the men too hearty. The music would be too loud, and the liquor would flow much too freely.

The garrison was a tight, confined little world, inbred, clannish, a hotbed of jealousy and intrigue. I had discovered that during these past two weeks. Far, far away from England and certainly not a part of the country they occupied, the English here had nothing to fall back upon but themselves. It was easier for the men, for they had military matters to keep them occupied, but it was extremely hard on the women. Those without inner resources of their own found it a hard go. They thrived on gossip, on petty intrigues and rivalries, and none of them were in the least interested in India itself. They considered the natives rather simpleminded children who had to be disciplined with a firm hand—"They make wonderful servants, don't you know, but, really, they must be kept in their place!"

With the exception of occasional forays into the village to examine the exquisite silks and trinkets on display at the bazaars, they kept aloof and apart from anything un-English.

Dollie and I had paid calls and taken tea in cozy, over-furnished parlors, Sally rarely accompanying us, for she had her own interests. I had met most of the women on post, had smiled and pretended to be interested in their shallow gossip, had politely answered question after question about England, English theater, English fashions, and never once had one of them mentioned anything about India. We had gone to the polo matches, sitting on tiers of benches to watch English gentlemen in their white suits and pith helmets riding their horses, hitting their ball across the grassy field to shouts of "Well done!" and "Fine show!" and "Carry on, chap!" and beyond the field, below the slope, I could see the river and the native women with their pitchers and the water buffalo, and it had all seemed a kind of madness, for we were in the heart of India, yet we weren't, not really. These people lived in a world apart and India existed for them only as a source of constant irritation.

I found it difficult to understand their narrow-mindedness, their self-conscious superiority. My parents had loved India, had found it a place of infinite variety and fascination, as, indeed, did Dollie and Reggie, which was probably one of the reasons he had achieved his prominent position. As a child I had been taken on wonderfully exciting outings and expeditions to see temples and ruins, to watch native dances, to view Indian art, and I had absorbed all the rich flavor, all the exotic color and detail abounding on every side. These people on post were totally disdainful of the natives and their native culture, unconcerned with the dreadful poverty and suffering that was the daily lot of the majority. No, they were interested only in England and English ways and their roles as English citizens in a barbaric, uncivilized country.

Perhaps I was being too hard on them. Most of them had good intentions, and I knew there were any number of English men and women who were devoting their lives to alleviating the suffering around them and trying to help the natives with schools and hospitals and medicine. They were a small minority though, and none of them happened to be in Dahlkari.

We had been here for two weeks, and Dollie had been wonderful and warm and amusing, Reggie a delightful if somewhat grumpy host, but already I was bored and preferred to spend my time alone in my room with one of the books I had brought along. I could never fit into this kind of life. It had taken me only two weeks to discover that. In many ways the atmosphere here was even more stifling than that at school back in Bath. Dollie assured me I would buck up as soon as Lieutenant Stephens returned, convinced there was nothing wrong with me a bit of romance wouldn't cure. Lieutenant Stephens had returned this afternoon, Sally had informed me, and he would probably be at the dance. I was not the least bit interested, and that was certainly not the reason I had taken such care with my appearance tonight.

Sally came bursting into my room, breaking into my reverie. She wore her red dotted swiss, and with her tarnished gold curls all atumble and her brown eyes alight with excitement she looked like a fetching young hoyden, far too vital and aglow to be mistaken for a lady. Sally was a sore point with a number of women on post. They considered her an outrageous creature much too bold to be acceptable in proper society, but as she was a guest in Dollie's house none of them quite dared snub her openly. Sally found their attitude amusing and claimed she felt sorry for the "whole dull lot of 'em." It wasn't the women she was interested in, needless to say.

"You look smashing, Miss Lauren!" she exclaimed. "That dress—it's going to send a few eyebrows soaring, just you wait. How do *I* look? Do I look all right?"

"You look enchanting, Sally."

"Red's my color, I do believe. I'm ever so excited, Miss Lauren—" Sally had taken my place in front of the mirror and was adjusting the bodice of her dress, arranging it so that a fraction more bosom showed. "I intend to pay quite a lot of attention to that good-looking Sergeant Brown tonight, even if he *is* rather slow. That should show Bill Norman a thing or two."

"I thought you and Sergeant Norman were—"

"Bill Norman and I aren't *any*thing! Promised to take me to a café in the village, he did, and I was looking forward to it. He stood me up good and proper. I don't intend to take *that* kind of treatment from any man. No indeed."

"I understand he had guard duty that night."

"He could have switched out with someone easily enough," she retorted. "I expect he'll fume and fume. He and Sergeant Brown are great rivals, you know. Can't abide each other. There might even be a *fight*!"

Sally smiled her pixie smile, delighted with the idea. Poor Sergeant Norman was in for a tough time this evening, but I doubted he would take it lying down. The moment he had laid eyes on Sally he had marked her as his own, promptly and forcefully discouraging all rivals, and I suspected she had finally met her match. Good natured but stern, Norman was one of the few men she wasn't able to boss around, one of the few she wasn't able to treat in her customary cavalier manner. She candidly admitted that he was *the* most exciting man she had ever met, also the most infuriating.

"I suppose I'll *do*," she said. "If this dress doesn't do the trick nothing will."

"We'd better go on down now. Reggie will be champing at the bit."

"Probably so," she agreed. "He usually is. Such an old phony. He's not nearly as fierce as he pretends to be. Actually, he's quite a dear, even if he *does* tease all the time."

"He's very fond of you."

"We hit it off from the very first. I'm not *afraid* of him, you see, and he finds that refreshing."

Reggie was waiting in the front hall as we came downstairs. Lamps were glowing warmly, and there was a scent of beeswax and lemon. Wearing his full-dress uniform, our escort looked both impressive and formidable, his expression quite stern. Short-clipped brown hair fitting his skull like a cap, mustache freshly trimmed, he scowled, piercing gray eyes observing us as we moved down the final steps in a rustle of skirts. He deliberately took out his watch and scrutinized it.

"Now don't you dare scold," Sally warned. "It takes time to make ourselves beautiful, and you should feel honored to be escorting the two most glamorous creatures on post."

"Hump!" he snorted.

"I must say you look absolutely dashing in that uniform. It's s shame I'm so fond of Dollie. If I weren't, I just might *forget* myself, I admit it with no shame. I always did like a mature man."

"Go on!" Reggie said gruffly, but a smile played at the corners of his mouth and there was an undeniable twinkle in those severe gray eyes. "Saucy jade! Back in the old days you'd have been clapped in irons as a disturbing influence. Two of my best sergeants at each other's throats, half the men on post dreamy-eyed, unable to do their jobs properly."

"I can't help that," Sally said coyly. "At any rate, you're the lucky man tonight."

Reggie chuckled, unable to maintain his rigid façade. Kulloo came in with his sword and cape, and Reggie fastened the sword to the side of his sash, muttering that the thing was a damned nuisance. He swung the cape around his shoulders with a dramatic flourish and then stepped over to the hall table and picked up his tall, beplumed hat. These embellishments made him look even more impressive, and I could tell by the way he examined himself in the mirror that he was proud to cut such a splendid figure. Kulloo held the door open for us and we moved out onto the front veranda. I took one of Reggie's arms, Sally took the other, and the three of us went down the steps and started across the green.

It was a warm, lovely night, the deep gray sky frosted with stars, the green spread with velvety blue-black shadows and patches of misty moonlight that brushed the ground with silver. Lights glowed in windows of all the houses around the green, making soft golden squares against the dark. Insects hummed, and there was the smell of newly mowed grass. I could hear a group of children playing in one of the back lawns, supervised, no doubt, by one of the faithful ayahs. As we strolled across the green I remembered just such nights as this when my parents had gone to dances and I had been one of the children left behind. It seemed such a very long time ago. Remembering that exuberant little girl made me feel rather pensive.

"—fine fellow," Reggie was saying, "and I don't want you ruining him. Soldiers like Norman are rare indeed. One of the best men in the outfit, he is, rugged as they come, smart as a whip. Can't let a mere bit of skirt mess up a lad like that."

"Oh, I shan't hurt him," Sally promised.

"Good-looking rascal, too. Sober, levelheaded, or *was* until you came along. You behave yourself now, hear? I say, this damned sword is awkward. Never could abide 'em. All this fuss and bother! I'd much rather be home with my manuals."

"No you wouldn't," Sally teased. "You're really a show-off at heart, and just think of the impression you're going to make when you step in with two beautiful women. Your men will be *green* with envy."

Reggie chuckled again, delighted with Sally, delighted with himself. We had left the green now and were passing along rows of barracks. Through the opened windows I could see spartan bunks, a few desolate-looking men in undershirts polishing boots and shining brass. We passed a sentry. He gave Reggie a smart salute, and as we passed I saw him looking at Sally and me with a lonely, heartsick expression. He was extremely young, as were most of the enlisted men out here. I wondered if he had a girl back in England who wrote to him. Touched by that longing look in his eyes, I hoped so.

"You're awfully quiet tonight," Reggie said, squeezing my arm. "Looking forward to the dance?"

"I—I suppose so."

"You look lovely tonight. Did I tell you that earlier? Meant to, at any rate. Dollie and I are ever so proud to have you here, you know. You're like the daughter we never had."

"Thank you for saying that, Reggie."

"Oh, I bluster and boom a lot, but I have an occasional moment or two every now and then when I'm as human as the next chap. Not often, though. Can't afford it! Have to keep the whole show running smoothly. Mustn't let 'em catch me off guard."

"I'm sure you do a magnificent job."

"I don't know about that. It's been pretty sticky of late—"

Reggie cut himself short, and I could tell that he was

thinking about the Thuggee situation, too tactful to mention it under the circumstances. Shaded by tall trees, surrounded by neat gardens, the mess hall loomed up ahead, sounds of merry festivity pouring out into the night. Tall French windows opened onto the shadowy veranda, golden light streaming out, and through them I could see men in uniform and elegantly begowned women moving about. Selected members of the military band were tuning up their instruments, awaiting our arrival. The dance couldn't begin, of course, until the commanding officer arrived. As we stepped onto the veranda, I braced myself mentally for the ordeal ahead, determined to put on a good front for Dollie's sake.

Our entrance was undeniably spectacular. As soon as we stepped through the door someone yelled "Attention!" and all the men snapped to, all noise and activity ceased. All eyes were upon us. Reggie seemed to swell with pride, not merely because of his position but because he had an attractive young woman on either arm, one in red, one in creamy white. He nodded a bit grandly and said "As you were," then removed cape and hat and gave them to the young subaltern who rushed over to take charge of them. People began to talk and laugh and move about again, the frozen tableau melting into a kaleidoscope of color.

Dollie had done herself proud. The mess hall had been cleared, wooden floor polished to a high sheen, armchairs and small sofas and potted ferns situated around it. The rafters were hung with streamers of colored paper and balloons that bobbed in the breeze coming through the opened French windows. The band was half concealed by banks of fern at the far end of the room, and there was a "social area" at the other end, long, linen-covered tables laden with a lavish buffet, with crystal punch bowl abrim with ruby red punch afloat with orange slices, crystal cups surrounding it. There was a long bar as well, row upon row of bottles, turbaned native servants to wait upon the guests.

"At last!" Dollie cried, rushing over to us. "I was beginning to think you'd decided not to come! Lauren, dear, your gown is stunning. So simple, so stylish! Hello, Sally. Hmmm, that dress is certainly *red*, isn't it? Reggie, you have no idea how *frantic* I've been."

Dollie threw up her hands, flushed, excited, all abustle with energy and vitality. She wore a jade green silk dress festooned with rows of fine black lace, a spray of green and black plumes fastened to her hair. Her girlish ebony ringlets were already slightly frayed, her forehead slightly moist, but her vivacious brown eyes were all asparkle and there was a smile on her cherry red mouth as she took my hands and squeezed them. Impulsively, I gave her a hug.

"Everything looks marvelous," I told her. "You've done a fine job. It's all so festive."

"I've worked my fingers to the *bone*! I'm already exhausted, and the evening hasn't even begun. Do you really think it looks nice? The punch is rather flat, but it's just for teetotalers. There's a case of champagne on ice. Reggie, you'll start the dance with Lauren, of course. Oh, I see you're wearing your *sword*! I hope it won't interfere."

"I imagine I can manage," he said patiently.

"There're several people you haven't met yet, Lauren, but you can meet them later. I *hope* there's enough food. I had my heart set on pâté, but I had to settle on cheese spread. There're glazed hams and a side of beef and turkey and ever so many cakes. The liquor, now, there's plenty of that. I just hope—"

"It's all going to be fine," Reggie told her. "Lauren, my dear, shall we get this thing started."

He took my hand and led me toward the dance floor, people parting to make way for us. There was a moment of silence and then the music began and smoothly, with great dignity, Reggie slipped his arm around my waist and we began to dance, all alone on the vast polished floor. Streamers and balloons swayed overhead, and people stood all around in small groups watching us. The band was even worse than I had expected it to be, and I was exceedingly nervous, uncomfortable under all those stares, but Reggie was superb, ever so calm, ever so poised, an expert dancer. Sensing my nervousness, he looked into my eyes and gave me a jaunty little wink, his mustache twitching as he grinned. I smiled, and I relaxed, and soon other couples joined us and the dance floor was filled with dancers: men in polished black boots and tight white trousers and neat red jackets, gold braid asparkle, women in colored gowns with skirts that swung and swelled, billowing like petals in the breeze.

Reggie danced the second dance with Dollie, and I danced with a dark, talkative captain who held me too tightly and stumbled every now and then. I danced with a lieutenant with sandy hair and soulful eyes, with a sergeant who was as stiff and rigid as a marionette, with another lieutenant, this one sober and severe and silent. Though the band was deplorably bad, it was highly enthusiastic, and the music was loud and brassy. I smiled. I made polite comments. My feet began to hurt. I felt flushed. I felt as though I couldn't endure another waltz, another polka, but I did, and it was almost an hour before I finally begged off and, unescorted, went to fetch a glass of champagne.

Everyone was merry. Everyone was having a good time, determinedly so, as though it were their duty. They might be exiled in the wilds of a barbaric country, but they could still carry on in grand style. As I moved toward the tables I saw the pale, too tall Prunella Dobson talking with one of the matrons. Her gown was a severe gray, her spectacles gold-rimmed, her dull brown hair worn in a tight bun at the back of her head. Prunella disapproved of dancing. She disapproved of almost everything, I had discovered, and I felt rather sorry for her, giving her a warm smile when she happened to look up and see me. Taking a glass of champagne from the native servant, I moved over to stand near one of the windows. The cool night air breezing in was ever so welcome, and I prayed no one would ask me to dance, at least for a while.

I sipped the champagne, watching the dancers. With her tarnished gold curls flying, her vivid red skirt swirling, Sally was easy to spot, dancing a vigorous polka with a good-looking sergeant. He had lively blue eyes and short-clipped brown hair, and he was obviously enchanted with the bubbling vixen who danced so gaily, smiled so brightly. I didn't know who he was, but he definitely wasn't Sergeant Norman. Probably Sergeant Brown, I reasoned, the chap she planned to use to make Norman jealous. Sally was in her element, had been having a glorious time ever since we arrived, and I almost envied her. She and the sergeant swept around the floor, now visible, now hidden behind other couples, now bouncing into sight again. Both of them were totally immersed in the dance and in each other.

"Disgusting sight," Sergeant Norman said grumpily.

I turned, startled. Sergeant Bill Norman was standing beside me, resplendent in his uniform, his expression extremely stern. Tall and powerfully built on lean, muscular lines, he had strong, clean-cut features and dark, reddish-bronze hair that tended to be unruly. His eyes were a deep, intense blue, honest eyes that reflected his mood. Sergeant Norman wasn't really handsome in the traditional sense, but he was a healthy, virile specimen, and there was a certain boyish quality and a raffish charm I found most engaging. Good-natured and ordinarily easygoing, he looked quite put out at the moment with his lower lip thrust out, those blue eyes smoldering with anger. A lock of bronze hair had fallen across his forehead. He brushed it back impatiently.

"Hasn't danced with me once," he said, "not once. Been avoiding me all evening. She's danced with Jenkins, with Anderson, with Taylor, and she's danced with that scoundrel Brown five times. I counted. If she thinks I'm going to stand back and—" He shook his head, the last part of the sentence an inaudible mutter.

"You mustn't let it bother you," I said, smiling. "She's only teasing, you know."

"Oh, I'm onto her games. Tryin' to make me jealous, she is. I'm well aware of that. Thing is, Miss Lauren, I *am* jealous. I wanna grab that cocky Brown by the throat and squeeze till he croaks. I just might do it, too!"

He looked down at his large, capable hands. I could well imagine them performing the deed. Sergeant Norman muttered something else, and that errant bronze lock tumbled down on his forehead again, emphasizing the boyish quality I found so engaging.

He might be stern and stalwart, he might be fearless on the field, but he was quite vulnerable in matters of the heart. He sighed, exasperated.

"She wants a spanking, that one," he told me. "In all my twenty-seven years I've never encountered such an exasperating female, and I've known a few of 'em in my day, Miss Lauren, I may as well confess it. I thought I knew how to *handle* women, but this one—she wants a good, hard spanking. A man can take just so much."

Blue eyes grim now, he stared across the dance floor at Sally and his rival. The music stopped. Everyone applauded. Some of the couples left the floor, moving toward the tables. Sally and Sergeant Brown waited for the next set to begin, chatting pleasantly. Sally brushed a speck of lint from his jacket, letting her fingers rest against his arm for a moment, and he bent down to whisper something in her ear. She laughed, glancing over at Sergeant Norman and me. Sergeant Norman stiffened as she waved at us. The band swung into a lilting waltz, and Sally and her partner were off again. Sergeant Norman clenched his fists.

"The ladies like me," he said. "No need my pretendin' they don't. I reckon I don't need *her.* I say, uh, you wouldn't like to dance, would you, Miss Lauren?"

I hadn't the heart to refuse. I handed him my empty champagne glass. He set it down and led me onto the floor with a murderous look. He slung an arm around my waist and squeezed my hand tightly and propelled me into the midst of the dancers. Propelled is the only word. Sergeant Norman danced as other men might play Rugby football, and I might have been the football. It was most invigorating, to say the least. As we spun around the floor he kept looking over his shoulder, trying to locate Sally and Brown, and when the music stopped at last we were quite near the offending couple.

"Thank you, Miss Lauren," Norman said curtly.

"It was—my pleasure," I replied, breathless.

He gave me a terse nod and moved briskly over to Sally and Brown. She smiled at him, but Norman ignored her, turning to Brown and muttering something I couldn't hear. Brown drew himself up, his handsome face hardening, lively blue eyes suddenly dark and menacing. Sergeant Norman placed a hand on Brown's shoulder and gave him a forceful push. Brown stumbled backwards, almost falling, and before he could recover himself Norman had seized Sally's wrist and was marching briskly toward one of the French windows, Sally tottering along behind him. They disappeared onto the veranda, and after a moment Brown went after them with fists clenched, his face fierce and determined. A young lieutenant stepped up and asked me to dance. I smiled at him and nodded, rather amused by the little drama that had taken place, wishing I were able to see the sequel out in the gardens.

When the dance ended the lieutenant asked me if I would care to have a plate of food, and I said that would be lovely. He was a pleasant young man, and I enjoyed chatting with him as we ate. We had just finished when Dollie hurried over, looking flushed and elated. The lieutenant excused himself. Dollie took a glass of champagne and drank it thirstily. Her dress was rather crumpled, the plumes in her hair beginning to droop. She hadn't missed a single dance, and I could tell that she was enjoying herself immensely.

"It's a raging success," she confided. "*Everyone* says so! Even Reggie's enjoying himself, dancing with *all* the ladies, cutting quite a dashing figure. This is doing him *good*. He's been so tense lately. I'm going to have another glass of champagne—there! It's delicious. Will you just *look* at Prunella Dobson! That dress must have been her grandmother's. She hasn't danced once, has done nothing but drink that hideous punch and look disapproving. That girl's so *pious*!"

"She's probably very sweet once you get to know her."

"Sweet, my foot! She has the disposition of a lemon. I declare, look at Sergeant Brown. He's just stepped in from outside. I wonder what could have happened. He looks positively *dusty*, and isn't that a cut on his jaw? He keeps rubbing it."

"I imagine Sergeant Norman is responsible," I said.

"Oh dear, are those two at it again? They had a fight last week, you know. There they were in the middle of the polo field, trying to choke the life out of each other. These boys! They're so *play*ful."

Brown brushed off his jacket and marched over to the bar. He downed a bourbon in two gulps, then asked for another. Most of the men had been making regular trips to the bar, and some of them were beginning to show it. A number of the ladies had been drinking the champagne steadily and with considerable enthusiasm. No one but Dollie and I seemed to notice the somewhat battered Sergeant Brown.

"Look, there's Sally," Dollie said. "Over there, beside the ferns. She's with Sergeant Norman, and *they*'ve just come in, too. Oh my, he seems to be giving her what for! Regular lecture, it looks like, and she's as meek as a lamb. I rather fancy Bill Norman's just the man to straighten her out."

"He seems a nice fellow," I remarked.

"A bit of a devil with the ladies when he was

stationed in Delhi, I understand, but he doesn't drink, doesn't smoke those dreadful cheroots, either. He's hard as nails with his men, and they all look up to him. There aren't many like him. He's ever so stern, yet there's a certain shy charm."

"A boyish quality," I said.

"Exactly! Sally seems to have cast a spell over him—they were fighting over her on the polo field, you know. I do hope she has the good sense to hold *on* to him."

"The courtship's likely to be rough and tumble, but I imagine she'll let him win her in the end. Sally's as smitten with the sergeant as he is with her, although she'd never admit it."

"Romance," Dollie sighed. "It's wonderful. Oh, to be a girl again! I led them all a merry dance myself, dear. Until Reggie came along. I took one look at him and it was all over—he never knew what *hit* him! I must say, I've never regretted it. Neither of us will see fifty again, but we're as happy together as we were twenty years ago."

Dollie finished her champagne, a thoughtful smile on her lips, brown eyes pensive. I felt a great rush of affection for her. She had been like a sister to my mother, and she had been like a mother to me. I considered myself fortunate to have Dollie in my life. Reggie, too. Dollie toyed with one of the black lace ruffles on her jade silk skirt, glancing around the room. Her eyes came to rest on a woman standing in front of one of the windows across the room, and she tugged my arm.

"Valerie Simpson," she said in a hushed voice. "The one I was telling you about."

I looked at the woman in question. Valerie Simpson was an exceedingly attractive brunette with a sulky

102

pink mouth and a petulant look in her languorous gray eyes. Her rather dark complexion and the abundant raven locks falling carelessly about her shoulders gave her an exotic look. Her dark blue velvet gown was much too low at the neckline, too tight at the waist. Half a dozen thin gold bangle bracelets dangled on one wrist, and she wore earrings of beaten gold. I thought she looked like a moody gypsy, a lovely creature who was undeniably sensual and preoccupied with men. She would wear musky perfume, I knew, and she would be totally indifferent to any other woman.

"She's—quite stunning," I said.

"Do you really think so? Much too flashy, I'd say. There's always at least one woman like Valerie Simpson on any military post. She's caused ever so much talk. She won't take part in any of the social affairs unless there are *men* about, never pays a call, keeps to herself. I can't imagine Michael getting involved with her. I don't know that he *was*, mind you, I just know that she set her cap for him, and when a woman like that makes up her mind to have a man she usually *has* him. After a while Michael started deliberately avoiding her, and that's when she took the overdose of laudanum."

"You don't believe it was accidental?"

"I doubt it, dear. Women like her thrive on melodrama. They're always acting out scenes, living on nerves and emotion. The men always find it tiresome after a while, particularly men as levelheaded as Michael."

"I understand that Lieutenant Stephens and his men arrived back at the garrison this afternoon," I remarked casually.

"They did, dear, and I can't imagine why Michael

hasn't shown up yet. It was late when they got in, of course, and I expect they were bone weary, but he *knows* how I wanted him to be here. Don't you fret. I imagine he'll show up eventually."

"I shan't fret at all," I told her.

Dollie gave me a knowing little smile, tapped my arm and then looked extremely flattered when a nice-looking, bashful young sergeant stepped up and asked if he could have the honor of this dance. She was as enthusiastic and radiant as a schoolgirl as he led her onto the floor, definitely the belle of the ball. I hadn't missed Lieutenant Stephens at all, I told myself. I had wondered why he wasn't here, true, but I had been much too occupied to dwell on it. Dollie seemed determined to match the two of us, and I resented that. I had seen the man once, just once, and with women like Valerie Simpson around he was hardly likely to be interested in a young and inexperienced girl just out of school.

"Thinking of me?" he inquired.

"I—" I blushed, unable to continue.

"You were," he said. "Good."

I had been lost in thought as he approached, and now he stood before me tall and even more handsome than I remembered. Excessively handsome, I had remarked before, and it was true. With that dark blond hair and those deep blue eyes, that cleft chin and wide, beautifully shaped mouth, he was like a virile Adonis, dazzling in his uniform. He smiled, amused at my obvious discomfort, and I was furious with myself as I felt the blush burning on my cheeks.

"Sorry I couldn't get here sooner," he remarked. "I wanted to write up my report first thing, get that out of the way, and then it took quite a while to get rid of the dust and grime."

"I—I hadn't given it a thought."

"Oh, come now. Let's not pretend. Dollie's been after you about me ever since you arrived, singing my praises. Am I right? Right. She's been singing *your* praises ever since she learned you were coming to Dahlkari. She made up her mind to match up the two of us quite some time ago, and she is a very determined woman."

"Really, Lieutenant Stephens—"

"I'm an agreeable chap. It's *time* I settled down. I must say, though, I was a bit taken aback when I first saw you. You looked like some pathetic urchin, dress in tatters, face streaked with dirt, hair all tangled. Not a very promising sight, I'll have to admit."

"I don't imagine I was," I said stiffly.

"Dollie had assured me you were a raving beauty, but I had my doubts. I still had them tonight, remembering that tattered waif, and then I came into the room and saw you standing over here and every doubt vanished. Dollie was right. She usually is."

I didn't know whether to be angry or amused. I wanted to laugh, and I wanted to lash out with a barbed remark. I did neither. I summoned all my composure and looked up into those dancing blue eyes with a cool, level gaze. Lieutenant Stephens smiled, that wide chiseled mouth curving up at both corners, and I smiled, too, unable to help myself.

"There," he said, "that's better. I'm really not a bad sort once you get to know me, and you shall get to know me."

"Indeed?"

"It's destined. Dollie ordained it."

The smile still played on his lips, and I felt myself responding to his charm. He had that in abundance, yet for all the light banter and playful gallantry there was still a certain reserve. I had no experience whatsoever with men, but I could tell that Lieutenant Stephens was at heart a serious, unemotional person, dedicated to his career. He was playing the gallant because it amused him to do so at the moment. It was not something he would care to devote a great deal of time to.

"I suppose we'd better dance," he said. "We've an awful lot of lost time to make up for."

"Have we, Lieutenant?"

"You've been here two full weeks. If I hadn't been gone we'd probably be engaged by this time."

He was teasing, and it meant absolutely nothing. It was what was expected of him. I let him lead me onto the dance floor, conscious of all the eyes upon us. People stared while pretending not to do so. The lieutenant nodded in silent greeting to various people as we moved past, as conscious as I of their curiosity, rather pleased by it. He was no doubt accustomed to being the center of attention, his personal magnetism and dazzling good looks making it almost routine.

He was a superb dancer, of course. He moved with a lithe, confident grace, holding me securely about the waist, his hand clasping mine lightly. He smiled, enjoying himself as we swirled to the music, and I returned the smile, relaxing for the first time. I had the feeling we were going to be friends. I had the feeling that was all he wanted, and that suited me nicely. We danced several dances together, and I let myself go, savoring the movement, the music, the man who guided me about the floor with such firm, expert precision. I was aware of swirling colors around us, aware of colored streamers and balloons bobbing above, aware of the strength of that arm wrapped so securely about my waist. I felt lightheaded and rather dizzy after the fifth dance, and when the lieutenant suggested we step out into the gardens for a breath of fresh air I nodded gratefully.

"I'd like that," I said.

"You look a bit flushed. I'd like to think I've overwhelmed you, but I suspect it's the heat."

"It—it is rather warm in here."

Clasping my elbow lightly, Lieutenant Stephens led me through one of the French windows and out onto the back veranda. We moved slowly down the length of it, pools of light alternating with stretches of shadow, voices and music spilling out in bursts as we passed the windows. We moved down three flat wooden steps and along a flagstone path, and gradually the sound of music was replaced by that of crickets and rustling leaves. We reached the foot of the gardens and stopped near a tamarind tree. I could smell exotic blossoms, strong and fragrant in the warm night air, and in the moonlight I saw a tiny lizard scurry across the path.

Lieutenant Stephens still clasped my elbow. He released it now with a murmured apology and stood looking toward the mess hall, half concealed by the trees and shrubbery we had passed along the way. The sky was an opaque purple-gray, gilded with moonlight, the gardens etched in black and gray and tarnished silver, romantic indeed, the music muted by distance. Michael Stephens was silent, lost in thought. In the misty silver-blue light his face was all smooth, flat planes, deeply shadowed, and he seemed remote, quite different from the teasing gallant of a short while ago.

107

Several moments passed before he finally sighed and looked at me, lips curling in a thoughtful half smile.

"You must be very tired," I said.

"Exhausted, actually. We rode most of the day. You must forgive me. I'm not doing my part. I'm supposed to sweep you into my arms and kiss you until you swoon with rapture."

"I shouldn't if I were you."

"You wouldn't swoon with rapture?"

"I'd probably slap your face quite viciously."

"I say, that wouldn't be cricket."

"Wouldn't it?"

He laughed softly. "Actually, I doubt if you would. Most women enjoy being kissed by me. You'll enjoy it, too, once I get around to it. And I *shall* get around to it," he added in a teasing voice.

"But not tonight," I said firmly.

He grinned, and I liked him immensely, feeling once again that we were going to be friends. Dollie had planned to throw us together from the beginning, and both of us were sensible enough to make light of a situation that could have been most embarrassing.

"You know, you're quite an unusual girl," he said. "Not at all what I expected. I expected a naïve, simpering schoolgirl, and I find a cool, intelligent and most independent young lady who clearly knows her own mind. Not at *all* what I expected," he repeated.

"Is that supposed to be a compliment? It sounds most unflattering."

"I meant it as a compliment. You're very refreshing, Miss Lauren Gray. Simpering schoolgirls bore me dreadfully, and I have the feeling you couldn't bore me if you tried. Would you really have slapped me?"

"I certainly would have."

"You don't find me completely irresistible?"

"I'm afraid not, Lieutenant."

"Most women do as a matter of course. It's rather a curse, you know, looking like a damned romantic hero and being a dull, conventional fellow at heart."

"I shouldn't say you were *dull*," I told him.

"No? I say, things are beginning to look promising."

He took my hand, and we began to stroll slowly through the extensive gardens behind the mess hall, the music a constant, muted background. I was completely at ease now, more relaxed than I had been all evening, and, no longer playing the teasing gallant, Lieutenant Stephens proved to be a most agreeable companion, thoughtful and polite. He asked me about my life, and I found myself telling him about my parents' death, about school life in Bath, about the books I had read. We stopped near a trellis heavily laden with honeysuckle vines. There was a long white bench, and I sat down gratefully, suddenly weary. It was the first time I had sat down all evening. Lieutenant Stephens stood with his feet legs spread, his arms folded across his chest.

"And so you graduated," he said. "What did you plan to do with yourself before you decided to come to India?"

"I—I rather thought I would become a governess. It was about the only thing I was suited for. I was relieved when Dollie's letter arrived. I wasn't really looking forward to going into service. I probably shall eventually."

"I seriously doubt that," he told me. He did not elaborate. Instead, he asked me what I had been doing with myself since arriving on post.

"I've made ever so many calls, drunk ever so much

tea, listened to an inordinate amount of gossip. I've watched the men drilling on the parade grounds and I've seen a polo match and, let me see—oh yes, I've arranged an awful lot of flowers for Dollie. She's not very good at it, you see, and she does love cut flowers in the house."

"In short, you've been wretchedly bored."

"Wretchedly," I admitted.

"We'll have to do something about that. Lieutenant Michael Stephens, at your service. Do you like to ride?"

"I adore it."

"I have quite a lot of free time in the mornings. We'll go out riding, let you see something of the countryside. You'll have to fend for yourself during the afternoons, but I rather imagine we can find a way to keep your evenings from being so boring, too."

"It's very kind of you to offer your—services, Lieutenant, but you really needn't, you know. Just because Dollie—"

"Dollie has nothing to do with it," he said in a stern voice. "Oh, I planned to be polite and attentive, just to humor her, but now—" He hesitated, and then he smiled that beautiful smile. "Now, Miss Gray, I've decided to sweep you off your feet."

I felt a warm glow, a curious swell of elation, not at all sure that he was teasing. Teasing or not, it was going to be nice to have an attentive companion, someone to take me for rides and help alleviate the tedium of life on post. The fact that he was over six feet tall and had the face and form of a blond Greek god made it all the nicer. Lieutenant Stephens took my hand, helping me to my feet, and we strolled slowly back toward the veranda. He still held my hand in a firm grip, and I still felt that subtle elation, something akin to contentment but much more exhilarating. It was enchanting to have a new friend. I was naïve and inexperienced enough to believe that's all he would be.

I was startled to discover that the music was no longer playing. When had it stopped? Although there were still voices and laughter drifting out into the night through the opened French windows, that noisy festivity was missing. When we entered the mess hall it was to find that at least two thirds of the guests had already departed, those that remained standing about in intimate little groups, talking. The dance floor was empty now, its highly polished surface deplorably scuffed, and the colored streamers and balloons drooped sadly, tattered looking. The bar was littered with empty bottles, the buffet tables desecrated. The Indian servants were stacking empty plates and gathering up glasses. I found it hard to believe we had been out in the gardens so long. It had seemed such a short time.

"*Here* you are!" Dollie exclaimed, scurrying over to greet us. "I was beginning to *wor*ry! Michael, you rascal, I didn't get to dance with you a single time. I'm terribly disappointed. Hurt, too. You'll have to be extra nice to smooth my ruffled feelings. The dance was a *splen*did success, I must say!"

"It was lovely, Dollie," I assured her.

"It began to break up a little while ago. Those poor, dear boys had been playing all evening without a break, and they were exhausted. Each one of them shall have the day off tomorrow—I've already informed Reggie of that fact—and I gave each one a bottle of port as well."

"Have you seen Sally?" I asked.

111

"I haven't seen hide nor hair of her since she first came in from the gardens with Sergeant Norman, and that was hours ago. I imagine they went *off* together. Lauren, dear, you look exhausted, and there's still so much to *do*. I must stay and supervise the clearing up, naturally, and Reggie's having a very important conversation with some of the men. I hate to tear him away. Michael, I wonder if *you'd* escort her back to the house?"

"With great pleasure," he said.

It was an outrageous ploy on Dollie's part, and I wanted to scold her. Lieutenant Stephens merely grinned, his deep blue eyes amused. He complimented Dollie on her success, bade her good night and led me out into the foyer, pausing to fetch his hat. I thought he looked rather weary himself. There was a tautness about his cheekbones, as though the skin was stretched too tightly, and faint grayish-mauve shadows were etched beneath his eyes. He brushed a thick wave of blond hair from his forehead, his mouth a tight line as he put his hat on and adjusted it. We left the mess hall and walked slowly toward the rows of barracks, all dark now, not a single light showing, the white walls gilded with moonlight and awash with shadows. Michael was silent, lost in thought again, and there was no sound but our footsteps and the silken rustle of my gown.

"It—it was quite presumptuous of Dollie to impose on you like this," I remarked. "I apologize for her."

"I'm grateful to her," he replied.

He lapsed into silence again. Michael Stephens was something of an enigma, I decided, certainly far more complex than he would seem to be at the first impression. He was undeniably self-possessed, calm, levelheaded, an efficient soldier. He had great charm, of course, when he cared to employ it, but I suspected he kept tight rein on his emotions and rarely did anything on impulse. He was ambitious, and perhaps he was a bit ruthless, but that wasn't at all unusual in the military personality. A good soldier had to be ruthless at times, had to maintain that steely control I sensed in him. I found him utterly intriguing already, and already I sensed he was going to become very important to me.

"You—you seem very preoccupied," I said quietly.

"Sorry. You'll have to forgive me."

"You were thinking about the expedition, weren't you?"

"I was, actually."

"Do—do you mind talking about it?"

"Not at all. It was a total failure. We visited over a hundred villages, interviewed hundreds of natives, and not a one of them knew a thing about the Thugs, not a one of them gave a satisfactory answer to our questions. They know, of course, but those not actually in league with the villains are too terrified to talk. We weren't given a single lead. Their cover is damn near perfect. It seems we'll never be able to break it."

"Perhaps this man Gordon—"

"Gordon's a fool," he interrupted, his voice severe. "He's a flamboyant, self-advertising opportunist who's managed to worm his way into the confidence of the military leaders. He hasn't accomplished a thing since he was sent out here. All he's managed to do is antagonize everyone on post. The man should be thrown out of the country."

"You seem to feel quite strongly about him."

"Everyone feels strongly about Gordon. He's a

rogue, a disgrace to England with those filthy books he's written, those vile translations. He acts so damned superior—the man makes me livid."

We had passed the barracks and were nearing the green. It was extremely late, but still a few lamps burned in the houses. The flagpole stood like a tall silver wand, casting a long black line of shadow across the ground. Michael had grown silent again after his outburst about Gordon. I could easily understand why the military personnel here at Dahlkari would resent the man, an outsider sent in to take over a job they had been unable to accomplish themselves. Michael felt very strongly about his failure to discover anything about the Thugs during the expedition, and that was probably the reason for this rather moody silence. He wouldn't take failure lightly. I felt certain he was accustomed to great success in everything he set out to accomplish.

As we walked across the green toward the house, I thought about the strange native with the harsh face who had come to our rescue, who had murdered to protect us. I had thought about him frequently during these past two weeks, wondering who he was, what had become of him. I kept seeing those dark, smoldering eyes, that cruel mouth unable to forget what he had done for us, unable to understand why he had gone off like that without collecting a reward. I wondered if Michael and his men had discovered any trace of him. I rather doubted it. Considering his present mood, I thought it unwise to ask any more questions.

We climbed the steps to the veranda and stopped in front of the heavy oak door with the fan of glass panes above it. A light was burning in the front hall, softly diffused golden rays streaming out through the panes.

Michael had maintained his silence, and he stood quietly now, looking down at me with a thoughtful, bemused expression in his eyes. I had a wild impulse to reach up and stroke that lean cheek, and I was alarmed at myself for even entertaining such a thought. I considered myself intelligent and self-possessed and quite above the shallow, romantic foolishness that had occupied the other girls back at school, yet at the moment I wasn't so sure of myself. I felt extremely vulnerable.

"I—I want to thank you for your kindness," I said. My voice sounded unusually stiff. "You've been very—" I hesitated, floundering.

"I'm afraid I haven't been very good company," he replied, "but I'll make it up to you. You be ready at nine tomorrow morning."

"Nine?" I had no idea what he was talking about.

"Our ride," he reminded me.

"Oh—yes. Yes, that will be fine."

"I'm looking forward to it, Lauren."

He placed his hands on my shoulders then and pulled me toward him. He looked into my eyes for a long moment, and I saw his mouth curving as he tilted his head to one side and leaned down to kiss me, and then those lips were covering my own ever so lightly. They lingered in a long caress, warm, pliant, pressing gently, and then he drew back. His brow was stern, but there was a hint of amusement in his eyes. I looked up at that handsome face, confused, at a loss for words. Another long moment passed.

"You didn't slap me," he said.

"I—I know I didn't, Lieutenant, but—neither did I swoon with rapture."

Lieutenant Stephens smiled. "You will next time,"

he promised. "Next time I shall definitely see to it that you do."

And then he turned and moved down the steps and toward the green, tall and splendid in his uniform, walking in brisk, confident strides. I stood there in front of the door. Moonlight spilled over the banisters, coating the wooden floor with silver. The old porch swing creaked gently on its chains. I watched him stride down the green, and my confusion mounted, mingling with emotions I wasn't ready to acknowledge. Michael Stephens disappeared, but still I lingered in front of the door, lost in thought. It was quite some time before I finally went inside.

Six

Sally and I stood in front of the stables, waiting for the men to join us. It was a glorious morning, the sky a pale bluish gray awash with brilliant silvery sunlight. Behind us the horses shuffled restlessly in their stalls, eager to be out on such a splendid day, and there was the smell of slightly damp hay and old leather and sweat. A week had passed since the night of the dance. I had seen Michael Stephens every single day. He had come to call on me at the house every single evening. We were going to visit the fabled ruined city of Karbala today, Sally and Sergeant Norman accompanying us. A huge straw picnic hamper sat at our feet, a blue and white checked cloth spread over the lavish lunch Olana had begrudgingly packed for us. I could hardly wait to be off.

I had heard about the ruined city, of course. Almost everyone had. It had been discovered quite by accident only a few years ago, and I had read an account of that discovery in one of the papers in Bath. It had caused a sensation among archeologists and, because of the nature of the carvings, had caused proper Victorians to recoil in horror. When I had learned that Karbala was a mere two hours' ride from Dahlkari, I had begun a persistent campaign to be taken to it. Michael had had considerable reservations, and Dollie had been most alarmed at the mere idea. Reggie agreed that Karbala was interesting indeed, although certainly not suitable for an impressionable young girl. I reminded him that I was quite grown up, and he said it still wouldn't be a good idea for just the two of us to go so far afield with the Thuggee situation being what it was. It was then that I suggested that Sally and Sergeant Norman come along. Surely with two armed men there would be no danger. The arguments continued all around, but I had finally won out.

Sally looked unusually fetching in a dusty-rose cotton dress. Although it had seen better days, it fit snugly at bosom and waist, pointing up her abundant curves, with a flared skirt. Freshly washed, her tarnished gold hair spilled to her shoulders in gleaming curls, fastened in back with a black velvet ribbon. Since the advent of Sergeant Norman she looked even more radiant, glowing with a new satisfied air that seemed to heighten her color.

"I can hardly *wait* to see those carvings," she said. "Bill assures me I'll be ever so shocked."

"I rather doubt it," I replied, teasing.

"I do, too," she agreed, "but I'm terribly curious. I do wish they would hurry. They're going to wear civilian clothes, by the way. Bill told me we'll have to tether the horses and walk part way, and it's rough going. They'll not want to ruin their good uniforms."

"I've never seen Michael out of uniform," I remarked.

"He'd look marvelous in *any*thing, but Bill—I'm not so sure. The uniform gives him a certain glamor. Without it he might look common as a potato. I told him so. He didn't like it a bit."

"You're not still fighting?"

"Oh, we fight every day, but I haven't seen anyone else, if that's what you mean. I wouldn't dare. He laid down the law to me the night of the dance—ever so masterful, he was, quite thrilling." She gave a wistful little sigh, her brown eyes dreamy. "You know, I think I may actually be *fond* of him."

"He's certainly kept you in line."

"That's because I want him to. It's ever so nice, having just one beau. Never thought I'd take to it, but then I never met a man like Sergeant William Norman."

"He keeps you *oc*cupied, too. I hardly ever see you."

"You've been rather occupied yourself. I'm very happy for you, Miss Lauren. Lieutenant Stephens is *such* a fine catch."

"I—I haven't caught him," I protested.

"No? It certainly looks that way to me."

"We're merely friends."

"Friends? Every morning he comes by for you and the two of you go riding—he hasn't missed a morning since the night of the dance—and then he comes round to the house every single evening and the two of you stroll in the gardens for hours. I suppose you just *talk*."

"That's exactly what we do."

"And that's *all?*"

"Of course that's all."

Sally shook her head. "It sounds dreadfully boring."

"It's—quite stimulating."

Sally made no reply, but she didn't need to. Her eyes told me exactly what she thought about such prim and proper behavior. It *had* been prim and proper. Michael had been charming and friendly and a wonderful companion on our rides, and, in the evenings, he had been attentive and polite and agreeable, but he had never kissed me a second time, had rarely taken my hand. I was relieved, or at least that's what I told myself. The evening of the dance had left me in a state of emotional confusion, and I still wasn't sure of my feelings toward him. I only knew that I looked forward to seeing him with keen anticipation, and in many ways this past week had been the happiest week of my life. Michael was giving me time, deliberately. I could sense that, and I both dreaded and eagerly looked forward to his next move, not at all certain what my response would be.

"You look unusually nice this morning," Sally remarked.

"Thank you," I replied.

"I like your hair done up like that. It makes you look older."

I had taken extra care with my appearance this morning, but then I had been doing that for a week now and no longer tried to deceive myself as to the reason. My chestnut hair was worn in a French roll on the back of my head, secured by a number of hairpins. I wore a long-sleeved white blouse with lace ruching, a wide belt of dark blue kid and a full riding skirt of powder blue broadcloth, my kid boots the same dark blue as the belt. I was pleased with the total effect and felt I did indeed look older, less like a schoolgirl.

"I *do* wish they'd hurry up," Sally said. "These men, you can never depend on them. I suppose they had to stop by the armory to check out their pistols. Bill said he wasn't at *all* in favor of this little outing, said it was downright foolhardy."

"That's nonsense," I told her. "The Thugs never attack English parties. It's only the native caravans they go after. There haven't been half a dozen English killed in the whole history of Thuggee."

"All I know is that the number was almost increased by two," Sally retorted. "Besides, these Thugs aren't like the others. The others had strong religious convictions, however grisly. These are the last holdouts, the most vicious of the lot. Although they still pay token allegiance to Kali, they're really just using it as an excuse to kill and loot."

"I can see you've been discussing it with someone."

"Bill says I have a *mor*bid interest in the matter, but, after all, I was almost strangled by the brutes. I want to learn all I can about them. Miss Lauren...." She hesitated, as though debating whether or not to tell me something.

"What is it, Sally?"

"You know that yellow scarf, the one the Thug dropped on the ground when that native stabbed him—I never gave it to Reggie. I never mentioned it. He was asking so many questions and carrying on so that I plain forgot it was in the pocket of my dress."

"I—I forgot about it, too."

"Anyway, a couple of days ago I took the dress out to see if it could be salvaged, and as I was examining it the scarf dropped out. It gave me *such* a turn."

"Did you give it to Reggie?"

There was a touch of defiance in her voice when she replied. "I folded it up and put it in the bottom of my wardrobe," she said. "No disrespect to Reggie, Miss Lauren, but he really hasn't been all that successful in flushing out these Thugs. I decided to wait and give the scarf to this man Gordon when he returns from his secret mission."

"Gordon?" I couldn't hide my surprise.

"I didn't tell Bill about the scarf, I didn't tell anyone, but from what Bill says about him I figure Gordon's the man who'll know what to do with it."

"You mean Sergeant Norman actually ad*mires* the man?"

"That's putting it mildly. You should hear him on the subject. Bill practically worships him, claims he's the brainiest and also the boldest, most daring man he's ever met. Oh, he admits Gordon's a bit un*usual*, has some peculiar interests, but he says he's undoubtedly a genius. If this Thuggee situation is ever cleared up, Gordon's the man who'll be responsible, Bill says."

"That's not an opinion shared by others."

"No one else likes him. They resent him being sent in from outside to take over a job they couldn't do properly. He in*timi*dates them—Bill says he's ever so cool and sarcastic, with a face like Satan incarnate. He and Bill struck up a friendship from the first, but Gordon makes everyone else uneasy."

Sally broke off when she spotted the men coming around the side of one of the buildings. They were talking in low voices. Sergeant Norman looked grim, and Michael seemed to be reassuring him about something. He indicated their pistols, and Norman shook his head and heaved his wide shoulders and looked resigned. They saw us then. Sally waved. Michael smiled at me, and I felt that little leap of happiness I always felt when I saw him again after being away from him for a period of time. I tried not to show it. Sally greeted her sergeant with cool disdain, informing him that we had been waiting in front of these smelly stables for fifteen minutes and when someone said *ten* she didn't expect them to come shambling along at ten-fifteen. Sergeant Norman told her to shut up. Sally was delighted.

Michael wore highly polished brown boots, snugly fitting tan doeskin breeches and a silky beige shirt with collar open at the throat and sleeves rolled up over his forearms, the tail tucked loosely in the waistband of his breeches. With the pistol hanging low on his hip in a brown leather holster, he reminded me of pictures I had seen of the American cowboys. He seemed more at ease than usual, the rather formal British officer replaced by a relaxed young man with windblown hair.

"Sorry we're late," he said. "We had to stop by the armory and check out our pistols. I hope you haven't been too impatient."

"Not at all," I told him, a shade untruthfully.

Michael took out his pistol and checked it, flicking the chamber open to make sure the gun was fully loaded.

"There—there isn't really any danger, is there?" I asked.

"The pistols are merely a precaution," he said calmly. "Norman here is convinced we'll all be massacred by the dreaded Thugs, but I've assured him that's nonsense. There've been no sign of them in the immediate area, and they're only interested in rich caravans to begin with. I wouldn't allow this if I thought there was even the slightest danger."

"I hope you're *right*, sir," Norman said glumly.

"Trembling in your boots," Sally taunted. "Big strapping fellow like you. Who'd have thought it?"

"You mind your tongue!" he warned.

Sergeant Norman was dressed in attire similar to Michael's, his shirt a coarse white cotton, breeches dark gray, black boots rather the worse for wear. Sally

123

eyed him appreciatively as he pushed a wave of reddish-bronze hair from his brow and called for the grooms to snap it up. They led out our horses, all saddled and ready to go. Sally and I both preferred to ride astride, disdaining the elegant but highly impractical side saddle. Sergeant Norman picked up the picnic hamper and secured it to the back of his saddle as Michael helped me mount the gentle chestnut mare I had been riding each morning. Sally complained that her plump dappled gray looked like a hack, but she swung nimbly up into the saddle nevertheless, and in a matter of minutes the four of us were on our way.

Michael and I rode slightly ahead, heading east, village and garrison both in back of us. There was no road as such, only a vast expanse of rough terrain covered with stiff brownish-green grass, bleak and empty, only an occasional tree with wind-tormented black limbs breaking the monotony. The wind was strong. Michael's locks flew about his head like short blond banners, his silky beige shirt billowing. I hoped my hairpins would hold the French roll in place. In the distance I could see a line of hills, green and dark brown and tan, all blurry in the haze of sunlight. We rode for several miles over this desolate area, horses moving at an easy pace, and gradually the land grew more verdant, greener, trees more profuse.

Michael drew his horse closer to mine, looking at me with a faint smile on his lips.

"Disappointed?" he inquired.

"I don't know what you mean. Why should I be disappointed?"

"I thought it might have been the uniform that dazzled you. I feared you'd take one look at me in these clothes and decide I was an unglamorous fellow not worth your time."

"I think you look quite dashing," I told him. "I'm not sure that I don't like you better without the uniform. You look less formal, less remote."

"Formal? Remote? Are you talking about Michael Stephens? I thought I was an engaging chap too whimsical for words. I see you've gotten some false impressions. I'll have to correct them. Today might be just the day for it."

"Indeed?"

"You're still going to swoon with rapture, you know. I imagine Sally and Sergeant Norman are going to want to wander off by themselves once we get to Karbala. Perhaps I'll have an opportunity to correct a few of those false impressions then—once we're alone."

It was light banter, nothing more, but I felt a nervous tremor inside, not certain whether it was dread or anticipation. Behind us I heard Norman give a loud guffaw, and I turned to see Sally clinging to the reins with one hand while trying to control her flying skirts with the other. The sergeant was grinning broadly, his blue eyes atwinkle. Sally controlled the unruly skirts and tucked them about her legs, giving the sergeant a look that should have felled him. Michael and I smiled at each other, and I was thankful for the distraction.

We rode past a small native village, a collection of wretched hovels, women in dusty saris working in stony fields, half-naked children running about as starved-looking dogs barked vociferously. Ironically enough, there was a rather magnificent old temple at the edge of the village. It looked like some bizarre wedding cake with hardened pink icing, a polished blue dome reflecting the sun rays. The columns were festooned with garlands of flowers. An emaciated old fakir clad only in loin cloth sat in the doorway, scrawny legs folded beneath him in the lotus position, his eyes glazed, an empty wooden bowl before him. I knew that he might well have been sitting there for years. Not a single person looked up to watch us pass, not even one of the children, but all were aware of us. I could sense their hostility, and those backs seemed to stiffen as the despised English galloped past on their expensive, well-fed horses.

Several miles beyond the village the vegetation grew thicker, and we rode under tall trees that blotted out the sky, flowering vines hanging from the spreading branches. It was cool and shadowy, not really jungle, but I saw a large gray monkey dart across one of the branches, and the birds cried out loudly. We finally stopped near a large, rushing stream, mangrove trees growing thickly on either side. There was a small clearing, and it was here that we dismounted. I was weary from the long ride, but not too weary to marvel at the immense flamboyant tree that towered nearby, trunk a tannish-gray, branches abloom with thousands of showy scarlet flowers. Karbala was at least another mile on the other side of the stream, Michael informed us, and we would have to leave the horses here and go the rest of the way on foot.

"There's a rough, rocky slope on the other side. It's a difficult climb for humans, impossible for the horses. The jungle beyond is extremely dense."

"If I'm going to climb rocky slopes and plunge through jungles, I want to *eat* first," Sally declared.

"I thought we'd lunch here in the clearing," Michael said.

"Haul down that hamper, Norman!" Sally ordered. "I do hope Olana packed some nice things. I wouldn't be greatly surprised if the old witch had filled the hamper with rocks. I thought she was going to throw a knife at me when I asked her to make some of those delicious honey cakes."

Temperamental or no, Olana had done herself proud with the lunch basket. Sally spread the blue- and white-checked tablecloth over the ground and proceeded to take out from the basket an abundance of delicious items: tiny sausages, sandwiches, hunks of cheese, fruit, even the famous honey cakes. Sergeant Norman had watered the horses and tethered them to trees nearby, and he returned with a wide grin and two rather dusty-looking bottles of wine he had smuggled into his saddlebags. The four of us sat on the ground. It was spongy and slightly damp, and above us the leaves rustled and birds darted. A monkey perched on a limb, jabbering quietly and watching us with greedy eyes as we ate, gradually inching closer. Sally tossed it a bun. The monkey caught it with a thin gray hand and scurried away in a burst of excited shrieks.

We all laughed. The food was marvelous, and the wine, which we drank from the bottles, was surprisingly cool. When the meal was finally over, I felt gloriously replete.

"Oh dear," Sally said, "I've got juice all over my fingers. I'd better go rinse them off in the stream."

"Go ahead," Sergeant Norman said lazily.

"By myself? What if I ran into a *co*bra? Get up, you big lout. You're coming with me."

Sergeant Norman groaned, brushed a spray of bronze locks from his brow and climbed to his feet, following with a lazy gait as Sally traipsed happily toward the stream, her dusty rose skirt swaying. Both were soon out of sight. Michael sprawled comfortably on his side, propped up on one elbow, long legs stretched out. I had never seen him so relaxed, so utterly at ease. He was like a different person. His lids drooped heavily over his eyes as he watched me put things back into the basket, and his full mouth lifted slightly at one corner. He looked like some superb, satisfied animal, and there was an aura of sensuality that hadn't been there before. I was rather nervous, for while I could cope with the polite, agreeable British officer, this new Michael disturbed me.

"They're likely to be gone for some time," he remarked.

"I shouldn't be surprised."

"Your Sally is quite uninhibited."

"She's—natural. I admire that. I don't pass judgment on her."

"You'll have to admit she's an unlikely companion for a prim young woman like yourself."

"Perhaps some people might think so. It's none of their affair. Sally has been like a sister to me. I'd defend her to the death."

I stood up, shook out the tablecloth and began to fold it up. Those deep blue eyes watched lazily, lids at half mast. I placed the folded cloth back on top of the hamper and brushed my skirt, wishing he wouldn't look at me like that.

"Your hair's coming undone," he said idly.

"Is it? All that wind, I suppose."

I reached up to push the hairpins back in place, and as I did so Michael stood up. He tucked the tail of his shirt more securely into the tight waistband of his breeches, and then he sauntered over to where I stood and turned me around so that my back was to him. I was startled when he began to remove the hairpins, too startled to protest, and I felt the heavy waves spilling to my shoulders as he removed the pins one by one. Dropping the pins into his pocket, he wrapped one arm around the front of my waist and, with his free hand, lifted my hair until the back of my neck was exposed. I closed my eyes, nervous, trying not to tremble. He murmured something I didn't quite catch, and then, leaning down, he placed his lips against the side of my neck.

"There are things we need to talk about," he told me.

"Are—are there? I really don't think this is—"

"You're stiff as a board. Relax. You're quite prudish, Miss Gray. So broad-minded about some things—about Sally, for example. Yet so very rigid. I've been wanting to—"

"Please, Michael, I—I'd rather you didn't."

"You just want an agreeable escort, is that it? You want a companion to take you riding, a cool, proper gentleman to walk with you in the gardens and discuss books and philosophy and never touch, never step out of character. Someone to use. Is that it?"

"You know that's not true. I just—"

"I'm very fond of you, Lauren. Were we back in England I would pay proper court and observe all the conventions, but time is very precious out here. Things happen quickly. If we were to announce our engagement tomorrow no one would be surprised."

He turned me around so that I faced him. There was a sleepy, indolent look in his eyes, and those wide, firm lips were slightly parted. Several blond locks had tumbled across his brow in disarray. His strong hands held my shoulders in a tight grip, and when he spoke there was a husky catch in his voice.

"I'm going to kiss you now, Lauren. I'm going to hold you tightly in my arms, and I'm going to kiss you until your head reels and every bit of that stiff reserve melts away, and you're going to enjoy it. You're going to hope I never stop."

"No, Michael." My voice was sharp.

"Don't pretend you don't want me to."

"Michael, please—"

He frowned, a deep line digging between his brows, and his eyes darkened. He studied me as though I were a problem he was trying to solve, his fingers gripping my shoulders all the while. I had to tilt my head back to meet his eyes, and my throat felt tight. I wished I could melt against him and welcome that firm, curving mouth and let him have his way with me, but something held me back, and it wasn't merely my rigid sense of propriety. I didn't fully understand it myself, and I knew that Michael had every reason to resent my stiffness.

"Why are you fighting it?" he asked. "You know it's inevitable. You know it from the first, at the dance, just as I did."

"I—I want to be sure, Michael."

"You're not?"

"I—I think I'm very fond of you. I haven't had much experience with this—this sort of thing. I've had no experience at all, really, and I want to—"

I paused, trying to find the right words, but they wouldn't come. I looked up at him with beseeching eyes, and after a moment Michael tightened his mouth and shook his head and let his hands drop from my shoulders. A parrot cried out raucously. Something scurried through the brush. Leaves rustled stiffly, and two tiny monkeys scampered across the bough of a tree nearby. Michael sighed deeply and stepped back.

"Forgive me. I shouldn't have rushed you."

"We've only had a week, Michael, and—it's been a wonderful week. I think it's been the happiest week of my life. All I ask is just a little more time."

"I understand."

"You—you're not angry?"

"Of course not," he said quietly.

"I'm sorry. I—"

"I'm entirely to blame," Michael said. Turning away from me, he ran his hand across his brow, sweeping back those tumbled blond locks. "I forgot myself. You just looked so damned appealing with your hair all falling loose like that—I should have realized you needed more time."

Sally and Sergeant Norman came back then, and I think Michael was almost as relieved as I was. He was calm and pleasant and as agreeable as ever, but there was a barely perceptible reserve that hadn't been there before, and that earlier relaxed, breezy manner was gone entirely. Would it have been so wrong to have let him kiss me? Hadn't I wanted him to do just that? Hadn't I? Wasn't I in love with him?

Sally chattered merrily about their adventure down by the river. She had lost her balance completely, had almost fallen in, and Bill had caught her *just* in time. Of course the water wasn't deep, but there was ever so much mud. Sergeant Norman wore a sheepish grin and looked very pleased with himself. He seemed to have completely forgotten his earlier apprehensions about the wisdom of this outing and was obviously enjoying

131

himself immensely. He and Sally were as carefree and enthusiastic as two children. I envied that zest, that natural, hearty acceptance of each other. Questions like those I had just asked myself would never plague either of them.

"Oh, you've taken your *hair* down," Sally exclaimed.

"It was—coming undone. All that wind. I—I decided I might as well take it down and be done with it."

Sally gave Michael and me a knowing look. "I *see*," she said, and I wanted to slap her.

"We'd better get going," Michael said. His voice was terse.

"Right," Norman agreed. "There are some rocks in the stream a little ways down. We can step across 'em to get to the other side. I'll just check the horses, see that they're in the shade."

A group of rocks did indeed form a ragged path across the stream, some of them as much as a yard apart, all of them wet and slippery. Sally vowed that she'd never be able to make it and contrived to look exceedingly helpless. Sergeant Norman shook his head in mock disgust, swept her up in his arms and stepped from one rock to the other, reaching the other side without mishap. Michael looked at me, and I told him that I was sure I could cross easily enough, not about to let him carry me. As it was, he went on ahead, turning to hold out his hand for me. I almost slipped once, but he held my hand tightly and I regained my balance.

On the other side of the stream the ground gradually rose, steeper and steeper until we were practically climbing. I realized that we were moving up one of the hills I had seen in the distance when we were riding.

Soon we reached a huge shelf of rock and earth that loomed up fifty feet or so. It was half covered with vines, small blue and purple flowers growing in the crevices. It looked impossible to climb, but Michael pointed out a large crevice that wound its way to the top. We began to climb, Sergeant Norman leading the way, Sally behind him, Michael bringing up the rear. It wasn't terribly difficult, for there were plenty of vines to hold on to, a wall of rock and earth on either side, but by the time we reached the top all of us were a bit soiled and dusty. I began to see why the men hadn't wanted to wear their good uniforms.

We had reached the summit of the hill. There was a clearing of perhaps twenty feet, then a seemingly endless stretch of jungle, much denser than any I had yet seen. Soon we were passing through dark green tunnels, trees close on either side, limbs a thick tangle overhead, vines hanging down in tangled clusters. There was no path as such, and we followed a rather tortuous course, Sergeant Norman forging on ahead with great confidence. Sally clung tightly to his arm, deathly afraid we would encounter a leopard. Or so she claimed. The sergeant greatly enjoyed playing the protective male, a role that suited him nicely.

Michael held the vines back for me and pointed out roots to avoid and once he caught my arm when I almost tripped, but he was silent and rather withdrawn. It was warm here, and damp, the air fetid. After we had been walking for some time the jungle seemed to thin out somewhat, the trees not so close together, vines not so thick. Far ahead I could see a blaze of dazzling sunlight and something gray. As we drew nearer I saw it was a wall, my first glimpse of Karbala. I felt a rush of excitement, for I had always been fascinated by ruins, and the temples and broken courtyards of Karbala were all that remained of a civilization so ancient it had no recorded history.

I recalled the article the Royal Geographical Society had published about Karbala. The ruined city had been completely covered by shrubbery and vines, literally hidden in the jungle for centuries, but most of these had been cut away now, and the ruins stood in a clearing of several acres, completely surrounded by jungle. The sunlight was almost blinding after being in the dim, heavily shadowed jungle. Sally blinked. I shaded my eyes. Both men suddenly looked ill at ease, Michael a bit too formal, Sergeant Norman bluff and obviously embarrassed. There were over a dozen temples and a labyrinth of fallen walls and courtyards, columns standing here and there, all crumbling and dust-coated, all of a crumbly gray stone streaked with the green and bronze of erosion. Everywhere there were carvings, and when I saw the nature of them I realized why the men were so awkward.

"Isn't it *pretty*?" Sally exclaimed. "I never was much one for ruins, to tell you the truth, not my sort of thing, but these are adorable. Look at all those intricate carvings, such detail." Sally paused, and her eyes grew wide in disbelief. "Miss Lauren, I declare! What are they *do*ing?" She was incredulous.

We faced a high wall, half of it fallen, a heap of crumbled gray stone at one end. There was a very dramatic frieze in bas-relief depicting a number of merry couples engaged in an age-old activity, the variety of positions quite astonishing. The figures were exquisitely done, the craftsmanship superb, although the female figures were slightly exaggerated, naked bosoms and hips rather too full. Certain portions of the male anatomy were likewise exaggerated. I tried hard not to blush, telling myself that I was intelligent enough to be objective and could view the ruins without letting my Victorian upbringing blind me to their beauty and importance. Sally was not quite so cool. She pranced nimbly over to the wall, peered closely at one of the couples and gasped.

"Goodness me! I never knew people did *that*. It's quite an education. Folks back then were certainly resourceful."

"Do you see why I didn't want to bring you here?" Michael asked.

"I've seen worse in museums," I replied coolly, quite untruthfully as well. "We came to see them. Shall we proceed? There's no need to stand here and—gawk like day-trippers."

Michael smiled for the first time since we had left the stream.

"You're indeed full of surprises," he remarked. "I expected you to recoil in horror, perhaps even swoon."

"That would be silly indeed, wouldn't it?"

Sally had recovered herself. She pretended a blasé disinterest in the carvings, although I could see her curiosity was lively indeed. She looked a bit alarmed when Michael and I began to walk away and asked if it wouldn't be better for us all to stay together. She would clearly be more comfortable with another woman around, for once not so eager to be alone with her good-looking sergeant.

"I'll take care of you," he said. "Come on, I'll show you around."

"I'm really not all that interested in a bunch of old carvings. Quite uncivilized they are, too. Mercy me, surely that isn't two *elephants*? You let go of my hand,

135

Bill Norman. I'm quite capable of walking about on my own. Don't you be getting any ideas!"

Michael and I walked around the wall and into the labyrinth. Once the initial shock was gone, I was better able to appreciate the artistry of the carvings, but I was still embarrassed and fought hard to conceal it. Crossing a courtyard of uneven gray stones, we stood before a large open temple with six spiraled columns supporting a roof that rose like a pyramid, hundreds and hundreds of figures adorning it. All of them were as active and versatile as those on the wall, a writhing mass of gray stone couples with explicit bodies engaged in explicit activity. I examined the temple with a studied calm difficult to maintain.

"You can see why the place hasn't become a great attraction," Michael remarked. "Most of the English pretend it doesn't exist."

"I think it's fascinating. Their culture was— obviously quite different from ours, but that's no reason why an intelligent person can't observe the ruins objectively."

My voice was slightly strained, and Michael was fully aware of my embarrassment, try though I might to conceal it. I was the one who had insisted on coming here over all objections, and I wasn't going to give him the satisfaction of knowing he'd been right to advise against it. None of my reading, none of my scholarly studies over the years had prepared me for anything like this, and I had thought I was quite well versed in primitive customs and immune to shock. It took a great deal of self-control to meet his gaze without looking away.

"Shall we continue?" he inquired.

"Of course. I want to see it all."

There were more temples, some of them fully standing, others tumbling down with piles of shattered stone about them, and there were more walls with bas-reliefs. Moving across another courtyard, we came upon a wall with three life-sized figures carved on it, two men and one woman. Although part of it had crumbled away, one of the men headless, the woman's right arm missing, it was by far the most explicit carving we had yet seen, and I tried to tell myself it was just ancient gray stone streaked with erosion and nothing at all to be alarmed about, but because the figures were life-sized it seemed all the more obscene. The men wore sandals and form-fitting jackets and leggings bunched up at the knee, the female in bracelets and a headdress that rose in a spire. I wasn't certain just what the three of them were doing, for it didn't seem humanly possible. I moved on rather hurriedly, and Michael chuckled. After the acrobatic trio in stone anything else was decidedly mild, and I was able to view the rest of the ruins without dismay.

The sun poured down in brilliant silver-yellow rays, bathing stone and dirt-streaked ground, intensifying the green of the surrounding jungle. A flock of vivid scarlet and blue birds flew over the ruins, and tiny yellow-green lizards scurried over the stones. Shock behind me, I began to enjoy myself as Michael and I continued to explore the ruined city. I tried to imagine the people who had lived here so many centuries ago, an uninhibited race who had lived and died before history was written. Frequently we heard a husky laugh or a trill of girlish laughter coming from another part of the ruins as Sally and the sergeant did their own exploring.

"Impressed?" Michael inquired.

"Very much so," I said. "Once—once you get over the surprise, the ruins are lovely. It's hard to believe people lived here hundreds of years before Christ. I wonder what became of them."

"I've no idea. Offhand, I'd say they died of exhaustion."

"Michael," I scolded.

"Sorry. I couldn't resist that."

We paused to rest in the shade of a crumbled wall near the edge of the jungle. I sat down on the stump of a column, spreading my blue riding skirt out and folding my hands demurely in my lap. Michael stood with his hands thrust into his pockets, his head tilted to one side. The tension between us had vanished completely. Leaves rustled nearby. One of the tiny jade lizards lolled in a patch of sunlight. I was tired, but pleasantly so. It had been a most unusual day, one I wouldn't soon forget. Michael looked at me with thoughtful blue eyes.

"I'm afraid I made an ass of myself back there by the stream," he said quietly. "I hope you won't hold it against me."

"Don't be foolish. Of course I won't."

"I don't ordinarily act that way, you know. Ordinarily I'm rather indifferent to feminine charms."

"Indeed?"

"I'm not saying I haven't had women. There've been a number of them in my life, but—well, it all seemed a lot of bother, not worth the effort. I was far more interested in making my mark in the world, advancing my career. I was never the aggressor, not once. The—uh—ladies always made the first move and, being an agreeable chap, I generally played along if the lady was interesting enough."

"You don't have to tell me all this, Michael."

"But I do, you see, I want you to understand. Valerie Simpson is a case in point. You've heard about that. You couldn't have been in Dahlkari for three weeks without hearing about it. She's supposed to have taken an overdose of laudanum because I rejected her." He frowned and kicked at a loose stone with the toe of his boot. "Valerie was bored with her husband, a complacent chap who couldn't care less what she does. She found me attractive, and she made a play for me—made several, actually. One thing led to another, and I began to see her."

I remained silent. Michael's frown deepened.

"As Lieutenant Colonel McAllister's aide, I have to spend quite a lot of time at the rajah's palace—diplomatic work, a bloody bore. I'm generally there for a couple of hours every other afternoon. As I couldn't very well visit Valerie at night when her husband was underfoot, I saw her in the afternoons—during my free time. She was very clinging, very possessive, resented my going to the palace instead of coming to her bungalow. I found her a nuisance from the very first."

"And so you broke off with her," I said.

"Rather brutally, I'm afraid. I told her I wanted nothing more to do with her. I'm confessing all this because—well, my relationship with Valerie is typical of all my relationships with women. As I said, I've been rather indifferent, not caring much one way or the other. I'm not indifferent about you, Lauren. I care a great deal."

"I—I see."

"Do you? I'm making a wretched mess of it, but what I'm trying to say is—"

Before he could finish there was a loud shout, quickly followed by the unmistakable sound of a

139

gunshot. I jumped to my feet. Michael stood there for a moment as though paralyzed, too startled to move, and then his face turned very grim and he jerked his pistol out of the holster and told me to follow him. He moved rapidly in the direction of the sounds, and I hurried along behind him, frightened, my heart palpitating.

"Halt, you devil!" Sergeant Norman shouted, and then there was another pistol shot. Michael seized my wrist and began to run, pulling me along with him. A couple of moments later we stumbled upon Sally and Sergeant Norman. She was pale and visibly shaken, and the sergeant's eyes were full of alarm. The pistol in his hand was still smoking.

"What happened, Norman?" Michael snapped. "What is it?"

"A native, sir. He was spying on us! A fierce-looking devil he was, too, crouching behind the rocks right over there at the edge of the trees. I don't know whether I hit him or not. There—there may be more, sir! I just saw that one, but there could be a whole pack of 'em."

"We must leave at once," Michael said crisply. "We must get the women back safely."

"My sentiments exactly, sir. The gunshots may have frightened those bloody devils off momentarily, but they could come back en masse. I think it might be the Thugs, sir. I *said* we shouldn't risk coming way out here like this. I had a feeling something was going to—"

"That'll do, Sergeant! We have no time to waste on words!"

His cheeks were ashen, his blue eyes frighteningly sober. I could see him struggling to maintain his calm, and he did so magnificently. Pistol gripped tightly in his hand, he told Norman that we must make for the jungle at once, that we'd have a far better chance to elude them once we were in its shelter. Norman gave a curt nod in agreement, and the four of us moved quickly past ruined temples with erotic carvings, past walls with pornographic bas-reliefs. We climbed over piles of stones, circled around barriers, and in a matter of minutes Karbala and the sunlight were behind us and we were moving down those long green tunnels again, moving as fast as possible in that density of trees and vines, for all we knew a pack of murderous Thugs in hot pursuit.

Sergeant Norman knocked vines out of the way and dragged Sally along by the wrist, and she made no protest at his rough treatment, stumbling along with golden curls atumble, her face still pale. I kept right behind them, out of breath, panting, remembering the horror, expecting a band of fiendish assassins to fall upon us at any moment with yellow scarves in hand. Michael brought up the rear, constantly looking back for signs of pursuit, but the jungle was so dense and the light so dim that he couldn't have seen them unless they were directly behind. Our crashing footsteps and Sergeant Norman's frequent curses drowned out any sounds our pursuers might have made. Slapping against branches, ducking to avoid hanging vines, I ran, keeping my eyes straight ahead, seeing Sergeant Norman's broad back and Sally's bouncing curls and her flying dusty-rose skirt. She stumbled. He jerked her back up. He shoved a curtain of vines out of the way and yelled "Bloody hell!" as a low-hanging branch slapped the side of his face, but he didn't falter for an instant, kept right on plunging ahead.

My lungs seemed about to burst. My heart was pounding loudly as though about to explode. In my panic I thought I could hear shouts of "Kali! Kali!" and

I could see those white turbans and those brutal faces and see the yellow rumals ready to be slung around our throats. I tripped over a root and fell to the ground. Michael lifted me up. He wrapped one arm around my waist and propelled me along, his pistol in his free hand. It seemed an eternity before we reached the great shelf of rock and earth. We moved down it quickly, stumbling, sliding, clinging to vines, and then we were in jungle again and moving downhill. Birds shrieked overhead, flying about in a frenzy of alarm, and a startled monkey screamed and leaped frenziedly from branch to branch.

Exhausted, ready to drop, we finally reached the stream. Sergeant Norman didn't bother looking around for stones to cross over on. Scooping Sally up into his arms, he dashed into the stream, boots making noisy splashes as he crossed. He tripped once and almost lost his balance. Sally let out a shriek as she swung perilously near the water, but the sergeant regained his balance and safely reached the other side. Following the sergeant's example, Michael gathered me up and started across in the same fashion. I clung to his shoulders, looking back at the line of jungle, still expecting a band of white-clad Thugs to burst into view. Michael sat me down beside Sally. Chest heaving, blond locks wildly disarrayed, he gave Norman a relieved look, and the sergeant sighed and shook his head.

"I think we've eluded them, sir."

"I'm not certain they ever came after us. I didn't see anyone behind us, but that doesn't mean anything. They could have been there, but if they were they've given up."

"It was a close call, sir. A very close call. I'm

convinced a whole pack of 'em were lurking around those ruins, just waiting for their chance. If I hadn't spotted that devil when I did. . . ."

Sally put her arm around my waist. She was amazingly calm now, and I thought there was a satisfied look in her eyes. I had the curious impression that she knew something the rest of us didn't know, but it could have been my imagination. I was utterly shaken. My lungs felt raw, and my heart was still beating rapidly. Sally gave me a squeeze and reached over to push a lock of chestnut hair from my eyes. The men ignored us, watching the other side of the stream with pistols held ready. Silently, Sally comforted me, and I finally managed to compose myself.

"That's it, then," Michael said. "There's no one following us."

"Looks that way, sir, but we'll not want to tarry, regardless. We must think of the women."

"Right. We'll head for the garrison immediately."

The men helped us mount, and soon we were riding away from the clearing. I turned back to have a final look at the flamboyant tree ablaze with scarlet flowers, knowing I would always remember it when I thought of this day. A short time later we had left the jungle behind and were once again riding over vast, empty terrain. It was only midafternoon. The sky was a pale, cloudless blue, and the air was clear, the breeze invigorating, and it seemed the other had never happened at all, that I had imagined that desperate flight through the jungle, that slide down the rocky crevice, the terror that had so completely possessed me.

We rode slowly, all of us exhausted, too exhausted for any attempt at conversation. We arrived at the garrison shortly before five, a bedraggled lot, the object of many stares. Sally was impatient to be alone with me. I could tell that she did indeed have something to tell me and could hardly wait to do so. We left the horses at the stables, and the men walked with us to the McAllister house, neighbor women lifting back lace curtains to peer as we passed. Dusty, disheveled, we looked as though all four of us had been in a brawl. Heaven only knew what kind of interpretation the gossips would put on it.

"I shall make a full report to Lieutenant Colonel McAllister," Michael said, "that goes without saying, but I think I should go inside with you and help explain things to Dollie. She'll be terribly alarmed."

Sally gave me a sharp look, her meaning quite clear.

"I—I think not, Michael," I told him. "I'm terribly tired, and Sally and I can handle Dollie. You really needn't come in."

"You're sure you don't want me to?"

I nodded and smiled. Michael creased his brow and looked uncertain. We told the men good-bye and watched them walk away, and then Sally took my hand and led me up onto the front veranda, her lively brown eyes full of excitement.

"It was him, Miss Lauren. It was the native."

At first I didn't comprehend. "The native?"

"Back there at the ruins. I got a good look at his face, and it's not a face you're likely to forget. It was *him* spying on us. There weren't any Thugs. There never were."

"But—"

"I tried to tell Bill, but he got all excited and jerked his pistol out and started *shooting*. I—well, I was afraid the men would go after him and—and someone would

144

get hurt, so I just kept my mouth shut, pretended I was terrified, too."

"Then—"

"There was just one man, and it was him, and he *was* spying on us. I wonder why. Why would he be watching us like that? Miss Lauren, I wonder who he *is*."

Seven

It was to be a very formal, very festive affair, and all the men wore full dress uniforms, the women their finest gowns. A caravan of carriages left Dahlkari early in the afternoon filled with stiff, resplendent officers and excited, chattering women, their full skirts ballooning in the seats. Ours was one of the last to leave, for Reggie had some paper work he wanted to clear away before he left, and Dollie explained that it wouldn't look good if we were to arrive too early. One paid obeisance to the rajah out of necessity, but one never appeared eager. There was a very fine line one had to draw with native royalty. One mustn't appear too cool, yet one mustn't seem too cordial either.

It was a lovely day, clear and sunny, the sky like a bolt of soft blue silk unfurled above. Dollie, Reggie and I rode in an open victoria with tan leather upholstery, the most splendid vehicle on post. I occupied the seat facing them, with plenty of room to spread my skirts out, while the driver perched on a high seat in front, urging the two chestnuts on at a brisk pace. As only officers and their women had been invited, and as it was Sergeant Norman's afternoon off, Sally had elected not to come with us, claiming she had better things to do than poke around an old palace and try to chat with a bejeweled heathen. She and Bill were to

146

spend the afternoon at the bazaar in the village. As Reggie's representative at the palace and a favorite of the rajah, Michael had left shortly after noon to be on hand to help the rajah greet his first guests.

"Thank goodness the weather is fine," Dollie remarked. "I was afraid it might rain."

"I was hoping it would!" Reggie snorted.

Dollie made a face at him and opened her ruffled purple parasol. Her purple taffeta gown was adorned with black velvet bows, a rather overpowering garment that she nevertheless succeeded in dominating. Reggie was even more impressive than he had been on the night of the dance, boots shining, tight white trousers spotless, tailored scarlet jacket festooned with gold braid. One white gloved hand toyed with his monocle, the other held on to the side of the carriage as we bounced and jostled over the rough road. I wore a soft white silk gown with tiny blue flowers scattered over the bouffant skirt and adorning the low-cut bodice. The gown had come from Paris, and Dollie had declared it just the thing for the garden party.

"Michael has often mentioned the rajah," I said. "I'm eager to meet him."

"He adores entertaining his English friends." Dollie told me. Reggie gave a little groan at the last two words. "Well, that's what he calls us," she continued, "his English friends. I think it's rather sweet. He's really giving this party in your honor, you know, dear. He likes to meet all the new arrivals at the garrison."

"Particularly the female ones," Reggie said grumpily. "The rogue has an eye for the ladies, Lauren. He was educated in Oxford, if you can picture that, and prides himself on his English ways. He likes to flirt with the English ladies. Outrageous, I call it."

"*I* think he's charming," Dollie protested. "He's a bit *wi*ly, true, and I've no doubt he's devious, but I've rarely encountered such fine manners."

"Fellow's a pain in the neck," Reggie grumbled.

"You're just in a bad mood today," Dollie told him. "I wager it's that Gordon fellow. You're *always* in a bad mood when he's around."

"Has Robert Gordon returned to Dahlkari?" I inquired.

"Came swaggering in yesterday," Reggie replied. "He condescended to stop by my office to say he was back. Cool as you please he was—fellow disappears for a month and casually strolls into the office, says he's back and then saunters off to his quarters to write those bloody reports. It's enough to put you off your feed."

"Will he be at the garden party?"

"Oh, dear," Dollie said, "I *hope* not. He despises the rajah even more than Reggie does. He claims all that wealth should be distributed among the people—"

"That's the only thing Gordon and I agree about," Reggie interrupted. "The radicals claim the *British* are exploiting India—building schools and hospitals and bridges and roads and planning a railroad and trying to build industry and *help* the blighters—yet a handful of sleek potentates live in luxury that staggers the imagination. Sahji Bandi, now, our host for the afternoon and the chap who 'rules' the district—he's got enough wealth in that crumbling palace of his to feed every native in every village in the whole bloody district for the rest of their natural lives. That's no exaggeration. And he's not even one of the *rich* rajahs!"

"Now don't get yourself worked up," Dollie scolded. "We have to display a pleasant front, dear. You know that."

"I know," he grumbled. "Chap expects us to jump at his beck and call, expects the Viceroy himself to pay homage. He's got his own police force, twenty men or so, I'd wager, not a man more, and every time there's trouble of any kind in one of the villages the military has to work hand in glove with those swarthy demons, can't make a move on our own."

"It *is* his district, dear," Dollie reminded him.

"And he'd find it damned difficult to manage if we weren't here to do the job for him—twenty men indeed! Take the Thuggee situation. The rajah didn't even *know* about it, claimed he didn't at any rate. He graciously consented to let us conduct our investigations, but he expects a full report on all our activities. Damned cheek, I call it! That's why he and Gordon don't get along. Gordon won't let *any*one know what he's doing. Flatly refuses to tell the rajah what he's up to. Sahji Bandi has made an official complaint to the Viceroy—not that it'll do him any good. Gordon'd tell the Viceroy himself to go to hell if he happened to feel like it."

"I believe he used those very words to the rajah," Dollie remarked. "Shockingly undiplomatic."

"Tickled me when I heard that," Reggie said. "I don't have any use for Gordon, mind you, but when I heard what he said to that crafty old tyrant it did my heart good. The fellow's got cheek if nothing else. Sahji Bandi lolls around on his satin cushions smoking his hookah, fingering his jewels, pretending he can tell us what we can or can't do. Makes my blood boil just to think about it!"

Dollie twirled her parasol. "Well, dear, you have Michael to handle the rajah for you, and a fine job he does of it, too. You're fortunate to have an aide who's

149

such a splendid diplomat. He and the rajah get along swimmingly," she informed me. "Michael has just the right touch. Reggie complains, but he rarely has to deal with the rajah directly, just an occasional meeting now and then."

"And these damned parties!" Reggie complained.

"It *is* a party, dear," she replied. "Please try to remember that. I know *you* don't care anything about it, but some of us would like to have a nice time. Do stop grousing now. It's a lovely day, and the rajah always puts on such a *show*."

We had entered the Royal Parkland now and, thanks to elaborate irrigation over the decades, the land made a startling contrast to the area surrounding it. The grass was a deep, rich jade, and enormous teak and mahogany trees cast soft blue-gray shadows on the ground. I was startled to see a herd of deer milling about. The rajah had gone to Magdalen College at Oxford, Dollie said, and he had been so impressed with the famous deer park that he had imported these animals over to add an English touch to the palace grounds. The carriage rounded a bend, and then I saw the palace itself and the incredibly beautiful lawns, and a few moments later a stern-looking native servant in white silk trousers and turban and a marvelously brocaded pink silk jacket was helping us alight from the carriage.

The palace wasn't nearly as large as I had expected it to be, yet it was still spectacular, all white marble with domes and minarets and mosaics of blue and green and gold. There were lavish gardens with ponds and fountains, and the teak and mahogany trees shaded the rolled green lawns where striped tents and marquees had been set up. Beautifully gowned women strolled about twirling their parasols, talking with handsomely uniformed officers, and native servants in those lovely pink jackets presided over tables covered with spotless linen cloths, tables piled high with heavily ornate English silver containing exotic and colorful food. Other servants circulated with trays of champagne, and a native orchestra painfully rendered traditional English tunes in an octagon-shaped white wooden gazebo unmistakably English with its fussy ginger-bread trim. Tame deer mingled among the guests, begging for bits of cake. It was all the most incredible combination of Victorian stuffiness and Oriental splendor.

The rajah stood on the front steps of the palace with a resplendently uniformed Michael beside him to help greet the guests. Two servants stood behind them holding aloft an enormous square-shaped canopy of gold brocade embroidered with pearls, tassels of pearls dangling from the edges. Dollie strived to look cool and dignified as we strolled toward the steps, but she couldn't quite contain her excitement, lively brown eyes taking in all the splendor with considerable zest. Reggie screwed his monocle in his eye and held his shoulders ramrod stiff. The rajah's face was inscrutable as he watched us approach, but Michael wore a warm smile, looking so handsome it almost took one's breath away.

"Lieutenant Colonel and Mrs. McAllister, Your Highness," Michael said, "and this is Miss Lauren Gray."

Dollie made a little half curtsy, her purple skirts crackling, and I followed her example. Reggie gave a curt nod and extended his right hand with deliberate brusqueness. A faint smile played on the rajah's lips as

151

he shook the gloved hand, but his dark eyes remained expressionless. A rather tense moment followed, but Michael quickly leaped into the breach, displaying that smooth diplomacy Dollie had mentioned earlier.

"Was I not right, Your Highness? I've been telling him all about you, Lauren. I told him you would be the prettiest girl at the party. He said he would judge for himself."

"Indeed so," the rajah said. "My friend Lieutenant Stephens is correct. I am honored by your presence, Miss Gray."

It was the first time he had spoken. His voice was deep and husky, yet there was a curious lilt that gave it a honeyed quality. Rajah Sahji Bandi was almost as tall as Michael, lean and muscular, his skin a dark mahogany. He wore soft white leather boots, and his formfitting trousers and tunic were of exquisitely brocaded white silk, as was his turban. A necklace hung across his chest like a cobweb of fine silver, ablaze with dozens of ruby pendants, some of them as large as grapes. There were matching silver and ruby bracelets fastened about his wrists. The jewelry merely emphasized his excessive virility, for here was a man who was unmistakably male. He had a seamed, harshly handsome face, deep lines on either side of a full, curling mouth, his nose a powerful beak. His glowing black eyes were disturbingly arrogant, yet he was a magnificent creature, crackling with magnetism.

"I am pleased to be here," I said politely.

"And where is the other young English miss? The one with the hair like old gold?"

"Sally? She—she couldn't attend, I'm afraid."

"I hear about her. I hear about you both, am most eager to meet you. My friend Lieutenant Stephens is a lucky man indeed. You must enjoy yourself, Miss Gray. Later perhaps we can have a conversation."

"I'd be delighted, Your Highness."

"I'll join you later, Lauren," Michael told me. "We're expecting a few more guests."

"Isn't he *some*thing?" Dollie whispered as we moved away. "Did you see those *rubies*? He was wearing emeralds last time—emeralds and pearls set in gold. You handled yourself so *well*, dear! So cool and composed. I'll confess, he always makes me awfully *ner*vous."

"I don't like the way he looked at her," Reggie told his wife. "I do wish that dress of yours wasn't cut quite so low, Lauren. I'm not a prudish man, not particularly, but—"

"Oh, hush!" Dollie told him. "It's the *fash*ion. My gown's cut just as low—well, almost as low. Bosoms are quite the *thing*, Reggie. Lauren looks divine."

Reggie stroked his neat mustache, scowling. "All the same, you watch yourself, girl. That fellow has a reputation. These heathens keep their women under lock and key, keep 'em covered up head to toe. Because our women follow the fashion and—uh—display their charms, these randy Indian males sometimes get the wrong impression."

"I'll keep that in mind," I said dryly.

We joined the other guests strolling about the lawns, moving past tables and striped tents. The huge trees cast soft shadows, and for once it was not overly warm. A native servant approached us with a heavy silver tray laden with glasses of champagne. Reggie took one for Dollie and me, declaring he wanted something a mite stronger himself. All around us voices rose, the officers' sober comments mingling with the women's flighty scraps of conversation. The native band chugged and churned out English melodies like Sunday afternoon amateurs giving a park concert, the music a cacophony of discordant noise in the background. Birds of brilliant plumage flitted about the trees, and water splashed in the magnificent white marble fountains inlaid with mosaics.

"I'll just go find some port," Reggie said gruffly. "There's bound to be some around somewhere."

"Mind you don't have too much," Dollie called after him. "He does so hate these affairs, always did. Oh dear, there's Prunella Dobson wearing a gray gown. *Silk*, but still gray. I hope you don't mind what Reggie said about *your* gown, dear. He didn't mean anything by it. He's just terribly stuffy about such things."

"Is the neckline really so daring?"

"Well, dear, they *do* go to extremes in Paris, but if I were nineteen and had a figure like yours I'd wear it that low, too. Gone are the days, alas! Michael admired your dress, and that's all that really matters."

"Did he?"

"You didn't *no*tice? You know, dear, I fancy he's going to ask you a very important question any day now. The lad's quite smitten. It's as plain as day."

I made no reply, and we continued to stroll about the grounds, pausing now and then to chat with various people, then moving on. One of Dollie's close friends rushed over to impart a fresh piece of gossip, and left them at it, walking on by myself, strangely discontented, not knowing exactly why. A servant came over to take my empty champagne glass. I took a fresh glass from the tray, sipping the bubbling brew as I continued to stroll. Pausing beneath one of the tall, slender mahogany trees, I was surprised to find my glass already empty. I looked back at the palace. The white marble minarets and domes were silhouetted against the pale blue sky, the intricately detailed mosaics gleaming in the sun. Michael and the rajah still stood beneath the golden canopy, greeting late guests.

I gave a little start when something cool and moist touched my arm. It was one of the deer, a lovely spotted tan creature with soulful brown eyes. I stroked its head, smiling when it tried to nibble one of the tiny blue flowers sewn on my skirt.

"You mustn't do that," I scolded. "I haven't anything for you to eat, I'm afraid. You'll have to look elsewhere."

As though understanding every word, the deer wandered away, joining the dozen or so others ambling among the guests. I leaned against the trunk of the tree, slightly dizzy from the champagne. I shouldn't have drunk it so quickly, I thought. Couples strolled past, and I nodded when necessary and smiled politely. Dollie was still deep in conversation with the captain's wife, and I was vaguely aware of Reggie standing with a group of men in front of one of the tents. There was laughter and animation, gaiety all around, full skirts rustling like colored petals, gold braid shining in the sun, and it all seemed to blur and grow hazy before my eyes, receding as my mind wandered elsewhere.

I thought about the native who had rescued Sally and me, who had mysteriously appeared at the ruins a week ago, spying on us. Who was he? What had he been doing there? The man was obviously a bandit, a fugitive, and that was one of the reasons neither Sally nor I had told anyone that he had been the man Sergeant Norman had fired at. After what he had done for us, we both felt curiously protective toward him, and both of us had been most relieved when the group of soldiers Reggie had sent to Karbala came back to report they had discovered no signs of anyone about the ruins. The native had disappeared once more, but I had a persistent feeling that I would see him again, and soon.

The leaves of the mahogany tree rustled, and flecks of gold sunlight danced among the shade surrounding me. The natives in their pink jackets were beginning to serve food, removing the heavy silver covers from chafing dishes, arranging delicious smelling Indian delicacies on fine English bone china. Nightingale tongues? I shouldn't have been surprised. I gazed at my empty champagne glass, wishing it were full again, knowing the sparkling wine would afford only a temporary escape from the confusion and indecision that had been bothering me all week long.

Michael was in love with me. He had been about to declare himself that afternoon at Karbala, his "confession" a prelude. *What I'm trying to say is—"* he had begun, and then Sergeant Norman had shouted and fired his pistol and Michael had never been able to finish his statement. He had not brought it up again. During the past week he had been polite, agreeable, charming, but he had been preoccupied, too, spending more time than ever here at the palace helping the rajah arrange the party. Twice he had been unable to accompany me on my morning ride, and he had spent far less time at the house in the evenings. I understood, and I was relieved, for I didn't want him to ask me that important question, not just yet. He was in love with me, but I wanted to be certain about my feelings toward him before I was required to answer the question that seemed inevitable.

I was fond of him. I thought I might be in love with him. I couldn't be sure. I knew so little about love, but from those books I had secretly devoured I understood it was supposed to be a shattering, exhilarating sensation, a highly charged emotion that left one shaken, unable to eat, unable to sleep. The heroines had all been ready to throw aside everything—wealth, position, respectability—to elope with their rakish gypsy lovers, their brooding, mercurial highwaymen. They would have gone through fire to be with their men, and there had been nothing mild, nothing pleasant about the emotions they experienced. When you fell in love you were supposed to know immediately. It was supposed to be as though a bolt of lightning had struck you. There was never any doubt, any indecision. That was the way it was in the books. Was it that way in real life?

Perhaps if I had let him kiss me as he had planned to do in the clearing by the stream, I would have experienced some of those wildly passionate emotions. Perhaps it was all my fault. I was bookish. I was scholarly. I was cool and dignified. Perhaps I was incapable of feeling such heady emotions. Somehow I doubted that. Somehow I suspected that deep down inside, beneath the cool exterior, I had a nature as passionate and responsive as any of those volatile heroines.

A native servant approached with a tray of champagne. I shook my head and gave him my empty glass. Grim and silent, he walked toward a cluster of guests. I didn't see Michael anywhere about. I wondered where he could be. He was everything a woman could ever hope for, I was certain of that. I enjoyed being with him. He made me feel wonderfully alive. When we were apart, I missed him, and I felt a fresh burst of joy each time I saw him anew. I must love him. It was pure folly to expect a bolt of lightning. If that suspected passionate nature had not been awakened, it was because I hadn't given him the opportunity. I sighed, wishing I were older, wishing it all weren't so complex and confusing.

"You don't enjoy the party?"

The husky, honeyed voice startled me. Lost in thought, I hadn't heard the rajah approach, and now he stood before me in all his splendor, rubies blazing like drops of blood against the white silk. The dark eyes, expressionless before, were filled with polite concern. I was embarrassed, at a loss for words. The rajah smiled, and when his full mouth curved up at the corners like that his face didn't seem nearly so malevolent. He made a gesture with a beringed hand, indicating his other guests.

"They all eat the food and talk and listen to the English music my men play in their honor. But you do not. I watch. I walk among my guests and speak to them and wish them enjoyment, and you stand here under this tree all the time, looking sad. I notice."

"I—I was thinking, Your Highness."

"I say to myself, I shall have a conversation with the young Englishwoman my friend Lieutenant Stephens is so fortunate to have met. She looks sad, I say. Perhaps she is feeling neglected because the handsome lieutenant must greet the guests and then must go inside the palace to confer with my chamberlain on a matter of business."

"I—wondered where he was," I said haltingly.

"I confess, the matter of business is not an important one. It could wait until another day, but, I tell myself, with the handsome lieutenant on hand, the young Englishwoman will not wish to have a conversation with me. So I send him into the palace to keep him away for a while. It is devious, no?"

The rajah smiled again. Hard, arrogant, undoubtedly ruthless, he nevertheless exuded a great charm, a warmth of personality I couldn't help but respond to. He wished to be friendly, and I knew full well that he was ordinarily aloof with all the English. I smiled back, embarrassment melting away.

"I am flattered you would go to such lengths, Your Highness."

"I ask myself, what would amuse the beautiful Miss Gray during the absence of her lieutenant. She does not chatter with the other women and she does not eat the food or enjoy the music. How can I amuse her? I ask myself if she would perhaps like to see the palace rooms."

"That would be a marvelous treat," I said, genuinely pleased.

"My palace is not as grand as some, but there is much fine furniture, many fine chambers. It shall please me to show them to you. I will add that not many of the English have been so honored, merely to show you how much I am impressed with Lieutenant Stephens' lovely young friend."

"I am indeed honored, Your Highness."

The rajah nodded, very formal now, and crooked his arm. I placed my hand on the brocaded sleeve, and we slowly made our progress toward the palace steps. It caused something of a sensation. People stared quite openly. Conversations halted in midstream. The music seemed louder than ever, a faltering *om-pah-pah* accompanying our steps. I knew it was extremely

159

unusual for the rajah to show such open favoritism, and I must admit it gave me a thrill to be walking up the steps with my hand on his arm, moving into the cool, sumptuous interior.

The hall was exquisite, the floor blue and white marble tile arranged in floral patterns, the walls ivory and gold, archways leading off into adjoining chambers. The rajah led me into one of the large, open rooms, and I marveled at the lattice work, the screens of beaten gold. We strolled into another room even more impressive, the white walls traced with gold in intricate patterns, and we passed into yet another, then another, and I saw delicate silver and gold filigree work and inlaid ivory, blue tiles and amazingly beautiful carpets, draperies of the finest, purest silk like spun air tinted with color.

It was amazing, each room a marvel, each containing jewel-encrusted artifacts, sumptuous chests, furniture of gold and silver and ivory, and there were mosaic murals of semiprecious stones, but the rajah passed by these without comment. Amidst all this staggering splendor there was, incongruously enough, an abundance of dark, heavy, heavily carved English furniture, all of it hideous, all of it second-rate, the sort of pieces one might find in a gloomy suburban mansion. The rajah was inordinately pleased with it, pointing with pride at the ponderous sideboards, the abominable wardrobes, the stiff-backed chairs with their red plush cushions and tarnished gold fringe.

"I am up to date, you see," he remarked. "I do not live in the past like a number of my fellow princes. I attended the college at Oxford, you know. I am proud to speak English and appreciate the English things."

"I can see that you do," I remarked.

"When I am at Oxford, many look down on me because my skin is dark, but still I admire the English. Does my dark skin bother you, Miss Gray?"

I found the question rather disturbing. "Of course not."

"At Oxford, I had a friend. She had golden hair. She serves the ale in one of the pubs, and she is most friendly. I take her from the pub and give her many fine gifts. She does not mind that my skin is dark. When I leave England she is very sad."

I examined a small silver box encrusted with emeralds that sat on one of the ebony tables, slightly uncomfortable. The rajah apparently saw nothing wrong in telling me about his white mistress. I felt sure he hadn't meant to embarrass me.

"You admire the box?" he inquired.

"It's quite lovely."

"It is yours," he said.

I looked up at him, startled. He was watching me very closely, those dark eyes inscrutable. There was an animal quality about him, and I sensed the savagery lurking behind that polite, formal façade. I remembered what Reggie had said, and I grew more uncomfortable. Surely I had misinterpreted his gesture. He had mentioned the barmaid and his gifts to her, and then he had offered me the emerald box, and . . . and there was no connection. Surely not.

"I—I couldn't accept it, Your Highness."

"No?"

"It wouldn't be—proper. The box is very valuable."

"I see. You are, then, very proper?"

I nodded and attempted a polite smile. The rajah stared at me for a moment, his face a mahogany mask, impossible to read, and I wished I had not been so eager to come with him on the tour. I wished, too, that I was wearing something a little less fashionable and more modest. Could he possibly think that because I was wearing a low-cut gown, because I had told him his dark skin did not bother me.... No, no, I was imagining things. I must be. There were vast differences in our cultures, true, but the rajah surely couldn't think that meant I would welcome anything improper.

"You must see the pool," he said.

He led me into another chamber, one thankfully free of Victorian furniture. The walls were a gleaming white, sunlight streaming through the arched windows covered with pearl latticework, and steps led down into an enormous pool of glistening silvery water so clear I could see the blue and gold mosaic designs at the bottom. Watery reflections danced on the walls like silver shadows, and the long yellow silk draperies hanging over the ivory-columned archways stirred in the soft breezes like thin, translucent yellow wings, the rich color shimmering in the sunlight. The rajah pointed to one of the archways.

"My women live in that section," he said. "My beloved wife died many years ago, but I have several concubines, all of them plump, all of them fond of jewels. It amuses me to toss handfuls of precious stones into the water and watch the women dive for them. They usually fight, alas, and I must be very stern with them."

I made no reply, and he looked at me with those dark, glowing eyes. His manner was as polite, as formal as ever, but I had the impression that he knew very well that it wasn't fitting to speak of concubines in front of an English girl, that he had done so deliberately. The faintest suggestion of a smile curled on his full lips, and

I was uncomfortably aware of the silence and the fact that during the tour we had not as yet encountered another person. Maintaining my composure at considerable expense, I stepped over to one of the archways and fingered one of the draperies.

"I've never seen silk so fine," I remarked, "and the color is beautiful, such a rich yellow."

"It is my own yellow," he informed me. "The dye is specially made for me. They also make a royal blue and a crimson that you will find nowhere else in India."

He had padded silently across the floor until he was standing directly behind me. I turned, alarmed by his nearness. It must have shown on my face, for he frowned.

"You are uncomfortable, Miss Gray?"

"We've been gone for quite some time, Your Highness. I think perhaps we should rejoin the guests now."

"But there is much you have not seen. You have not seen the Throne Room nor the official reception chambers. Nor have you seen my private quarters. They are the most elaborate in the palace, as is fitting. There are many rich items to behold."

"Perhaps I shall be able to see the rest of the palace another time," I said, gracious, I hoped, but firm.

The rajah hesitated a moment, studying me intently, and then he nodded.

"It shall be my privilege, Miss Gray." His voice was smooth and formal. "Perhaps the lieutenant will bring you back to the palace soon."

"I shall look forward to returning."

He crooked his arm again, and I placed my hand on it. He was silent as we moved down a long hallway, the white walls adorned with blue, black and gold mosaics depicting a tiger hunt. Moments later we were moving down the front steps again in splashes of bright sunlight, and I felt a wave of nervous relief. We joined the other guests. I thanked the rajah politely for the honor he had done me. He nodded and moved toward a group of guests in long, lordly strides, and I stepped over to one of the tables to fetch a much-needed glass of champagne.

I was shaken, much more so than I cared to admit to myself. I drank the champagne quickly, and then I took a second glass and turned to look at the crowd. Couples were strolling all over the grounds, some of them far away, looking like dolls in the distance. I saw Reggie across the way, deep in conversation with three officers, and Dollie was sitting with a group of women in a circle of white wicker lawn chairs under one of the shade trees, all of them with plates in their laps, gossiping avidly as they ate. Michael was nowhere in sight. He must still be in conference with the chamberlain, I thought, and I was relieved, for I didn't want to talk to anyone just yet, afraid I would betray myself.

I knew I mustn't let anyone know what had happened. Reggie was already adamantly set against the rajah, and if he were to think that Sahji Bandi had even hinted at anything improper it could, I knew, lead to serious diplomatic problems. I had thought Reggie amusingly stuffy when he critized my gown and told me to be wary of the rajah, and like a fool I had let the man take me into the palace, away from the other guests. I had been calm enough when the rajah had made his subtle proposition—for I knew now that that was exactly what it had been—but as I thought about it now, as I remembered the look in his eyes, I could feel a delayed reaction setting in. I finished the second glass of champagne, shuddering inside, trying to maintain my composure.

The sunlight was too bright. The music was too loud. Everyone else was enjoying the party, much less dignified and formal than they had been earlier on. The champagne and plentiful hard liquor were responsible for that. Colored parasols twirled. Voices were shrill. Dishes clattered. The music played and played, and I thought my head would split. I moved through the crowd, smiling, pretending to enjoy myself, and then I circled around one of the striped tents and passed a splashing fountain and walked over richly green grass toward the four teak trees growing on a small slope in the distance. Several deer were grazing on the grass. They lifted their heads as I moved quickly past, my full skirts swaying back and forth like a white silk bell. Finally I was beneath the trees and the dreadful music wasn't so loud and I was alone at last, away from the others, free to relax.

Or so I had thought. I had been standing there only a few moments when I smelled the burning tobacco and saw a plume of blue-gray smoke writhing around one of the trees and floating off into the air. A man was standing on the other side of the trees, smoking one of those evil-smelling black cheroots. I could sense his presence now. He couldn't have helped hearing my approach nor the sigh of relief I had uttered upon reaching this sanctuary. Why hadn't he shown himself?

"Damn!" I muttered. It was a word I rarely used.

"Such language," he said.

I hadn't realized I had spoken loud enough to be heard. A blush tinted my cheeks as the man stepped casually around one of the trees and looked at me with mocking black-brown eyes, and then the blush must have vanished for I know I turned pale with shock and surprise. I couldn't speak. I could do nothing but stare at him, amazed, alarmed, disbelieving.

"Relax," he drawled. "I shan't bite you."

"You," I whispered. I felt weak, dizzy.

He wore shiny black boots and a beautifully tailored creamy white linen suit and a loosely knotted emerald green tie. His head was bare, thick raven locks untidy, tousled by the wind. The face was exactly as I remembered it: cruel, ruthless, the face of a killer. The hypnotic black-brown eyes observed me coolly beneath hooded lids, and the lips curled sardonically at one corner.

"Surprised, Miss Gray?"

I stared at him, still unable to speak.

"I do hope you're not going to faint," he said dryly.

"I don't faint," I told him. My voice was tight.

"I shouldn't think so. Any young woman who can carry on so splendidly in the middle of a jungle after witnessing a massacre isn't likely to swoon at the sight of me. Pity, rather. I should enjoy reviving you."

"You—you're Robert Gordon," I accused.

"Guilty. I confess it."

I could feel hot anger rising up inside, eclipsing all other emotions. I stared at him in outrage and dismay.

"You spoke English all the time!"

"Indeed," he confessed.

"And —and you let me make a fool of myself! You let us think you were some kind of—" I gasped, unable to continue.

"Brigand, ruffian, brute, rapist, white slaver. I freely admit the first three labels might apply, but I've never committed rape, and I definitely don't sell young girls into bondage. I can't recall all the things the two of you called me during our little adventure, but it was certainly interesting to hear you speculate."

"We were terrified of you!"

"Perhaps. It served its purpose. Had you known I was English you would have given cries of relief and gone to pieces, giving in to the hysterics both of you were holding at bay so superbly. I knew we had a difficult time ahead of us. Two brave, determined young women constantly alert, constantly on guard were much easier to manage."

"That was despicable!" I cried.

"Is that fair?" he asked. "After all, I did save your lives. I should think you'd show a little more gratitude."

He flicked an ash off the tip of his long black cigar and took another drag. Smoke curled about his harsh, deeply tanned face, and he narrowed his eyes against it. I thought of all the things Sally and I had said about him. He had understood every word. He had been laughing at us. My anger mounted, and I wanted to pound on his chest with balled fists. I had rarely experienced such tumultuous emotion, and it left me helpless, composure shattered, dignity gone.

"How *could* you? We were stranded in the middle of nowhere, paralyzed with terror, not knowing *what* you intended to do to us, and you—you were British all the time! You let us babble on like fools. You shoved Sally around brutally and treated us both like imbeciles and—"

"Guarded you with my life," he interrupted. "Fine thanks I get for it, too, I must say."

167

"You were prowling around at Karbala as well. Sergeant Norman thought you were a Thug. He almost *killed* you!"

"Poor shot, Norman. He fired twice, never came anywhere near me. I'll have to speak to him about that. Chap needs a bit more practice if he's going to qualify as a real marksman."

"You let us rush off into the jungle like terrified cattle, thinking a whole band of assassins might fall upon us at any minute. I've never run so hard in my life."

"The exercise did you good, I dare say."

I swung my hand back, ready to slam it across his face. Robert Gordon caught my wrist, gave it a savage twist and slowly lowered it to my side. I winced at the pain, biting my lip, and he released me, shaking his head in silent admonishment. I could feel tears welling up inside, and I was horrified they might start flowing. Desperately, I fought them back, and the anger fled, replaced by confusion and frustration and other emotions I couldn't identify. Gordon took another long drag on his cigar and released the smoke and then, dropping the cigar to the ground, crushed it under his heel.

"I'd gone to considerable risk to save your lives once before," he remarked, "and when I learned you were going to Karbala I decided I'd best tag along, make sure that nothing happened. Despite what your upstanding young lieutenant might believe, the whole area is infested with Thugs. It was a foolhardy venture. Your idea, I believe."

"How could you possibly know that?"

"I know almost everything that goes on at the

garrison, Miss Gray. I could give you a thorough account of everything you've done since the day you arrived, although I'm afraid it would prove quite dull."

I had the tears under control now. At least I wouldn't suffer that humiliation. I struggled to summon some kind of composure. Never before in my life had I experienced so many different emotions in so short a time. Never before had I encountered anyone so disturbing.

"How could you possibly know what I've been doing?" I asked coldly.

"I have my sources, Miss Gray. Knowing things is my business."

"Then you really *are* a spy?"

"If that's what you choose to call it. I'm a government agent attached to the military, a useful chap who can do things your average soldier boy can't."

"Like posing as a native."

"Among other things, yes."

"If you work for the military, why aren't you in uniform now?"

"Wearing a uniform could cause unnecessary complications," he informed me. "Because of the nature of my job it's often necessary for me to give orders to men who considerably outrank me. Were I wearing the uniform of a captain, say, or a mere first lieutenant, they would find it both difficult and galling to obey me. As I wear no insignia, no one here knows my rank. Makes my job a bit easier."

"Apparently you need all the help you can get," I replied. "From what I've heard, it appears you've had a remarkable lack of success."

"You've heard that, have you?"

"I've heard a lot of things about you, Mr. Gordon, all of them highly unflattering."

He made no reply, but a disdainful half smile curled on his lips. Cool, arrogant, mocking, he gazed at me with heavy lids drooping over those dark, hypnotic eyes, and I experienced yet another emotion, one that shocked me profoundly. When he had been disguised as a native, he had reminded me of one of the improbable heroes who charged through the pages of those flamboyant romances I had read back at school. I had felt his potent magnetism then, and it had horrified me even to recognize it as such. In his civilian clothes, his hair untidy, the emerald tie loose and flapping, he bore an even more striking resemblance to those unprincipled rogues who caused such stormy upheavals in the hearts of all of those heroines with flowery names. The man was infuriating, insufferable, but he had magnetism so strong it was almost like a physical force.

"It seems I have quite a task ahead of me," he remarked idly.

"Oh?"

"Wooing you, winning you. I've made up my mind to marry you, you see. Can't have a wife who harbors such ugly ideas about me."

"Of all the outrageous—"

"Never thought I'd care to marry," he interrupted, still speaking in that idle, casual tone. "I lead an unsettled, frequently uncomfortable life, travel a lot, intend to do much more in the future. I need a woman who'll be willing to pay, pack and follow, who has a taste for adventure as strong as my own. A woman, in short, who can trek through jungles and face sandstorms and savages and endure all sorts of hardships without whining. Never thought I'd meet her. Most of the pale, puny English misses I've met wouldn't last a week. Then I met you, Miss Gray, under highly unusual circumstances. Took me no time at all to realize I'd finally found the woman I'd been looking for."

"I—I've never been so insulted in all my life!"

"Insulted? I've just paid you the highest compliment a woman can receive. You're one in a million. Oh, you're cool and conventional enough on the surface, but there are depths yet unplumbed. I spotted that immediately. You're remarkably intelligent, and you have spirit and stamina and, incidentally, a face and form to make a man seethe with lust."

I slammed my palm across his face, hard, and this time he made no attempt to stop me. My palm stung viciously, and I could see the imprint of my hand glowing on his cheek, but Gordon merely smiled.

"I can see this has come as a shock to you," he told me, "but I dare say you'll grow accustomed to the idea. There's really no use fighting it, Lauren. I've made up my mind to have you, and one way or another I always get what I want."

I was trembling with rage, unable to speak. I wanted to slap his face again. I didn't. I turned and moved quickly down the slope, my cheeks burning, my heart pounding. My skirts swayed wildly, and I almost lost my balance. The deer looked up, startled. The dreadful music grew louder and louder. My head was spinning. My pulses were leaping. Never before had I been so thoroughly shaken. Never had I felt such emotional turmoil. It was almost as though I had been struck by a bolt of lightning.

Eight

"I was absolutely fascinated," Sally said. "He was wearing black trousers and this billowing Indian robe of dark maroon, all embroidered with leaves in black silk, and, Miss Lauren, he was smoking a *hookah*! It gave me a turn when I saw him, I don't mind telling you. There he was, big as life, looking just as sinister and mysterious as he did when he came riding up to us in the desert."

"Surely you didn't visit that man's quarters *alone*?" I asked sharply. "Really, Sally, there are limits—"

"Of course I didn't," she interrupted. "Bill went with me. He and Bill are good friends—I think I told you that. Anyway, he was ever so polite and gracious, told us to sit down on a pile of cushions, offered the hookah to us. I took a puff. Made me quite heady. You should see his rooms, Miss Lauren—Indian cushions on the floor, books and papers everywhere and the *most* unusual curios, all jumbled together. There were drawings, too, whole portfolios of 'em. I looked at some—they made what we saw at Karbala seem tame! He's writing a study of Eastern sexual customs."

"Sally!"

"Oh, it's ever so scholarly, has to do with anthropology. I can't imagine anyone actually *publishing it, but it seems there's a firm in Germany anxiously awaiting the manuscript. He's writing it in German, by the way. I guess that makes a difference."

It was the morning after the rajah's fête, and we were out in the back garden. Sally had scampered off immediately after breakfast, the yellow rumal in her pocket, and I had moped around listlessly, irritated by Dollie's bright banter and bits of gossip, in a thoroughly foul mood. I had finally come outside to get some sunshine and try to compose my thoughts. Sally had come prancing out a few minutes ago, brimming over with excitement at her visit with Robert Gordon.

"We didn't stay long," she told me. "Bill had to report for duty at ten-thirty. I gave Gordon the yellow scarf and told him how I'd gotten it, and he just nodded, frowning a bit. Bill was astonished, I must say. 'You mean you're that native who—' he began, and Gordon cut him short and said he was to keep his mouth shut about it. Said I was to keep *mine* shut, too. No one knows but just the four of us, Miss Lauren. Gordon says it's important no one else knows. *You* haven't told anyone, have you?"

I shook my head. I hadn't mentioned it to anyone. I had rejoined the garden party and had several more glasses of champagne, and when Michael had finally come out of the palace I had been very charming and just a little tipsy. He had been amused and slightly alarmed at my condition, insisting I eat something, walking with me over the grounds until my delightful haze was gone and I was depressed and silent. Apparently no one had noticed me standing under the trees with Gordon, and I hadn't told anyone about meeting him. Although there was to be a spectacular fireworks display as soon as the sun went down, an event eagerly anticipated by the guests, I told Michael I

173

had a frightful headache, and he had driven me back to the garrison shortly after five. I had had a restless evening, a sleepless night, and Sally's enthusiastic chatter about Robert Gordon wasn't helping my present frame of mind one bit.

"I told him I didn't think you had," Sally continued. "I told him you were in a wretched state last night after the party, wouldn't eat anything and just mooned about in your room. For some reason, that seemed to *amuse* him. He asked if 'the upstanding young lieutenant' had come by this morning and I said no, he hadn't, and you weren't in any mood for riding anyway."

"You *do* talk a lot, don't you?" I snapped.

Sally paid no mind to my bad humor. She was so eager to talk about Robert Gordon that she probably didn't even notice it.

"Fancy, Miss Lauren, it was him all the time. All those things we said about him—he understood every word! I told him it served him right, pretending not to speak English like that."

"I think it was horrible of him."

"Not really, not when you stop and think about it. He explained why, and I must say it makes sense to me. If we *had* known he was English, we'd have been much less cautious. It's rather funny, actually. Remember how you tried to explain things to him? 'Dahl-kari. Mc-Al-lis-ter pay many rupees.' I'll bet he had a laugh over *that*."

"I'm sure he did."

"Gordon said you and he had a nice long talk yesterday."

"Nice is hardly the word for it."

"Why didn't you *tell* me you'd met him at the garden

party? Letting me go off like that, knowing the shock I had in store."

"I don't recall that you told me where you were going."

"I guess I didn't, come to think of it. I didn't want Reggie or anyone to overhear. Still, I should have thought you'd have told me about it last night. When I came into your room, eager to hear all about the party, you nearly snapped my head off, told me you were in no mood for chitchat. You weren't yourself at all."

"I'm sorry, Sally."

"I guess it was the shock of seeing him like that," she said thoughtfully, "and then all that champagne you drank. Oh, did I tell you he gave me my pistol back? He did. He told me to hold on to it, never leave the post without it. Between you and me, Miss Lauren, I think he's *on* to something."

"Really?"

"Reggie claims he hasn't accomplished a blooming thing, but I have the feeling Gordon is just biding his time. I think he knows a great deal and is waiting to get the proper evidence. He asked me so many questions about the caravan and all, and now and then he would look fierce and give a sharp nod, as though he had known exactly what I was going to say. I think he's much nearer flushing out these Thugs than anyone suspects."

"That well may be," I said stiffly.

"You don't like him, do you, Miss Lauren?"

"Not at all."

"He admires *you*. I could tell by the way he talked. He asked me a lot of questions about you, too, things that had nothing to do with India or the Thugs. He asked me about the school in Bath, how you got along

175

with the other girls, what you did in your spare time. He asked me if you'd had any beaux, and I said no, not that I knew of. I told him you spent most of your time with your nose in a book. He seemed quite pleased."

"I'll thank you not to ever discuss me with Robert Gordon again, Sally. I—I can't abide the man!"

Sally gave me a peculiar look. "I must say, Miss Lauren, I've never seen you react quite so strongly to anyone before. Hmmm. Makes you stop and *won*der."

"What do you mean by that?" I demanded.

"Noth-ing," she said carefully. "Nothing at all. Well, since you're in such a snappish mood and not at all *friend*ly this morning, I think I'll go up and start on my dress. I bought the most gorgeous bolt of silk in the bazaar yesterday. It'll make a smashing gown. Bill and I had a great time yesterday, incidentally, but I'm sure you wouldn't be interested. I'll see you later."

She moved nimbly back into the house before I could stop her and apologize. I knew I was in a foul mood, and I knew why, but it wasn't fair to take it out on Sally. I felt remorse now, on top of everything else, for I knew I had treated her shabbily. I strolled toward the line of gray banyan trees with their exposed, twisted roots. Tall purple hollyhocks grew in a bed in front of them, and a gorgeous white cockatoo perched on one of the limbs, surrounded by vivid green leaves. It ruffled its feathers, unperturbed by my approach. It was a dazzling morning, awash with streaming silver sunlight, but it might as well have been gray and gloomy for all the good it did me.

He had been jesting. Of course he had been. He hadn't meant a word he had said. He couldn't have meant it. Upset by my experience with the rajah, I had fled the party, seeking a few moments of solitude, and then he had stepped around the tree and I had been startled, shaken to the core to see that harsh, familiar face. I had overreacted. I had been rude and haughty and, yes, horrible to him, and in order to get his own back he had said those incredible words, hoping to unsettle me even further. He had succeeded brilliantly, his reward the sight of me fleeing down the slope in a state of near panic. How he must have enjoyed that. How he must have laughed when I stumbled and almost fell.

Disguised as a native, working undercover to track down the Thugs, Robert Gordon had rescued us when we were stranded in the middle of desert sand and dense belts of jungle, and later on he had risked his own life to defend us, killing two men in the process. Standing now in the shade of the banyan trees, I could see the curtain of vines parting, and I could see the Thug and the yellow rumal stretched tightly between his hands, and the whole scene played itself again in my mind: his murderous cry and that arm slung around his throat, cutting it off, his mad puppet dance as the arm tightened, the flash of knife in the moonlight, the body crumpling to the ground as the native released it. It had been horrible, but if Gordon hadn't appeared when he did I wouldn't be standing here now with the leaves rustling and sunlight striping the lawn and throwing long blue-gray shadows across the back veranda.

Robert Gordon had saved my life, and instead of thanking him, instead of showing my gratitude, I had flown at him in a rage because he had maintained his cover and let us both think he was a native brigand. I had acted like an idiot. I fully realized that, and I probably owed him an apology. He wasn't about to get one. I intended to make every effort to avoid the man, and if by chance I encountered him I would be civil out of necessity. I would be cool and polite and remote. I would maintain my dignity and let him see that I had quite forgotten that absurd speech about finally finding a chattle to pack his things and pay his bills and follow him across wild and dangerous uncharted territories.

A woman would be insane to marry a man like that, I told myself. He would make her life an unmitigated hell. He would be much more interested in his explorations and his writings than in her, and if he didn't openly abuse her, he would neglect her terribly, noticing her only when she failed to do something right, failed to be the meek, subservient slave he seemed to require. Granted there might be great adventure, great excitement. There might even be moments of shattering happiness when he decided to toss her a bone now and then, for, like those gypsies and highwaymen and ruthless vagabonds, he would be a superb lover, but the bliss would be short-lived and he would be off to discover some lost city and she would be left to pay the bills, pack the provisions, hire the porters and follow after.

"You're in a very thoughtful mood."

Startled, I looked up. Michael smiled.

"Michael. I—I didn't hear you come out."

"So I noticed. I hope that dreamy expression means you were thinking about me."

He smiled a warm smile, and I was glad the question wasn't one that really required an answer. Dreamy expression? Whatever could he mean? He was wearing his uniform and, as always, looked spectacularly handsome in the glossy black knee boots, the clinging white breeches and superbly tailored red jacket with gold epaulettes at the shoulders. Although the smile continued to play on his lips, he seemed preoccupied, as though there were something very important on his mind.

"I didn't expect to see you this morning, Michael."

"Nor did I expect to drop by, but—well, there's been a new development, Lauren. I'm afraid I've come to say good-bye."

"Good-bye?"

"I'm off on another expedition, leaving in a couple of hours as a matter of fact. I don't know how long I'll be gone. It could be two weeks, could be three."

"But—"

"Gordon has reported strong Thuggee activity around one of the distant villages on the very outskirts of the district, up near the tiger country. He claims they have a camp hidden somewhere in the jungle, claims they're in close contact with the villagers, most of whom are relatives of the assassins in the hidden camp. It has to be checked out thoroughly. I'm taking a full two dozen men with me."

"But, Michael, you're Reggie's aide. Your work is primarily diplomatic. Isn't there someone else who could head the expedition? I don't understand why *you* have to go."

Michael frowned, a deep crease forming between his brows. He looked very stern. "This damned diplomatic work—catering to the rajah, keeping relations smooth between the palace and the garrison—it's frustrating to a man of action, a man who wants to *do* something."

"What you do is very important," I protested.

"It isn't the same thing. I'm a soldier, not a civil

servant. I was trained to fight."

"You're just recently returned from one expedition—"

"And I botched it up terribly. We didn't find a single lead, and the mission went down on the books as a total failure. I need to make up for that. I need to prove that I can do something besides drink endless cups of tea in reception rooms and charm a dissolute native prince into tolerating our presence in his district. I intend to make this mission a complete success."

"Will it be dangerous?"

"Quite likely," he said. "If what Gordon says is true, it could be very dangerous. I've got to go, Lauren. Surely you can see why. Gordon himself recommended me for the job."

"*Gordon* recommended you?"

"McAllister was against me going, particularly with this bloody tiger hunt coming up, but Gordon told him I should be given another chance, said I'd try twice as hard as anyone else simply because the other mission was such a failure. I resent the man, don't like anything about him, but I have to be grateful to him. If he hadn't put his word in your guardian wouldn't have allowed me to head the mission."

"I wish you weren't going, Michael."

I meant that sincerely, and Michael heard the sincerity in my voice. I could tell that it pleased him. He looked at me with those vivid blue eyes, and I could see the tenderness in them. Impulsively, I reached up and brushed a lock of dark blond hair from his forehead. I let my fingers rest for a moment on his lean cheek. Michael stepped closer, the corners of his mouth tightening. He wanted to take me into his arms. He was struggling with himself to keep from doing so.

180

"You'll miss me?" he asked.

"You know I will. I'll miss you, and I'll worry."

"Will you?"

"Every day," I told him.

"I'm very glad to hear that, Lauren." His voice was low.

"How could you have doubted it?"

He was standing so close I could see the tiny pink scar on his cheek where he must have cut himself shaving. I saw the intense blue eyes and the high, flat cheekbones and the beautifully shaped mouth: firm, pinkish-tan, curving tensely now as he ached to kiss me. I had rebuffed him that afternoon by the stream, but I knew I wouldn't rebuff him now. I wanted to be in love with him. I wanted him to kiss me with passionate abandon and drive everything else out of my mind. I wanted him to sweep me off my feet as he had teasingly promised to do.

"I'm in love with you," he said.

"I—I know, Michael."

"I've never felt this way, never knew I *could* feel this way."

Michael frowned again. He stepped back, thrusting his hands into his trouser pockets. The fringe on his epaulettes swayed and shimmered. He turned and stared at the back of the house, his face in profile. I didn't know whether I was relieved or disappointed. I was fond of him, so very fond, but that wasn't enough, and I wanted him to take the initiative and force me to feel those emotions locked up inside. He was handsome and virile and strong, decent and honest and stable, everything any woman could wish for in a man, and I felt certain he could set those emotions ablaze. I hadn't given him a chance before. Now that I was willing to, he

181

was understandably reluctant. It was my own fault.

"I don't want to rush you," he said gruffly. "I did that once before, and I don't want to make the same mistake twice. You said you wanted to be sure, Lauren."

"I—I know, Michael."

"When I get back, I'm going to ask you a question, and I want you to be prepared to answer it. I'm hoping the answer will be yes. I want you to think about that while I'm gone."

"I will," I promised.

He turned to face me, and his expression was severe, almost belligerent.

"I know you don't like the military life," he said, his tone still gruff and severe. "I know you think it's stuffy and dull and too confined, and perhaps it is, but I'm not going to be a soldier all my life. I have plans, big plans."

"Do you?"

"I'm not prepared to talk about them yet, but. . . ." The crease between his brow deepened into a tight line. "I believe I can make you happy, Lauren. I'm hoping you'll give me the chance."

He was extremely uncomfortable. I could see that it had taken a great deal for him to declare himself like this. Scowling, he looked more like an angry little boy than a tender suitor, and I found this endearing. At that moment the white cockatoo began to squawk loudly, making a dreadful racket. Michael gave a start and then looked as though he wanted to throttle the bird. I laughed in spite of myself, and after a moment Michael laughed, too, and, taking my hand, led me toward the back veranda.

"I have to get back at once," he said. "There are still a great many things to do before we set off. I didn't actually have the time to come by in the first place, but I couldn't leave without seeing you."

I opened the back door, and we walked toward the front hall. "I'm so glad you did," I said. "I would have been crushed if you hadn't."

"I'm hoping to be back for the tiger hunt."

"Tiger hunt?" This was the second time he had mentioned it.

"Hasn't anyone told you about it? The rajah's going on one of his celebrated tiger hunts in two weeks, and he's asked the commander and a party of twelve from the garrison to accompany him. The commander is to select the twelve, but the rajah especially asked for you and Dollie and 'the other English miss' to be included in the party."

"I—hadn't heard."

"The commander doesn't want to go, of course, but he realizes that a refusal would be a gross insult to the rajah, could cause a serious strain on relations between palace and garrison. The commander fussed and fumed, but in the end he saw there was no way out."

"He accepted the invitation?"

Michael nodded. "Most reluctantly, though. I imagine he'll tell you all about it later on."

"I imagine he will."

We were standing in front of the door now. Michael hesitated for just a moment, more uncomfortable than ever, and then his mouth grew tight and his blue eyes were suddenly resolute. Roughly, abruptly, he pulled me into his arms and kissed me vigorously. I was startled, but I made no attempt to push him away. One arm wrapped around my waist, the other curled around the back of my neck, he made a sudden swerve, bending me at the waist and swinging me around until I was almost leaning over backwards, his mouth over mine all the while. When he finally released me, I was breathless, too stunned to speak.

"Think about that, too," he said brusquely.

And then, before I could reply, he opened the front door and stepped out onto the veranda and pulled the door shut behind him, leaving me alone in the hall. I was still dizzy, still out of breath, not knowing what to make of that sudden lunge or my own reactions to it, but I would definitely think about it.

As I had been so uncivil to Dollie in the morning, I could hardly refuse to go to the village with her that afternoon. Laden with food and clothes and medical supplies, she made periodic visits to the needy families of Dahlkari, a bright, chatty Lady Bountiful who distributed her parcels with jolly good will and a merry smile, totally unlike the rigid, tight-lipped missionaries and other organized do-gooders determined to do their "duty" and leaving a wake of resentment behind. Although none of the other women on post would accompany her on her charitable missions, all of them contributed parcels, frequently under duress. It was one of the rare times when Dollie used her position as the commanding officer's wife to bully the others into doing her will.

The open carriage jolted uncomfortably. As we left the post and started down toward the village, the corporal who served as our driver tugged on the reins to slow the horses. The parcels heaped up on the seat opposite us slipped and slid about, one of them tumbling to the floor. I bent down to put it back in place. Dollie sighed, the girlish black ringlets on either

184

side of her plump face jiggling comically. She wore a blue and maroon striped dress, her black kid boots peeking out beneath the voluminous skirts. A befringed blue shawl was wrapped around her arms, and she held a large blue parasol over one shoulder. I settled back beside her, my lilac skirt rustling. The carriage bounced on down the slope under a sun-drenched pearl-gray sky, yellow heat waves shimmering.

"One does what one *can*," Dollie remarked, eyeing the bouncing parcels on the seat opposite. "It frequently seems so hopeless—all this poverty and starvation on every side, disease, malnutrition. Of course the natives of Dahlkari have it much better because of the garrison. There's a great deal of trade—the men are always buying things to send home, and the bazaar is the largest in the district. Dahlkari's far more prosperous than the average Indian village."

As we rode past the river I looked at the water buffalo wallowing in the thick brown mud. The women in worn, dusty saris moved by with their inevitable pitchers, and a group of naked children were splashing in the water, half hidden by reeds. We passed a crumbling white religious temple and a line of sunbaked hovels. The corporal on his high seat in front tugged on the reins again, slowing the horses down as we reached the village proper.

"Many of the natives work as servants for the English," Dollie continued, "and Doctor Hendricks and his assistants tend all the sick—the beds at the infirmary on post are generally filled with ailing natives. Nevertheless, I'm afraid it's just a drop in the bucket. They resent us, and I suppose that's only natural."

185

The street we were moving down was narrow and congested, filled with beggars and filth and exotic shops. Stacks of woven baskets stood beside bamboo bird cages filled with dejected, brightly colored birds. Hawkers cried their wares. Children raced alongside the carriage, hands held out hopefully. Dollie reached into her maroon silk reticule, withdrew a handful of coins and tossed them to the children. They began to scream, scrambling in the street on hands and knees as the carriage moved on.

"It doesn't do any good, I'm afraid, but I can never resist it. Can you feel the hostility? As I said, they resent us dreadfully, and why not? We live up there in comfort and seclusion, while down here they struggle to exist. Our men spend a lot of money in the village, but I fear they don't always conduct themselves like gentlemen. There are frequent brawls in the cafés when they've had too much to drink, and then there are those terrible houses—some of the girls are barely in their teens, their hands and feet painted vermilion, eyes lined with kohl. It does no good to put such places off limits, dear. Men are men, particularly *mili*tary men. If it weren't for the houses there'd be even more trouble."

"I can imagine," I replied, not at all shocked.

"There are certain things one learns to accept," Dollie said regretfully, "and then there are others that must be stopped. Before we arrived in Dahlkari anyone caught stealing, be it merely a piece of fruit from one of the stalls, had their right hand chopped off. We put a stop to that, against considerable objections from the rajah, I might add. There are other, even more brutal practices we abolished, like suttee, for example— burning the widows on their husbands' funeral pyres. There was even more opposition when we put a stop to that, from the natives themselves. It's a religious practice, you see. In many cases the widows are eager to join their husbands in death."

"And if they're not?"

"They're bound and gagged and hurled into the flames anyway. It gives one the shivers just to think about it!"

We passed a street lined with shabby cafés, strands of beads dangling over the doorways, bizarre music and the noise of clattering dishes pouring through the windows along with the flies. Beggars squatted against the walls, many of them missing arms and legs, some sightless, all wearing tattered rags begrimed with filth. This street was congested, too, a solid mass of moving humanity who grudgingly stepped aside to let the carriage pass. The din was incredible, the stench appalling. I was beginning to see why the other wives weren't eager to accompany Dollie on these missions.

"Only a week or so before you arrived Reggie had to send some men down here to stop a suttee," she continued. "He heard about it just in time. The relatives of the deceased had already prepared the pyre down by the river, a huge stack of wood. The torches had already been lighted, and the widow was weeping and wailing and tearing her clothes. The poor woman would have gone up in flames if the men hadn't arrived when they did. As it was, she fought them viciously when the pyre was lighted, trying to break free and hurl herself into the fire. We can't allow anything that barbaric, even if it does have to do with their religion. Suttee has been officially abolished all over India, but I'm afraid it's still a common practice."

Leaving the congested business district, we drove past grim gray and brown hovels with unprotected windows and doors. Whole families lived inside, frequently with their animals. Dollie explained that Blossom, the maid, kept her informed about those villagers who were particularly in need of provisions, and she tactfully suggested that I remain in the carriage when we made our stops, afraid I might find the squalor within difficult to take. We made stop after stop, Dollie bouncing in and out of the carriage with spirit undaunted. As we waited for her to come out, several native men skulked around, eyeing the parcels with unabashed greed, but the robust young corporal's menacing countenance held them at bay. When all the parcels were finally delivered, Dollie informed me that she wanted to stop by and visit with Blossom's family for a while.

"Why don't you visit the bazaar, dear? It's fascinating, I can assure you. The corporal can leave the carriage in front of Blossom's house. Now that the parcels are gone no one will bother it. You couldn't possibly go without an escort, but Burke will be glad to act in that capacity. You can come back for me when you've seen enough, then we'll return to the garrison."

"I'd love to see it, but I wouldn't want to impose on the corporal."

"It'll be a treat for him, too, escorting a pretty young girl about. Isn't that right, Burke?"

"Indeed it is, ma'am," the corporal replied.

"Watch him, Lauren," Dollie teased. "He's got quite a reputation as a ladies' man. Handsome brute like him, it's no *won*der."

Burke grinned, and a few minutes later I found myself walking with him toward the bazaar that occupied several acres in the center of the village. In his early twenties, he was tall and sturdily built, a taciturn fellow with dark brown hair and a humped nose that had obviously been broken. His wide mouth was grim as he escorted me through the crowd, his dark gray eyes glaring a warning at anyone who dared get too close. Burke was exceedingly conscious of his responsibility, I thought, rather amused by his fierce demeanor.

The bazaar was indeed something to behold, hundreds of stalls forming a maze, the paths in between crowded with prosperous looking natives and a number of soldiers from the garrison enjoying their afternoon off. As Corporal Burke and I entered the maze, I marveled at booths heaped high with mangoes and coconuts and melons, some split open to reveal the juicy red pulp. Meat hung on racks with flies abuzz. Live chickens were strung up by their feet squawking and struggling. There were stalls displaying exquisite silks of rainbow hue interwoven with gold and silver thread in delicate patterns, stalls with fancy leather work, with bowls and platters of chased brass, with rack after rack ashimmer with jewelry. The noise was deafening, the atmosphere charged with excitement, people arguing, haggling over prices, exclaiming over the beauty of various items. I was startled to see a skinny, dingy white cow ambling casually down one of the aisles, people stepping aside to make way for it. We were soon in the middle of the maze, a constantly changing kaleidoscope of sight and sound. The corporal kept close beside me, patient with my enthusiasm, shoving aside anyone who got in our way.

"Must you be so rough?" I asked him.

"You've gotta watch these rogues," he said sternly. "They'd steal the clothes off your back if they could. You've gotta be firm with 'em, show 'em you won't tolerate any nonsense."

Burke obviously wasn't about to tolerate any. A rugged specimen who carried himself like a pugilist, the humped nose giving a belligerent look to his face, he was merely watching out for me. I realized that, and I realized that what he had said about thievery was undoubtedly true, yet I wished he weren't quite so zealous about his responsibility. His rough manner could only make the natives resent us even more.

We turned a corner and started down another aisle lined with dozens of stalls, and it was then that I saw Gordon and Valerie Simpson. He wore the same white suit he had been wearing at the rajah's party, and she was wearing a deep garnet dress, her lustrous black hair tumbling loose. They were standing in front of a stall displaying jewelry. Mrs. Simpson was examining a silver bracelet while Gordon smoked a cheroot with a bored expression. I stopped abruptly. The corporal asked me what was wrong. I pretended to examine a pair of leather slippers on the stall in front of me, but I kept my eye on the couple at the end of the aisle. She held up the bracelet for his approval. Gordon gave a weary nod and took the money out of his pocket, paying while she fastened the bracelet around her wrist. She wrapped her arm possessively around his, and they moved on, her garnet skirt swaying provocatively. Corporal Burke was so intent on protecting me that he hadn't seen them. Not at all keen on encountering the couple face to face, I gave the corporal a nervous smile and suggested we turn around and walk in the opposite direction.

"Anything you wish, Miss Gray," he said patiently.

It was outrageous, utterly outrageous. How dare they flaunt their liaison so openly. Dollie had told me a number of the wives had tried to captivate Gordon when he first arrived, that he had refused to give them the time of day. He was obviously giving Valerie Simpson considerably more than that. Men didn't buy silver bracelets for women without good cause. When had he taken up with her? He'd only been back for two days. They had probably had something between them before he left on his secret mission.

The woman was little better than a trollop, I thought furiously. She had pursued Michael and made a fool of herself over him, and now she was clinging to Gordon's arm as though she owned him. She was precisely the kind of woman a man like that would take up with: darkly beautiful, moody, totally amoral. They were welcome to each other, I told myself. I couldn't care less what Robert Gordon did as long as he kept out of my way.

"Something wrong?" Burke inquired.

"Wrong? Of course not."

"You look upset."

"You must be imagining it, Corporal," I said, much too sharply.

"Sorry," he replied.

"I—I didn't mean to snap like that. Please forgive me."

Burke shrugged his broad shoulders and curled his mouth as though to indicate his failure to comprehend the vagaries of women. We continued to move slowly through the noisy, colorful bazaar, and I tried my best to put Gordon and the Simpson woman out of my mind. Another fifteen minutes or so passed, and I paused in front of a stall displaying exquisite handwork. I spotted a small green silk bag embroidered with gold and yellow birds, red and tan flowers. It was lovely, and as it cost less than an English pound I

decided to buy it for Sally as a peace offering. Sensing
my interest, the obese proprietor in turban and robe
began to babble and make excited gestures. When I
indicated the bag, he shook his head and pretended it
wasn't for sale, hoping no doubt to obtain a higher
price. Corporal Burke heaved a sigh and told me I'd
better let him handle it. I stepped aside, and he began to
berate the proprietor in amazingly fluent native dialect.

The two men argued vociferously. I was extremely
embarrassed, even though I knew such arguments were
customary, a sale rarely being made without some kind
of verbal bout. Burke appeared to be threatening the
proprietor's life, and the plump native shrieked and
waved his hands and seemed to be calling on Allah to
protect him from such villainy. It was as this was going
on that I first had the feeling that someone was
watching me. As I stood there beside the stall I could
feel a pair of eyes directed on me, a sensation so strong
it was almost like a physical touch. I turned around to
see a tall, slender Indian youth in a jade silk tunic and
white trousers standing by one of the stalls at the end
of the aisles. He quickly dropped his eyes and, melting
into the crowd, turned the corner before I could get a
look at his face. Why had he been staring at me so
intently? There had been something vaguely familiar
about him, I thought. Where had I seen him before?

"Here we are, Miss Gray," Burke said, handing me a
neatly wrapped package. "I knocked the bugger down
to almost half what he was asking in the first place."

I took the money out of my reticule and gave it to
Burke. He handed it to the proprietor with a satisfied
grin. The proprietor made an ugly gesture and
muttered something under his breath. Burke chuckled,
pleased with himself.

"My friend Sally will be terribly pleased," I remarked.

"It's for her, is it? I reckon she will be."

"You've met Sally?"

"I met her the day she arrived," Burke confessed. "I was hoping I might have a chance with her, and I had my eye on her, just like all the other enlisted men. Then she met Bill Norman, and the rest of us gave up. Norman's a great pal of mine. If he weren't...."

Burke shook his head, and I smiled, warming to him considerably. We continued to move along the aisles, viewing the merchandise, listening to the incredible uproar. Burke nodded grimly when we happened to meet any of the other English soldiers, but I could tell that he was pleased that they had seen him with me. I had almost forgotten the Indian youth when I felt someone staring again. I didn't turn around. I told myself that I must be imagining it. The sensation persisted, even after we had turned a corner and started up another aisle. I stopped in front of a stall covered with brilliantly hued carpets, and when Burke saw the expression on my face he immediately sensed that something was wrong.

"What is it, Miss Gray?"

"Don't—don't turn around, but I—I'm sure someone is following us. While you were arguing over the bag I felt someone staring, and I saw an Indian youth."

Burke pretended to examine one of the carpets, frowning, fingering the weave, and he glanced ever so casually in the direction we had come. "What was he wearing?" he asked under his breath.

"White turban and trousers," I said, "and a jade green tunic. I think it was silk."

The words had hardly left my lips before he was

charging back down the aisle like an angry bull, heading for the Indian youth who stood paralyzed, apparently too startled to move. I saw his face clearly, and I could feel my cheeks turn pale as I recognized him. Corporal Burke shoved a native out of his way, knocking over a pile of woven baskets, and it was then that the handsome Indian youth darted away like a frightened deer, racing down the aisle with Sergeant Burke in close pursuit. I heard Burke yell, saw him make a flying tackle, bringing the boy down. They rolled and tumbled on the ground between the stalls, punching, jabbing, quickly surrounded by a crowd of shrieking natives. The boy fought viciously, but he was no match for the corporal's superior strength. Burke pulled him to his feet, thrusting his left arm up between his shoulder blades in a brutal twist. I heard the lad cry out, and then the crowd of native men closed around them, shoving and pushing. A moment later I saw the youth tearing through the crowd. Racing around the corner of the aisle, he disappeared from sight.

The natives crowding around Burke quickly moved off in different directions, leaving him standing there between the stalls with a look of amazement on his face. Stunned, he shook his head, unable to understand what had happened. There was a cut on his jaw, and the skin on his right cheekbone had been scraped. I hurried toward him, afraid he might have been seriously hurt. He looked at me with confused gray eyes.

"I had him," he said. "I had his arm twisted up behind his back, and then I wrapped my arm around his throat to make sure he couldn't get loose. I was just getting ready to question him when—" He shook his head again, his brows pressing together in a frown. "I don't know what happened. Three or four natives seemed to pounce on me at once, and then the little bugger was free and tearing off into the crowd. It all happened so fast I couldn't even tell which of those yammering heathens were on me."

"Are you all right?"

"I'm fine," he growled. "I just feel so bloody clumsy, losing him like that. Once Ted Burke has someone, he doesn't usually get loose."

"It—it isn't important," I told him. "He just seemed to be following us. I don't suppose it meant anything."

"That lad was guilty as hell of something. I could see it on his face. He wouldn'ta put up a fight like that if he hadn't been up to something. Damn it, I had him, had him good and proper."

"Don't worry about it, Corporal. You—you did your best."

"I'm sorry, Miss Gray. If those natives hadn't fallen on me like that I woulda been able to squeeze a few answers out of him. There wouldn't be any point in trying to find him now."

I pulled a clean handkerchief out of my reticule and handed it to him. He dabbed at the cut on his jaw. I was relieved to see that it was very minor, hardly a scratch. I suggested that we go on back to the carriage, and Burke sullenly agreed, disgruntled with himself for his failure to hold on to the boy. On the way back to Blossom's house I told him it might be better if we didn't mention the incident to anyone, as it really wasn't of any consequence. Burke nodded, maintaining his brooding silence. When Dollie came out he climbed up on his seat without a word. She didn't notice anything unusual, and I was thankful for that. I showed her the bag I had purchased for Sally. Dollie exclaimed over it and twirled her purple parasol and chattered pleasantly as the carriage moved slowly through the congested streets and out of the village.

I hardly heard a word she said. I nodded now and then, and I pretended to listen, but Dollie might as well have been talking to the wind. Although I was careful to conceal it, I was still thoroughly shaken by what had happened. Ahmed. The youth Burke had tackled was Ahmed. It couldn't have been him, I told myself. It couldn't have been. Ahmed was dead. He had been murdered by the Thugs along with Yasmin Singh and all the others. I recalled that handsome, arrogant young face, that slender physique, and I knew I hadn't been mistaken. He had even been wearing the same clothes he had worn that last day, the jade silk tunic, the white trousers. Ahmed was very much alive, and he had been spying on me this afternoon in the bazaar. What could it mean? What on earth could it mean?

Nine

I knew I shouldn't have gone out riding without an escort, but there was so much on my mind that I had felt I simply had to get away by myself for just a little while. I had left the house immediately after breakfast without telling anyone of my plans, had gone directly to the stables and asked the groom to saddle the chestnut mare. For over an hour I had been riding wildly over the grassy plains with the wind tearing at my hair and stinging my cheeks. Exhausted now, I dismounted and led the mare toward a cluster of large rocks with a gnarled tree growing beside them, spreading a thin patch of shade. The sky was a pale yellow-white, and from the position of the sun I figured it must be after ten.

"There, girl," I said, tethering the mare to the tree. "We'll rest for a while."

I stroked her jaw and gave her a lump of sugar I had brought along for her. She whinnied in delight, stretching her neck. The vigorous exercise had stimulated me, and I felt keenly alive, all lethargy vanished. I sat down on one of the tannish-gray rocks, relishing the solitude. All around me the land stretched in bleak monotony broken only by an occasional twisted tree or a pile of boulders like this one. I could see the line of hills in the distance, and the heat waves were already beginning to shimmer visibly. I might have been the only person in the world.

I thought about what had happened yesterday in the bazaar. I had discussed it with Sally, and she had been incredulous. If Ahmed had escaped the massacre, why hadn't we seen him the next morning? I must have been mistaken, she assured me, and I had finally had to agree with her. The Indian youth I had seen had borne a striking resemblance to Ahmed, true, and he had been wearing similar clothes, but it simply couldn't have been him. I had never seen him close up. He had been built like Ahmed, had had the same handsome, arrogant features, but he had probably been some sly village youth who had been watching me hoping he might have an opportunity to snatch my bag, afraid to come too close because of Corporal Burke. I realized that was the only explanation, and Sally agreed.

I spread out my blue riding skirt and leaned back against the rock. It was so peaceful here, so calm. It was good to be away from everyone. Breakfast had been uncomfortable, Reggie complaining vehemently about having to go on the tiger hunt, Dollie trying to soothe him, telling him it would be an exciting experience for "the girls" and adding that the relaxation would do him a world of good. Reggie snapped that he wouldn't be able to relax a minute and complained that Michael should have been able to find some way to put the rajah off. Sally said she was personally looking forward to it. I kept silent, remembering my experience with the rajah and, like Reggie, not at all enthusiastic about going. Dollie asked Reggie if he had decided who would be included in the party. He grumbled and fussed, saying he would think about that later. Dollie said she certainly hoped Michael would have returned in time to go along, as his presence would help considerably.

I brushed a strand of hair from my temple, thinking about Michael and that passionate kiss he had given me yesterday morning. I remembered those fervent lips covering mine, those strong arms crushing me against his hard, powerful body. There had been nothing gentle about that kiss. It had been decidedly ardent, and it had proved that the cool, rather reserved officer could be as exciting a lover as any of those I had encountered in the pages of novels. He had been charming and gallant that first night at the dance, but it had been all on the surface, automatic, a role he played because it was expected. He had been preoccupied at the time and, with the exception of that afternoon by the stream, had treated me ever since with a warm, polite courtesy that was pleasant but hardly stirring. He had been holding back, but he hadn't held back yesterday. I had glimpsed a different Michael, bold, reckless, determined to take what he wanted.

I could never be happy as an army officer's wife. Michael knew that. He intended to leave the military. He told me he had plans, that he wasn't yet prepared to discuss them. I had sensed an undercurrent of excitement when he spoke about them. They were big plans, he had said, and I wondered what they could be, why he had been so evasive. He had said he could make me happy. I was beginning to believe he could. I missed him already. I missed that warm smile, that quiet manner, that attentiveness that made me feel so important. Having glimpsed a new side of him, I wanted to discover more. He was an enigma, complex, full of hidden depths that were vastly intriguing. I knew that when he returned our relationship was going to take on a whole new dimension. That rough, impassioned kiss had proved it. Michael was no longer going to hold back out of consideration of my feelings. He wanted me, and he was going to employ a dynamic approach to try and win me. I still wasn't certain about my feelings, but I was already anticipating his return, just as he had intended.

The horse began to neigh and move about restlessly. I looked up to see what had disturbed her. On every side the brownish-green grass waved in the breeze like a moving sea, and there was nothing else in sight but the occasional tree, the clusters of rock. Then I saw the horseman on the horizon, silhouetted against the yellow-white sky. I stood up, alarmed. As he drew nearer I recognized the magnificent black stallion. Robert Gordon tugged on the reins, slowing the horse to a walk. He stopped a few yards away, looking at me with dark, angry eyes, his mouth a severe line.

"What if I were a Thug?" he asked harshly.

"But you're not," I replied.

"What if I were a thief, a villain, a cutthroat?"

"Are you?" I asked sweetly.

"You're a bloody little fool, Miss Gray. I thought you had more sense. After all that's happened you come riding out here all alone. I suppose you didn't give a thought to what might happen."

"What I do is none of your business, Mr. Gordon."

"The commander must have been out of his mind letting you do something like this."

"Reggie knew nothing about it. I—I slipped off."

"I just happened to go by the stables to check my horse. I noticed the mare you always ride was missing, so I questioned the groom. When he told me you'd gone off without an escort, I could hardly believe it. I've been riding all over these bloody plains looking for you, imagining God knows what."

"Here I am, safe and sound."

"It's no joking matter!"

He was seething with anger. I could see him fighting to control it. He glared at me for a long moment, and finally he shook his head in exasperation. Swinging one leg over the saddle, he slipped off the horse with that pantherlike grace I had noticed when he was in his native disguise. He was wearing brown leather knee boots and a suit of corded tan tweed, the jacket hanging open to reveal a white shirt and the dull orange scarf tied loosely about his neck. A dark brown hat with a wide brim protected his face from the sun. As he moved slowly toward me he seemed to emanate power and authority, his presence so vital and commanding it was like an invisible force crackling in the air around him. He stopped a few feet away from me, resting his hands on his thighs.

"I could brutally assault you," he drawled. "I could strangle you to death. No one would ever know. You'd simply disappear without a trace."

"I trust those aren't your intentions."

"Don't get clever with me, Miss Gray. I just might forget myself and give you the thrashing you deserve for pulling something like this."

His anger was under control now, but there was an undeniable menace in his voice. I realized with horror that he was perfectly capable of carrying out his threat. I remembered the way he had shoved Sally to the ground and pulled me roughly over to the horse that day he had come upon us in the desert. Robert Gordon was no polite, considerate gentleman. He wouldn't hesitate to strike a woman. I glared at him rebelliously, defiant, refusing to be intimidated.

"You don't frighten me," I snapped.

"No?"

"Not in the least!"

"You're headstrong, impulsive and far too independent for your own good, Miss Gray. Most girls your age, with your background, are sitting in parlors with their embroidery."

"Are you implying that that's what I should be doing, Mr. Gordon?"

"God forbid."

"I've always had freedom to do what I wished. I—"

"I'll wager you can't even cook," he taunted.

"I've never had to," I informed him. "I've been far too busy translating the Latin poets and studying Greek philosophy. I happen to believe that women have as much right to an education as a man."

"Greek philosophy isn't going to do you much good when we're living in a tent in the middle of the Sahara desert."

I didn't deign to reply to that absurd comment. His anger had vanished completely now, and those dark, glowing eyes seemed to be filled with something akin to amusement. He stood there with his legs spread apart, hands still resting on his thighs, and a wry smile played on his lips. He was enjoying himself, enjoying my obvious discomfort. I couldn't be near the man without experiencing a whole series of tumultuous emotions, anger foremost among them. That arrogant, aloof, lordly manner made me want to lash out at him, and it took a great struggle to maintain any sort of composure when he looked at me with such cool mockery in his eyes.

"You don't even have a pistol," he remarked.

"Of course I don't!"

"What if there were a cobra coiled under that rock?"

I stepped aside gingerly, glancing back at the rock. Robert Gordon was considerably amused. I didn't find it at all amusing and told him so in no uncertain terms. He reached inside his jacket and pulled out a long revolver with a handle of polished horn.

"Ever use one of these?" he inquired.

"Certainly I haven't."

"If you're going to go gadding about like this, it's high time you learned. Here, take it."

"I wouldn't touch—"

He thrust the revolver into my hand, and then he stepped behind me and placed both his arms around me, guiding my hand with his own. I tried to pull away, but his arms tightened, holding me prisoner. There was nothing I could do but lean back against him.

"You hold it like this—" and he wrapped my fingers around the gun in the proper grip—"with your index finger on the trigger. Don't pull it! Not yet. You take aim, looking along the sight."

"The sight?"

"You *are* dim, aren't you?" He indicated the sight. "You hold it thus, until the sight is centered on what you want to hit—in this instance, the rock over there in the grass. Is it in your sight?"

"I think so."

"This isn't a game, Miss Gray. Your life could depend on this."

"Mr. Gordon, this is—"

"Shut up! All right, take aim. Got the rock in your sight? Now you squeeze the trigger."

I squeezed. The explosion was deafening. The chestnut mare reared up on her hind legs and squealed loudly. The more sophisticated stallion continued to nibble at the grass, unperturbed. The impact knocked me back against his chest. His chin rested just above my right shoulder. I could smell leather and tobacco and a strong, male odor of sweat and skin.

"Did I hit it?"

"Nowhere near," he replied. "We'll try again."

"This is utterly ridiculous. I have no intentions of—"

His arms tightened about me in a brutal grip, and he leaned forward until his lips were inches from my ear.

"You're going to learn to use a pistol, Miss Gray. In fact, you're going to become a crack shot. You may as well resign yourself. I'll keep you here all day if need be."

"You're hurting me!"

"Let's have another go at it. Take aim this time. That rock's no more than thirty feet away. You couldn't possibly miss it."

I did. I missed it three more times in a row, although the bullets did seem to be getting closer. Gordon was growing more and more impatient, and there was a distinct edge to his voice when he spoke.

"If you don't hit that bloody rock this time, Lauren, I'm going to believe you're deliberately *try*ing to miss it, and if I believe that I'm going to be very, very angry. Do you understand me?"

"Damn you! I can't help it if I keep missing!"

"You'd better not miss this time," he said ominously.

"I don't know how you expect me to hit anything with you holding on to me like this."

"Aim!"

I aimed. I pulled the trigger. The rock shattered, chips flying in every direction. I was startled—and vastly pleased with myself.

"*Now* are you satisfied?"

"Not at all. A child of five could have blown that rock to pieces the first go round."

He released me and, taking the pistol, carefully reloaded it and put it back inside his jacket, thrusting it into the waistband of his trousers. He had been holding me so tightly that I felt stiff and sore, and I felt curiously elated as well, pleased with my accomplishment. Although I would never have admitted it to Gordon, the lesson had been exceedingly stimulating.

"You'll do better tomorrow," he told me.

"Tomorrow?"

He reached up to adjust the brim of his hat, slanting it down on one side. It made him look quite dashing. With the pistol concealed under his jacket, he might have been a highwayman getting ready to pull a job. His expression was bored, his voice a casual drawl.

"Since you seem determined to take these morning rides, and since your soldier boy is no longer here to accompany you, I'm taking the job. We'll continue with the lessons each morning."

"And what will Mrs. Simpson have to say to that?"

"I was wondering when you were going to bring her up."

"I—I saw you with her at the bazaar yesterday."

"I saw you, too, and your expression was one of pure moral outrage. In answer to your question: Mrs. Simpson won't say a word. It's none of her business what I do."

"You bought her a bracelet—pure silver. She clung

to your arm like she owned you. She—"

"I don't intend to discuss Valerie Simpson with you, Lauren. I have my reasons for seeing her."

"I feel quite certain you have. It doesn't take a great deal of imagination to guess what they are. You can forget about escorting me on my rides, Mr. Gordon. I've just decided to give them up."

"You'll be at the stables at nine-thirty in the morning," he told me. "I'll be waiting. I suggest we start back to the garrison now before I do you bodily harm. I've exercised considerable restraint up till now, but I'm fast losing my patience."

Chin tilted haughtily, I marched over to the mare and untied the reins from the tree. Cool, dignified, ignoring him entirely, I put my foot in the stirrup and swung myself up, only I didn't go up. My foot slipped and I went down with considerable impact, landing on a particularly sensitive portion of my anatomy. Robert Gordon didn't say a word, nor did he make any attempt to come to my aid. He simply gazed at me with a bored expression. Catching hold of the stirrup, I pulled myself up and brushed off my skirt. If I had had the gun in my hand at that moment I would have shot to kill, and I felt certain I wouldn't have missed.

We returned to the garrison in silence, Gordon immersed in thought and apparently unaware of my presence on the horse beside him. When we reached the stables I quickly dismounted, handed the reins to the groom and hurried away without a word, picturing in my mind the anger and frustration Robert Gordon was going to experience the following morning as he waited and waited and I failed to appear. I had every intention of giving up the rides. I would find something else to occupy my time. The man was insufferable, and it was unthinkable that I should deliberately spend time with him. He could wait all morning long, but it would do him no good. I wouldn't be there.

As my riding skirt had been unfortunately soiled by my tumble, I was wearing a pale tan dress sprigged with tiny rust red and brown flowers and miniscule black leaves, a highly becoming garment that really wasn't at all suitable for riding. I had brushed my chestnut hair until it gleamed with silvery highlights, and as I approached the stables I was confident that I had rarely looked better. Robert Gordon was leaning casually against the wall, his arms folded across his chest, and he didn't seem at all surprised to see me. I gave him a cool nod, and, ignoring me, Gordon called for the groom to bring the horses.

In the days that followed, I was cool and exceedingly formal, treating him with a polite indifference frequently difficult to maintain. I was determined to retain my dignity at all costs. Gordon treated me with a curious combination of weary impatience and surly disdain, that mockery always lurking just beneath the surface. I could tell that he considered me a foolish girl, and that irritated me, but somehow I managed to keep my poise, even when he was berating me for being so awkward and clumsy with the pistol. At other times he was remote, deeply immersed in thought and completely ignoring me. His harsh face would be fierce then, his scowl causing a little hump of flesh to swell above the bridge of his nose.

Dollie was absolutely horrified when she learned that I was going out riding with him each morning. It was unsuitable, she claimed, most unsuitable. I told her that I had been out riding with Michael and failed to see how my riding with Gordon was any different. Why, the man was openly carrying on with Valerie Simpson, it was the talk of the post, and heaven only knew what terrible things he might do to an innocent young girl. Reggie's reaction was near apoplexy, and I found myself championing Gordon against both of them. For some reason their ardent disapproval made those early morning rides all the more exciting.

For it was exciting to be with him, I couldn't deny that. I never knew what he was going to say or do. He might nod coldly when I happened to hit a target, or he might scowl darkly and threaten to throttle me if I missed. He might tease me in a bored, lackadasical manner, or he might withdraw and brood silently, no doubt thinking about his work. On occasion he might tell me about the books he had written and the translations he had done, or he might talk about his trip to Africa at twenty-two, his journey to America and his experiences in the rugged frontier towns in the west. He had done so many things, been so many places, had such a vast, incredible store of knowledge about such diverse, unusual subjects. He was undeniably fascinating, this sojourn in India merely another bizarre chapter in an already remarkable life.

There was a truce between us, and we didn't argue at all, although he was unnecessarily rough and surly during the shooting lessons, determined I would become an expert shot. He taught me how to load the gun, how to clean it and take care of it. After I was finally able to hit targets he set up a considerable distance away, he began to teach me how to hit moving targets, gathering small, flat stones and tossing them in the air. I told him it was impossible, but Gordon would have none of that. I was secretly flattered that he was devoting so much time and attention to me, for he was extremely busy, sorting out information, making reports, frequently leaving the post for hours on mysterious trips to villages in the district. Nevertheless, he devoted at least two hours to me every morning. I wondered if Valerie Simpson had as much of his precious time lavished on her.

A week passed, ten days, twelve. Reggie had chosen the men who would accompany us on the forthcoming tiger hunt. In addition to Reggie, Dollie, Sally and I, there would be four other officers and four enlisted men. Sally was delighted that Sergeant Norman had been selected—she had been campaigning toward that end since she first learned about the hunt—and I was pleased that Corporal Burke would also be going along. There had been no word from Michael, and Reggie said it seemed unlikely that he would be back in time to accompany us. We might well run into him, though, he added, as Michael and his men were scouting the very area we'd be going to.

Two days before we were to depart, Robert Gordon and I met at the stables at the usual time and rode away from the garrison. I was wearing the sprigged tan dress again, and in his black knee boots, tight black trousers and thin white shirt with sleeves full gathered at the wrist, Gordon looked like a disreputable gypsy, a bright red scarf tied about his neck, his raven locks blowing wildly as we rode. After thirty minutes or so of hard riding, we finally reached a suitable spot and stopped, dismounting. Gordon tethered the horses to a scrawny tree while I stretched my legs, enjoying the pale blue sky, the bright morning sunshine, the miles and miles of empty land that isolated us from the rest of the world.

He gathered up several small, flat stones and, handing me the pistol, walked away from me, moving in long, lazy strides. He seemed terribly far away when he finally stopped. I indicated that I was ready, and he hurled the first stone up toward the sky. Quickly, I took aim and fired, and the stone kept right on sailing across the blue. I missed the second as well. I could see his expression. It was fierce. I frowned, disappointed in myself, knowing that I had been overconfident and therefore careless. When he hurled the third stone up into the air, I blasted it into tiny pieces that showered down like rain. He threw three more stones. I hit every one of them.

I was reloading the pistol when he rejoined me. His face was expressionless.

"Pleased with yourself, aren't you?"

"Very," I said.

"You shouldn't have missed the first two."

"No one's perfect, Mr. Gordon. Shall we try some more?"

"The lessons are over," he said.

"Over? You mean—"

"I mean you're pretty damned good. You've done extremely well. Just don't get so bloody confident. I want you to keep the pistol. I want you to keep it with you at all times."

"I couldn't accept—"

"Don't be coy, Lauren. Keep it. Keep it loaded. When you leave on that bloody tiger hunt, make sure you have it with you."

"You think there might be danger?"

"There's always danger," he said.

The reply was cryptic, not at all satisfactory. He had never talked about his mission before, and I had never dared question him about it, but I couldn't refrain from questioning him now.

"Do—do you think all this will be over soon?"

"The Thuggee situation? I have a couple of very strong leads. I think we'll shortly be able to end their activities once and for all. Your lieutenant and his men should be able to locate their camp in the jungle, and I believe I'll know the identify of the ringleaders in a few days."

"Is it true there might be a white man involved?" I asked.

"I'm certain of it," Gordon replied, grim. "There's no other way the assassins could have known about certain caravans secretly carrying military pay and supplies. He's probably a soldier, probably quartered at the garrison. He's been feeding them vital information. When I have that man, the spine will be cracked. He'll talk. I'll see to it."

"I don't understand how a white man could do anything so hideous."

"Easily. For money. A great deal of it. I'm sure he gets a generous share of the spoils."

"I—I've read a lot about the Thugs. I find it hard to believe they'd work with a white man. It's a religious thing. They believe they're doing it in the name of Kali, and—"

"At one time it was purely religious," he interrupted, "but that was in the beginning. This bunch—and they're the last left in India—murder for gain. Kali has little to do with it. If a white man can help them, feed them vital information, so much the better. These chaps are the sole survivors of a once thriving society—surviving because they're the toughest of the lot, the most clever, the most vicious. They've fled Sleeman

211

and his men from all over India, banding together in this area. Thuggee is merely an excuse for them to continue their villainy."

"Their—their main camp, their stronghold, is in the tiger country, isn't it? Hidden somewhere in the jungle. Michael and his men are looking for it, and Reggie said there was a chance we might even run into them. If that's where they have their stronghold, then this hunt could be—"

"All the men in your group will be fully armed," Gordon said dryly. "The rajah will have most of his police with him and dozens of servants as well. The Thugs rely on surprise and vulnerability. They wouldn't dare attack a party of that size, that heavily armed."

"Then why do you want me to take the pistol?"

"Purely as a precaution. And, too, we're going to be visiting a lot of dangerous places in years to come. I want you to get used to carrying a gun around with you."

I stepped over to the mare and placed the pistol in one of the saddlebags. "I trust you're not going to begin that nonsense again, Mr. Gordon," I said, my back to him. "I don't find it at all amusing."

"Nonsense? There's nothing nonsensical about it. You're going to marry me. I thought I told you so."

He spoke in a casual, matter of fact voice, as though he were telling me the time of day. I turned to look at him. He stood in that characteristic pose, legs spread apart, hands resting on thighs, waiting for me to reply.

"It—the weather seems to be changing," I said. "I think we'd better start back to the garrison."

Gordon nodded, unperturbed by my abrupt change of subject. The sky had indeed turned darker, blue gradually merging into gray, and the light was dimming as clouds began to build on the horizon. It was going to rain in a little while. As we galloped back over the plains, the wind grew stronger and the sky turned even darker, the gray tinged with purple. There was a rumble of thunder in the distance. We rode faster, and by the time we reached the garrison the sky was an expanse of dark purple-gray heavily laden with ponderous black clouds. We dismounted in front of the stables. I took the pistol from the saddlebag and managed to conceal it in the pocket of my skirt. The groom led the horses into their stalls, and Robert Gordon and I stood looking at each other. We had not exchanged a single word since leaving the site of the lesson.

"I'll walk you back to the house," he said.

"That won't be necessary, Mr. Gordon. I'm sure I can make it safely enough. I have the gun in my pocket."

"You're so damned obstinate," he told me. "It's a charming trait, up to a point. Beyond that point...."

"Yes?"

"We're going to fight a lot, you know. We'll probably have some bloody rows. The porters won't know what to think when I knock you down. They'll be even more dismayed when you kick me out of the tent and send a cast iron skillet flying after me. We'll never be a model of connubial bliss, but ah what times we'll have."

"You have a vivid imagination, Mr. Gordon."

I turned and moved briskly away. He came right along after me, seizing my elbow, forcing me to slow down. I tried to pull free. He tightened his grip until I winced.

"Why are you so angry?" he inquired.

"Angry!" I exclaimed. "Whatever gave you that idea?"

"There's no need fighting it, Lauren. It's inevitable. We're going to have a marvelous future together."

"You're the most infuriating man I've ever encountered!"

"And by far the most intriguing," he added.

"Let go of my elbow!"

"You'll behave? You'll walk sedately, like a well-bred young woman?" There was a touch of laughter in his voice.

"You've never walked me back to the house before," I said petulantly. "I don't know why you feel you should now."

"There are still some things I want to say to you."

"I don't want to hear them!"

"But you shall," he informed me.

We were walking along beside the parade ground now. It was surrounded by tall trees, and on its edge there was a small open gazebo where the military band played. Another rumble of thunder sounded. A streak of lightning tore at the sky like a jagged silver hand trying to rip it apart. Gordon slipped his hand down from my elbow and tightened his fingers around my wrist. I gave a startled little cry as he pulled me toward the gazebo. He ignored it. I stumbled on the steps, almost falling, and a moment later we were inside.

"This is scandalous!" I cried.

"It's going to start pouring down rain at any minute now. You don't want to get wet, do you? Relax, no one can see us. The trees make a perfect blind."

"That's what I'm afraid of."

"You think I plan to seduce you? It would be like

shooting a sitting duck. I may be the rogue you believe me to be, but I play fair. When the time comes, I'll initiate you into the delights of the flesh, but you'll be legally bound to me, I assure you."

"Everything they say about you is true!"

"Probably," he admitted.

"You're despicable!"

"I don't deny it."

"I happen to be in love with Michael Stephens. He—he's going to ask me to marry him as soon as he returns, and the answer will be yes. I suggest you go—go play your games with Mrs. Simpson. She's much more likely to appreciate them."

"Are you still fretting about Valerie?" he asked casually. "You've nothing to worry about there. I told you, I have my reasons for seeing her, and they're not what you think. She presents no threat to you."

"The whole post is talking about—"

"I've no doubt they are. People love to talk. I bought her a bracelet. I've visited her bungalow a number of times when her husband was out, and I confess I've slept with her. She finds me—"

"How dare you mention such—such matters in front of me! You have no breeding whatsoever. You're vile, uncouth, un—"

"And you're in love with me," he said. "That's one of the things I wanted to say to you."

I was stunned into silence. Gordon smiled that familiar wry smile and stepped over to lean against the wooden railing that surrounded the gazebo. It had grown even darker, and the wind caused the trees to bend and sway in frenzy. His dark locks swirled about his head. The bright red scarf at his neck fluttered, and the full gathered sleeves whipped against his arms. He gazed at me, a bemused look in his eyes, the smile still curling on his lips. A gust of wind caused my skirts to bell out. Long chestnut waves blew across my face.

"You can forget about Michael Stephens," he told me. "Stephens doesn't have a prayer."

"You know nothing about it, Mr. Gordon."

"You're still just a girl, Lauren. You're naïve, immature, unable to cope with your emotions, but that's to be expected. You've spent all your adult years in the stuffy, secluded atmosphere of a girl's school, an atmosphere hardly likely to prepare you for the world outside. Most of what you know about life you've obtained from books. You're amazingly intelligent in some ways, but emotionally you're illiterate."

"That's *your* opinion," I retorted.

"You don't know what you feel. You've had no experience to guide you. You were attracted to me from the first—when you thought I was a villainous native. You were shocked at yourself, recoiling in horror at the very idea. When you saw me at the garden party and realized I was English—"

"I think you've said quite enough!"

"There's no need to be afraid of the truth, Lauren, and no need to be ashamed of it, either. You may not want to love me—can't say I blame you for that—but there's no way you can change what's already—"

The air around us was suddenly a hissing, crackling expanse of blinding silver-blue light, and there was a shattering explosion of sound. The floor of the gazebo seemed to shake. I cried out, stumbling forward, and there was another, louder explosion as a tree limb nearby split in two and crashed to the ground. I was in his arms. He was holding me tightly, tightly, and I was trembling, terrified. My cheek was pressed against his shoulder, and his arms tightened even more.

"It was only lightning," he said, his voice so tender that I hardly recognized it. "It's all right. A bolt of lightning struck a tree limb. There's nothing to fear."

It had all happened so quickly: the blinding flash shimmering silver-blue, silver-gold, crackling in the air, the explosion, the wooden floor shaking. I had cried out, stumbling, and he had leaped toward me, gathering me to him, all in a matter of seconds, and now there was the smell of burnt wood and smoke and the rain began to fall, pounding on the roof of the gazebo, splattering on the ground, the wind sweeping gusts of spray across the railing. I don't know how much time elapsed. He stroked my hair, rocking me in his arms. I finally stopped trembling, and then I was aware of his lean, muscular body, the strength in his arms, his warmth.

"I—I'm sorry. I don't know—"

"Hush," he said.

Moments passed. Thē rain slackened, its fury quickly spent. It fell softly now, pattering quietly, and the wind was gone. I pulled away. Gordon did not try to prevent me. His arms loosened. I stepped back, looking up at him, unable to speak.

"I'm leaving this afternoon, Lauren," he said. "That's why today was our last lesson. I have a job to do."

"Another mission?" My voice was barely audible.

He nodded, his expression grim.

"You'll be careful?"

He ignored the question. "When this is all settled, when my job is accomplished, I'm coming back for you. You know that, Lauren, and you know why."

The rain stopped abruptly, as abruptly as it had come, and small rivulets spilled from the domed roof of the gazebo and made a gently splashing curtain all around. It shimmered for a moment and then disappeared, only a few drops dripping now. Gordon looked at me with dark, solemn eyes, and I felt helpless. Tremulous emotions rose inside, all so new, so confusing that I couldn't begin to identify them.

"You're still just a girl, as I said," Gordon told me, "but you're beginning to bloom. When the process is over, you're going to be a magnificent woman. I could see that at once. All the qualities are there—and, of course, you're already ravishingly beautiful."

"Don't," I whispered, "Please don't."

Gordon frowned, and then he shook his head, pressing his lips into a tight line. I knew that I had displeased him, and I was sorry. There was so much I wanted to say, yet I could find no words.

"The rain's over now," he said. "You'd better run along. There'll be time for us later, when I return."

"Robert—"

"Go!" he said gruffly.

I hurried away from him, moving quickly down the wooden steps and over the wet, spongy grass. I didn't look back. I didn't dare. At dinner that evening Reggie told us that Gordon had disappeared again on one of his mysterious missions. I slept little that night, thinking about what had happened, wondering when I would see him again. The next day was spent packing, for we would be gone at least a week and, Dollie claimed, the rajah would expect us to look our best every day. When we departed the next morning I had Gordon's pistol with me. I had no idea that in just a short while it was going to make the difference between life and death.

Ten

There were six huts in the jungle, flimsy wooden structures with verandas in front, woven grass shutters and roofs, mosquito nets draped like gauzy tents over the beds inside. The English party used these, Sally and I sharing one, Dollie and Reggie another, the remaining eight men using the other four. The huts stood in a small clearing that had been hacked out of the dense jungle, and they were completely surrounded by trees and vines and a thick tangle of plants. The rajah and his men had pitched their tents in a somewhat larger clearing a short distance away, a belt of jungle separating the two parties. I thought the arrangement rather odd, but Dollie assured me it was traditional. The English valued their privacy and much preferred sleeping in these huts which had been set up for their convenience a number of years ago.

Sally and I were in our hut, dressing for the rajah's celebration banquet after the first day's hunt. Bright yellow rays of sunlight streamed in through the opened windows, but we would soon have to light the oil lamps. Our hut was only a few yards from the trees, and we could hear the rustle of leaves, the shrill cries of birds, an occasional jabbering clamor when a monkey ventured near. Both of us were exhausted after a day spent crouching in a blind, watching a nervous goat move restlessly on its tether. It bleated loudly, eventually attracting the magnificent gold and black creature who leaped through a thicket to make his kill and was himself slaughtered, somersaulting in the air as the rajah's bullet struck him and landing in a thrashing heap only a few feet away from the terrified goat.

"I can't say I really cared for it," Sally remarked. "I felt so sorry for that poor goat—for the tiger, too, I may as well confess it."

"It all seems terribly barbaric," I replied. "I don't see how anyone can consider it sporting. The tiger didn't have a chance."

"I imagine the men see it in a different light."

"Undoubtedly," I agreed.

Having performed rather primitive ablutions with water the rajah's servants had sent over, both of us were in our petticoats. I sat in front of a tarnished, murky blue mirror, brushing my hair, and Sally was taking out her new gown, the one she had made from the bolt of silk she had purchased in the bazaar the day of the garden party. Insects hummed, and both of us were rather wary as Corporal Burke had shot a cobra last night in the hut he shared with Sergeant Norman. My pistol was on the table in front of me, and I had already assured Sally that I could use it.

Sally held the gown up in front of her. It was a sumptuous creation of emerald green, the silk embroidered with floral patterns in silver thread. "I've never had such a gown," she sighed, moving over to stand behind me in order to admire it in the mirror. "To think I made it myself. It took for*ever*, but it was worth it."

"You did a splendid job, Sally."

"Dollie said we should dress to the hilt tonight. She said the rajah would expect it. I. . . ." She hesitated a moment, frowning. "I don't know quite what to make of him. He's ever so polite and attentive, speaks in such a gentle, silky voice, but—well, he makes me a bit uneasy. I've seen him *looking* at me, looking at you, too. If the men weren't with us I'd be downright jittery."

"The rajah admires women," I said, deliberately casual.

"That's for sure," she retorted.

I made no further comment, and Sally moved over to her bed to put on her slippers. I hadn't told her about my experience with the rajah, hadn't in fact, mentioned it to anyone. He had been exceedingly polite to me since the morning of our departure three days ago, but, like Sally, I had noticed him looking at us at odd moments with disconcerting intensity. It had taken us two days to reach the site of the hunt, and he had provided lavish accommodations: sedan chairs for the women, silken tents for us to sleep in on the way, exotic food and wine, a battalion of servants to wait upon us. He was, without doubt, a superb host—even Reggie had to admit that—but I thought there was something devious about his manner. I had the feeling he was secretly mocking us even as he smiled and made friendly conversation and saw to every detail of our comfort. My encounter with him at the garden party had undoubtedly prejudiced me to a certain extent, but I still didn't think I was imagining the slyness or that thinly veiled contempt for everyone in the British party.

I had the curious feeling that something was afoot, that the hunt had been arranged with something else in

221

mind besides solidifying relations between garrison and palace. It wasn't anything I could explain, even to myself, yet the feeling was there, a vague uneasiness that had plagued me since the morning we departed. The rajah was gracious, his men friendly, his servants attentive, and everyone else in the British party seemed to be perfectly at ease, enjoying themselves. As soon as we reached the jungle, I had had the feeling that we were under observation, that unseen eyes were watching our every movement, and the feeling had persisted even during the hunt this afternoon. After the experience Sally and I had had it was natural enough that I should feel a certain apprehension, particularly as I knew the Thugs supposedly had their secret camp somewhere in this area, but that didn't explain it. This had to do with the rajah, with that sly expression that crossed his face now and then, as though he knew something no one else did. I tried to tell myself that I was letting my imagination run away with me, but it did no good. The feeling remained.

Leaving the dressing table, I helped Sally fasten up her gown, and she performed the same service for me a few moments later. My gown was sky blue silk, exquisitely simple, exceedingly elegant. When we joined the others outside in front of the huts, the men eyed us both with considerable appreciation. Sally was positively glowing, thrilled with her gown, thrilled to be garnering so much masculine attention. Dollie, in red velvet, eclipsed us both. She looked stunning, plump and lovely with her bobbing black ringlets and merry brown eyes, easily dominating the remarkable gown that would have overwhelmed a less striking individual.

"I see we're all *ready*," she exclaimed. "I must say

you men look handsome in your dress uniforms. Such a lovely custom, dressing up."

"In the middle of the jungle? It's bloody nonsense," Reggie snapped. "Here we are, surrounded by trees and vines and jabbering monkeys, a hundred miles from nowhere, and we're dressed like we were paying a visit to Buckingham Palace. We British are mad. I've always said so."

"Don't you start in now," she cautioned him. "We're going to have a splendid evening, and I refuse to let you be grumpy and spoil it for these youngsters."

"You'd be grumpy too if a scorpion had dropped in your shaving water."

"A scorpion!" Sally exclaimed.

"There I was, calm as you please, scraping away, and I heard a funny splash. There *it* was, thrashing about in my bowl of shaving water. It had dropped off the ceiling—as big as my fist, it was. As if that bloody cobra last night wasn't bad enough."

"I think we'd better *go*," Dollie said firmly.

As we started toward the pathway that had been cut through the jungle connecting the two clearings, Corporal Burke stepped up to take my arm. He had stuck close to me ever since we left the garrison, his manner as stern and protective as it had been the afternoon we visited the bazaar. I was rather flattered, but his proprietary manner clearly irritated the unattached men in our party, particularly the four officers. Burke paid them no mind, taking charge as though by right.

The sun had begun to go down, and the jungle was already beginning to fill with shadows. It pressed close on either side, and with three branches meeting overhead the path was more like a tunnel, only a few wavering gold rays of light sifting through the leaves. Sergeant Burke and I were in the rear, all the rest of the party ahead of us. I could hear Dollie's chatter, hear the men's voices as they talked among themselves. Sally let out a cry as a small snake slithered across the path. Sergeant Norman laughed huskily, delighted. I looked at the rustling green-brown walls that seemed to close in on us, and again I felt those unseen eyes.

"Is something wrong, Miss Gray?" Burke asked.

"N—no," I replied. "I—for some reason I'm just a bit uneasy."

"No need to be," he assured me. "I promised to take care of you—" He cut himself short, scowling.

"You promised? Whom?"

"I shouldn't have let that slip," he grumbled. "I may as well tell you now, though. I gave my promise to Gordon. You see, I—well, I sort of work for him."

"Indeed?"

"I was sent to Dahlkari two weeks before he arrived, as a kind of secret aide. I guess you might call me a spy. I keep my eye on everything that happens on post, report to him. I shouldn't be telling you this, Miss Gray, but since you're already so involved—"

"I see."

"I know you'll mention it to no one, not even the commander."

"Of course I won't."

"Gordon would be furious."

"Have you any idea where he is now?"

Burke shook his head. "He doesn't tell me any more than he tells anyone else. I just follow instructions, keep my eyes and ears open, report everything to him. He's convinced a white man is involved with the Thugs, pretty certain it's someone from the garrison—I'm not giving anything away, I know he's discussed it with you."

"He has. I think it's—the mere thought is shocking."

"He's pretty upset with me at present, Gordon is. Blames me for letting that Ahmed fellow get away."

I was startled. "Ahmed? He—he used that name?"

"Sure. I described the incident to him, described the lad I tackled. He said the chap was called Ahmed, said he'd been on the caravan with you. Gordon was furious with me for not holding on to him. The lad's a Thug, no doubt about it. He infiltrates the caravans, scouts around, finds out if there's money and where it is, then signals his colleagues. If he hadn't gotten away, we could have forced him to talk."

I found it hard to believe, but everything fit perfectly. I remembered Ahmed talking with the five strangers who had joined the caravan. He was the only one who had been friendly with them. Now I knew why. The night of the attack he had disappeared. Sally had looked all over for him, thinking he would lead us to the temple in the jungle. Ahmed had set us up. He might not have participated in the actual attack, but he was undoubtedly the one who had sent the Thugs back to murder us when he learned that the bodies of two English girls hadn't been broken up and tossed into the grave that had been prepared in advance. Just thinking about it made me shudder. Sergeant Burke gave my arm a squeeze.

"Don't think about it, Miss Gray. Gordon'll soon have this thing all wrapped up. I've complete confidence in him."

"You seem to be the only one who does."

"No, ma'am. Captain Sleeman has confidence in him, too. That's why he chose Gordon for the job."

I made no reply. We moved through the jungle, close on the heels of the rest of the party. The light had grown even dimmer. We would have to use lanterns on the way back from the rajah's encampment. Corporal Burke pushed aside a vine festooned with dark purple flowers. A white parrot flew across the path. I hadn't realized that so much distance separated the two camps. We must have come half a mile already.

"There are so few of us," I remarked uneasily.

"Lieutenant Stephens and his men are camped just a few miles away," Burke said. "One of his scouts spotted us this afternoon during the hunt. He reported to the commander. There're thirty men with the lieutenant, you know."

"I had no idea they were so near."

"None of us did until the scout appeared."

"Have—have they had any success?" I asked.

"I don't know," Burke replied. "The scout talked with the commander for half an hour, but the commander didn't tell anyone what he said. I just overheard him tell his wife that Lieutenant Stephens and his men were close by. He said Stephens might join the hunt in a day or so if it was at all possible."

I thought about Michael, and I wondered what I was going to say to him when I saw him again. Did I love him? I wasn't sure. I had missed him, yes, but not nearly so much as I would have had Robert Gordon not entered the picture. Did I love Gordon? How could I possibly love him? He was impossible, totally impossible, and Michael was so safe, so stable. Life with him would be predictable, perhaps, but it would be comfortable and secure. And he loved me. I was certain of that. He loved me, and that impassioned, tempestuous kiss proved that he could be as exciting as any woman could wish. My feelings about him were confusing, but I knew that if I didn't love him already he could make me love him. If I gave him the chance, he could drive every doubt from my mind.

I was still thinking about this as we entered the rajah's camp. It was twice as large as ours, and it had been transformed into an amazing, glittering wonderland. Colored lanterns had been strung up everywhere, spilling dazzling light. The horses, including the ones the British had used, were in a corral to one side, and the rest of the area had been covered with gorgeous Oriental carpets. There were over a dozen white silk tents fringed with gold, dominated by a huge golden tent the size of a small house. Servants in white silk uniforms moved about performing their duties, and the rajah's men, his "police," wore soft blue leather boots and splendid blue trousers and long-sleeved tunics, their turbans and sashes of silver cloth. Musicians were playing soft, melodious tunes, and the air itself was perfumed. It was a spectacular scene, incredibly beautiful. It was almost impossible to believe we were in the middle of the jungle.

The rajah stepped out of the golden tent to greet us. He was dressed in silver, his chest draped with a shimmering web of sapphires and diamonds, deep blue and silvery fires flashing as he moved. Diamond and sapphire bracelets encircled his wrists, and an enormous sapphire surrounded by diamonds was fastened to the front of his silver turban. These jewels alone must have been worth hundreds of thousands of pounds. He smiled and greeted each one of us personally, bowing to the women, shaking hands with the men, displaying his best English manners. When he stopped in front of me, I gave him a polite nod, refusing to make the traditional half curtsy. If he noticed, he gave no sign of it.

"You are enjoying the hunt, Miss Gray?" he inquired.

"It's been very interesting," I replied.

"You do not perhaps like to see the tiger killed?"

"I—I found it rather disturbing."

"You find it brutal? You are sensitive. That is as it should be. But the tiger is a predator, and if we did not have the hunt two or three times a year the tiger would soon kill all the other animals. It is necessary to kill, you see. It is not merely for sport."

"I understand, Your Highness."

The corpse of the tiger had been roped to a bar suspended on two poles by one of the tents. It hung limply, like an enormous tawny gold and black rag doll, a single scarlet stain marring the gorgeous pelt. I looked away, hating the sight of it. The rajah smiled again, but his dark eyes remained flat, inscrutable.

"I hear you learn to shoot," he remarked.

"I—yes. I have learned to use a pistol."

"Tomorrow, perhaps, you will share my blind. I will show you how to use the rifle. Perhaps you will shoot a tiger for me."

"I really don't think I'd care to, Your Highness."

"We shall see. Tonight, you enjoy. My musicians play especially for you. Native songs, soft and lovely, like you. Later on we shall perhaps have another conversation, like before."

He moved on to speak to one of the officers, and I felt a wave of relief. Corporal Burke came to stand beside me. With his short-clipped dark brown hair, his humped nose and tight, disapproving mouth, he looked formidable indeed. His gray eyes were hard as he watched the rajah move on. I knew he must have overheard everything that had been said.

"You want to watch him, Miss Gray," he said grimly. "He's altogether too interested in you. The fellow may be a bloody prince, but I still don't trust him."

"Neither do I," I confided. "I wonder how he knew about my learning to shoot."

"I shouldn't imagine there's much he doesn't know," the corporal replied. "The fellow's shrewd, and he's highly intelligent, has spies everywhere. Shall we wander around the camp?"

I nodded. The carpets were soft underfoot. Silken tents billowed gently. As we strolled, I saw tall ebony stands holding beautifully chased brass bowls filled with the burning incense that perfumed the air. Servants moved about quickly but unobtrusively, and the rajah's men in their sumptuous blue uniforms lingered about, observing everything with dark, impassive faces, not attempting to mix with the English party. I noticed that each had a long, gleaming dagger thrust in his silver sash, and each looked ready to use it at a moment's notice. A bird screamed shrilly in the jungle. The horses moved about restlessly.

"Do—do you have the feeling we're being observed?" I asked nervously. "I mean—from out there."

"I've had the feeling for the past two days," Corporal Burke retorted. "This afternoon while everyone else was occupied with the hunt, I did a bit of scouting of my own, couldn't find a thing. I reckon we're being watched, all right, but not by anything human. The jungle's full of animals, and animals are curious."

"You think that explains it?"

"I reckon so, Miss Gray. If it's the Thugs you're

worrying about, forget it. They prey on unsuspecting caravans, not heavily armed hunting parties. Those men of the rajah's would butcher 'em."

"They certainly look fierce," I remarked.

"They are," Burke said. "They do the rajah's dirty work for him, collect the taxes, dole out punishment, terrorize the villagers. If there's anything they like more than torturing a miscreant, it's coming upon some poor, defenseless young girl. When the rajah's men are about, the villagers hide their daughters."

"The rajah *condones* such conduct?"

"He encourages it. Fear's a mighty powerful weapon. It keeps the natives on their toes. As long as they're terrified, they don't grumble, they starve to death in order to pay for the rajah's jewels. It's always been that way, and it was even worse before the British arrived."

A short time later a brass gong sounded and servants pulled silken ropes that caused the front flaps of the enormous golden tent to lift, turning it into a gigantic marquee. The interior was lined with blue and white silk, there were piles of blue and silver and gold cushions to sit on and two long tables laden with silver dishes and a gorgeous array of food. The musicians stood in one corner, playing their soft music, and servants with huge plumed fans stood ready to fan the guests.

"Burke," Dollie scolded as we entered, "you've monopolized Lauren long enough. I shan't stand for any more of it! Now you run on, do. Lauren, dear, isn't this *some*thing? I told you it would be smashing. Even Reggie's impressed."

"You must all help yourselves," the rajah said. "It is

what you call the buffet meal, no? My cooks have prepared many delicacies to please you. Eat the food, drink the wine, be happy."

The rajah's men had entered the tent along with the English party, and soon there was a crowd around the tables. As I waited to get a plate, the rajah stepped up beside me, lightly touching my elbow.

"Your watchdog is very vigilant," he said, "but I see that he is busy getting his food now. Here, let me serve you, Miss Gray. It will be my pleasure. A plate!" he said harshly, and one of the men quickly handed him one and stepped aside. "The food is lovely, no? You are hungry?"

"Not—not particularly," I said.

"You are frightened of me? Because perhaps I make a blunder the last time we are together? We shall sit on the cushions and eat and have a conversation, and your friends will be all around us. Your young watchdog is looking at us already. He will fly at my throat if I touch you. You need not fear."

There was nothing I could do but let him fill a plate for me and lead me over to a pile of cushions. A servant followed with a plate of food for the rajah. I sat down on the cushions as primly as possible, and the rajah lowered himself beside me, half sitting, half reclining. He didn't try to emulate the English tonight, but, instead, ate with his fingers while we used knives and forks. The tent was noisy with the clatter of dishes and conversations in two different languages. Sally and Sergeant Norman sat on a pile of silver cushions in one corner, deep in conversation. There was a radiant glow about her I had never seen before.

"Your friend is happy," the rajah remarked. "She is

231

enjoying herself much tonight. The sergeant with the bronze hair and serious blue eyes—he is her special friend?"

"They are very good friends," I replied.

"He is indeed fortunate. She is beautiful—not like you, not cool and elegant, but of the earth. Earthy? A man would give you a rose and quote poetry in the moonlight. He would seize your friend roughly and treat her with lusty abandon. She would enjoy it."

"She would more likely double up her fist and give him a bloody nose," I said stiffly.

"She does not bloody the sergeant's nose. He is most familiar."

"I'm sure that is none of your concern, Your Highness."

The rajah smiled, not at all put off by my frank reply. He lolled back on the blue velvet cushions, supporting himself on one elbow, his long silver clad legs stretched out. His plate of food perched on a cushion. Gems flashed as he picked up a spicy chunk of meat and put it in his mouth. His smoldering dark eyes watched me as he chewed. I had rarely been so uncomfortable, he was like some magnificent, sensual animal, only the thinnest veneer of civilized manners covering the savagery that lurked just beneath the surface. He smelled of heavy musk, and his eyes seemed to undress me as his lips curled in what could only be called a lascivious smile.

"You are angry," he said in that husky, silken voice. "You do not like to talk of things of the flesh? You are frightened of them? That is because you are a virgin and have no knowledge of the pleasures the body is capable of giving. You are ripe to learn. The right teacher can open the doors to paradise."

I knew I couldn't make a scene, but I knew I couldn't sit there a moment longer. I smiled politely for the benefit of those around us. I set my plate down. My skirts rustled as I stood up and moved away from him, and it was at that very moment that we heard a great commotion outside. Conversation died abruptly. The musicians stopped playing. Through the open front of the tent we saw a frothing brown horse stumble across the carpets, several of the rajah's servants trying to restrain it. The soldier riding it was deathly pale, his face streaked with dirt, his uniform covered with dust, one sleeve half torn off. He reined the horse sharply, and when it reared up he tumbled off, falling in a heap onto the thick carpets.

Pandemonium prevailed. Everyone rushed out, talking excitedly. Reggie bellowed for quiet. Several of the rajah's men had drawn their daggers. The soldier staggered to his feet and tried to salute as Reggie rushed over to him. I recognized him as Private Stanton, one of the men who had left with Michael. His cheek was bleeding from a small cut, his blue eyes looked glazed, and his short blond hair fell in an untidy fringe across his forehead. He stared at Reggie, his throat working as he tried to speak, but no words would come. He stumbled. Reggie caught him in his arms, holding him securely.

"Disaster, sir. Dead—all of 'em. Murdered."

"What is it, Stanton? What's happened?"

"It was mealtime—in the camp. Everyone relaxed—at ease—there'd been so sign of the Thugs any-where—"

Stanton's voice broke. He shook his head, and there were tears in his eyes. Dead silence prevailed in the rajah's camp now, all eyes focused on the tormented young private who tried valiantly to control himself. Reggie released him, and Stanton stepped back.

"The men were eating their food, talking, laughing. Lieutenant Stephens was in his tent. I—I had gone to see about the horses. They fell on us all at once. One minute there was the clatter of mess kits and the sound of talking and laughter and then the whole camp was swarming with them, all of them yelling and cracking those yellow scarves."

Stanton took a deep breath. He shoved the blond fringe from his forehead and looked around at all of us, and then he shuddered. Reggie squeezed his arm, willing the youth to continue.

"We didn't have a chance. There wasn't time for a single man to seize his gun. There were too many of them—two or three falling upon each one of our men. They—it happened in minutes, our men thrashing and kicking and dying as those demons—" He cut himself short, and his light blue eyes were filled with anguish. "They didn't see me over by the horses. I knew there was nothing I could do—I didn't even have my gun with me. Then they saw me. They came running. I jumped on the nearest horse. They tried to pull me off. One of them grabbed my arm, almost tore my sleeve off. I kicked him in the face. Another one tried to jump up behind me. I knocked him away. I rode, and they ran after me—they were on foot, but they almost had me, too, a pack of 'em swarming around the horse."

"Easy, fellow," Reggie said gently. "Just take it easy."

"Rutherford—Johnny Rutherford, my best mate, he—he was telling one of his funny stories. His eyes were full of laughter, and he was grinning like he always does when he's got an audience hanging on his

234

every word. He was standing there, telling his story, and then three of them were upon him and that scarf was tightening around his neck and his eyes were popping out and he was fighting for his life. I saw him die. I saw them all die. It couldn't have taken more than three or four minutes—I wanted to help 'em. I wanted to *do* something, but there was nothing, nothing—"

"We understand, lad."

"My only thought was riding for help. I knew you were camped out here. I heard the scout telling Lieutenant Stephens where you were. I thought—I had the crazy idea I could ride for help, but they were dead before I even got out of the camp with a dozen Thugs running after me."

"Here," Dollie said.

Without any of us noticing she had stepped back into the tent to fetch a goblet full of wine. She gave it to Stanton and watched as he drank it, and then she slipped her arm around his waist and led him toward the tent, all of us stepping aside to make way for them. She sat him down on a pile of cushions and perched beside him, slipping one arm around his shoulders and taking his hand.

For a long moment no one spoke. The English wore expressions of horrified dismay, but the rajah's face was an inscrutable mahogany mask. None of his men showed the least emotion.

"We can't leave tonight," Reggie said in a carefully controlled voice, "but we'll have to start back as soon as there's light in the morning."

"But of course," the rajah replied.

"There's nothing we can do for those poor lads. We'll return for the bodies later. The thing now is to get back to the garrison as quickly as possible."

"My men will be ready to depart at dawn."

"We'll go back to our huts and pack. Those devils must know Stanton reached us. They wouldn't dare risk another attack tonight, knowing we'll be alert. All the same, I'll post a guard. I suggest you do the same, Your Highness."

The rajah nodded. "Now I shall have my servants light the lanterns to carry back with you. Most grievous, a tragedy. All those fine young English soldiers murdered, including my friend Lieutenant Stephens. We shall avenge it, I promise."

I was in a daze. Michael was dead. I couldn't believe it. I couldn't accept it. I knew I couldn't let myself think about it or I would lose complete control. Sally was holding my hand, looking at me with dark, concerned eyes, and I remember telling her that I was all right. Then we were moving along that narrow pathway through the jungle again, and the lanterns flickered like giant yellow fireflies, making the leafy walls seem all the darker and more ominous. No one spoke. Our footsteps crunched on the rough ground. Twigs snapped. Some animal in a nearby thicket cried out. I gave a start, stumbling. Corporal Burke held my arm in a brutal grip, his face a stern mask. We were in the middle of the group this time, Sally and Sergeant Norman directly behind us, the other two enlisted men in front, supporting the still badly shaken Stanton between them. I don't know how long it took us to reach the clearing, but it seemed an eternity.

We stood in front of the huts, still silent, all of us watching Reggie, waiting for instructions. He was superbly calm now, and when he spoke his voice was crisp, full of authority.

"You will go to your quarters and pack, get

everything ready so we can leave immediately at first light. I suggest you change clothes tonight and sleep in what you'll wear tomorrow. Sleep. God knows it won't be easy, but tomorrow is going to be a rough day, and all of us are going to need our strength. I feel sure there's no immediate danger, but, just the same, I'm going to keep two men on guard all night. We'll take it in two-hour shifts. Norman, you and Burke will take the first shift. Bates and Herlihy will relieve you."

Sally and I returned to our hut. While she lighted all three of the lamps, I closed and locked the door, closed and fastened the flimsy woven grass shutters over the two windows that opened onto the small front veranda. I was calm. I knew I had to be. Later, when this was over, when we were out of danger, I would grieve, give way to the emotions welling up inside, but it was a luxury I couldn't afford at the moment. I took off the blue silk dress and packed it away, changing into a blue- and tan-striped cotton frock. Lifting the mosquito netting aside, I sat down on the bed to fasten up my kid boots.

Sally was still in her petticoat, holding her sumptuous emerald gown in front of her with a resigned expression.

"I have a feeling I'll never wear it again," she said.

"That's a foolish thing to say. You—you mustn't think that way."

"It did the job," she replied. "He asked me to marry him, just up and asked me as we were sitting on those cushions. I said no, of course, said I'd never consider marrying a military man. Then he grinned and told me he was leaving the army, being demobbed just six weeks from now. He's saved enough to go into business for himself, and he owns a little house in Chelsea—his

237

aunt left it to him. He wants to be a *printer*, can you imagine that?"

"I'm sure he'll do very well for himself. What did you say then?"

"I told him I'd think about it. Naturally I'll say yes eventually, but it'll be lovely having him per*suade* me. This—this was the loveliest evening of my life, and then...."

"Let's not discuss it, Sally. We—we must pack."

"I'm worried. I may as well confess it. They—they're just supposed to attack unwary caravans, and then they massacre a whole group of English soldiers. Reggie says there's no danger, but—he just says that. I could tell he was just trying not to alarm us."

"Maybe so, but—we've got to be strong, Sally."

"You're right, of course. At least *this* time we're surrounded by men. We came through before. We'll come through again. Personally, I intend to be bright and brave and put on a good front for the men tomorrow. They're going to need all the encouragement they can get—"

Sally changed into her old dusty-rose frock and put on a pair of brown kid boots. We finished our packing and made everything ready, and then we blew out the lamps and stretched out on our beds. Sally said she knew she wouldn't be able to sleep a wink, not a wink, but both of us were exhausted and a short time later I could tell from her breathing that she had indeed fallen fast asleep. Moonlight seeped in through the cracks under the shutters, tracing silver patterns on the floor, and the walls were thick with shadows. The camp was still, silent. I could hear jungle noises. All the creaking, rustling, slithery sounds seemed to take on ominous, threatening new meanings as my imagination peopled the jungle with stealthy figures all in white.

You must stop this, I scolded myself. You must go to sleep.

I tried not to think of Michael. It did no good. I could see that handsome face, the wide, mobile mouth, the solemn blue eyes, the errant lock of dark blond hair that always seemed to be spilling over his brow. I remembered his touch, his smell, and I remembered the gravity in his voice when he spoke of his love for me. He would never ask that question now. I fought the emotions sweeping over me, knowing that if I gave in to them I would never be able to face the ordeal ahead. Michael was gone. The passionate promise of that last, tumultuous kiss would never be fulfilled. If only I had given him the sign he had so eagerly awaited. If only I hadn't held him off . . . How I wished now that he could have left for his expedition confident of my love.

Try though I might, I was unable to sleep. Resting on top of the covers fully clothed, I turned this way and that, trying to make my mind a blank, but it was futile. I thought about all that had happened since Sally and I had left Bath. I was no longer the same person. That stiff, stubborn, inexperienced young girl seemed a stranger to me now.

I heard low voices outside as the guard was changed, then the sound of Burke and Sergeant Norman returning to their hut next to ours. Norman was indeed a fine specimen. He would make a superb, if somewhat strict husband, exactly the sort Sally needed. I had no doubt they would be extremely happy together, two strong, vital, red-blooded people who were very much in love. I was pleased for them both.

Time passed. Still I was unable to sleep. Now that my eyes had grown accustomed to the darkness, I could see everything inside the hut clearly, the misty moonlight turning the rough wooden floor the color of old pewter, spread with long black shadows from the furniture. Sally moaned softly and stirred in her sleep, throwing out one arm. The transparent tent of mosquito net billowed. A stream of moonlight reached the wooden table between our beds, washing it with silver. The pistol rested on top of the table, cleaned, oiled, fully loaded, ready to use. If the occasion arose, would I be able to use it? Could I actually shoot someone with it? Would I be able to take a human life?

Drowsy now, praying for sleep, I thought about Robert Gordon. I wondered where he was, what he was doing. He was probably somewhere in the area, probably wearing his native disguise. . . . I saw him in the flowing tan and white burnoose, the hood pulled up over his head, looking like some fierce Arab sheikh, and he had hold of my wrist and was dragging me across the sand toward a billowing tent. We were inside, and he was holding me in a tight grip and I struggled, beating at his chest, and he told me it would do me no good, that it was inevitable, and then he wrapped his arms around me and it was raining and we were in the gazebo and he was wearing the gypsy outfit and I wanted never, never to leave those arms because I was truly alive only when I was with him and he was my fate, my destiny. . . .

I awoke with a start, galvanized into a state of total alertness in a matter of seconds, not the least vestige of drowsiness remaining. There had been some noise. . . . I sat up, my blood cold, and I was startled to see Sally sitting on the side of her bed, the mosquito net thrown back. The room was flooded with moonlight. It was almost as bright as day.

"I—I was dreaming," I said. "Something woke me—"

"I thought I heard a—a funny noise," Sally whispered.

My heart seemed to have stopped beating, and that icy coldness inside was chilling. I heard a soft, barely audible thud on the veranda as though someone had swung lightly over the railing. Sally gave a little gasp, her cheeks pale. I stood up, seizing the gun. Sally stood behind me, and I could feel her body tremble. We listened, and there was no more noise. I was beginning to think I had imagined it when the shutters covering one of the windows began to rattle.

"Miss Lauren—" Sally said hoarsely.

And then the shutters flew back and the man leaped up on the sill. He was dressed all in white, and he held a yellow rumal stretched tautly between his hands.

Eleven

He crouched there on the windowsill, ready to spring into the room, and he was like something from a nightmare, his dark face stamped with hatred, the eyes burning, the lips spread back, teeth bared. He stared at us for perhaps three seconds, and then he popped the yellow rumal and coiled his body for the leap. I swung the pistol up from my side and aimed and pulled the trigger. The hut seemed to rock with the blast. I saw a bright red blossom explode in the direct center of his forehead in the brief instant before he toppled over onto the veranda. It had happened in less than a minute, in a matter of seconds.

I felt nothing, nothing whatsoever. I heard shouts, screams, the deafening explosions of guns firing, firing, and I threw open the door and rushed onto the veranda, instinctively, without thinking, and I saw the white clad figures swarming over the camp. I took aim. I fired. I saw the Thug leap into the air with arms and legs thrown out, and then he fell in a heap, blood gushing from his temple. I fired again, again, never once missing, and vaguely I was aware of Burke and Norman and all the others, all of them firing, the noise incredible, causing my ears to ring, the area around the huts dense with smoke, orange fires streaking, bodies flying in a grotesque, frenzied dance of death.

Reggie was standing several yards in front of his hut, firing his pistol rapidly, turning this way, that, bodies falling around him, and then I saw Dollie rush out of the hut with another pistol. She was still wearing that remarkable red velvet gown. Quickly, she and Reggie exchanged pistols, and she turned to rush back inside to reload the one he had been using. It was then that I saw the Thug standing on the edge of the roof of their hut. He dived toward Dollie, flying through the air like some treacherous bird, and he would have landed directly on top of her if my bullet hadn't caught him in midair, the impact of it sending him crashing against the veranda. He hit it with such force that one of the columns broke in two, causing the roof to sag down. Dollie rushed on into the hut without a pause.

A Thug leaped toward me, screaming, cracking the yellow rumal between his hands. I fired, and there was nothing but a loud click. The gun was empty. I turned and stumbled back into the hut, slamming the door behind me, locking it. I saw Sally standing at the foot of her bed, her face chalk white, one hand hidden in the folds of her skirt, the other spread across her bosom. I hadn't moved two yards across the room before the Thug hurled his body against the door. It came tumbling down with a loud bang, the Thug on top of it. I stared in horror as he climbed slowly to his feet, looking at me with insane eyes.

I shook my head, backing away from him. His lips spread in a terrible smile of anticipation as, slowly, deliberately, he moved toward me. Still holding the empty pistol, I stumbled, falling back against the wall. The Thug yelled. He swung the yellow rumal in the air and hurled himself at me, and then his body jerked back convulsively and his eyes widened with shock as the bullet from Sally's pistol splintered his spine. Tumbling to the floor, he landed on his side and began to thrash around in a circle, kicking his legs, spinning like a gigantic insect. Sally fired again, and the side of his face exploded like a pulpy red plum. His body jerked violently, then went limp.

"He—he's dead," she said hoarsely. "I killed him."

The pistol in her hand was still smoking. Dazed, incredulous, Sally stared at the broken, bloody thing on the floor.

"I brought the pistol—just like Gordon told me. He told me never to leave the post without it. I—I didn't think I could use it."

"Give it to me, Sally. Here. Take this one. Reload it. Do you know how to do it?"

"I—I think so. Bill showed me once."

"The bullets are in a box in my bag. Hurry, Sally."

Clutching Sally's pistol, I rushed back out onto the veranda. A Thug was climbing over the railing. I shot him between the eyes. I saw Private Stanton across the way. A Thug charged him, and even as Stanton fired at him another Thug fell upon him from behind, slinging his rumal around the private's throat. Stanton dropped his pistol and threw his arms up to tear at that tightening yellow scarf, and then Corporal Burke leaped on the Thug strangling the private, and all three of them went down together. Through the smoke I saw Stanton stumble to his feet, rubbing his throat. He shook his head, momentarily dazed, then quickly retrieved his pistol and continued to fire. Burke was astride the Thug on the ground, choking the assassin to death with his bare hands. When the Thug went limp, Burke leaped up, seized the pistol he had thrust into his waistband and fired at a Thug who was about to sling a rumal around Reggie's throat.

It went on and on. I emptied Sally's pistol, and then she was beside me with my own gun, fully loaded. I took it from her, gave her the other, and she rushed back inside to load it. I shot another Thug, another. The ground was littered with bleeding bodies, dozens of them, it seemed, as though some furious giant had scattered handfuls of them from above. Bullets streaked. Smoke billowed. People yelled. It seemed there weren't so many of them now, only a few when before there had been multitudes. The bodies continued to pile up. The ground ran red with blood. Then only half a dozen or so assassins remained. Realizing they were defeated, they raced into the jungle, Burke and three others in hot pursuit. We heard the loud crackle of gun shots and anguished yells, and finally there was silence.

The smoke gradually lifted. I stood in front of the hut, dazed, in a trance, and Sally stood beside me, gripping my hand tightly. The ground in front of us was covered with bodies, at least twenty-five of them, all twisted in crazy angles, blood still streaming from some of them. Four of the bodies were English. Lieutenant Jones was dead, his neck broken, his dark brown eyes open wide in amazement. Captain Barber was dead, too, and Sergeants Bates and Herlihy, the two men who had been on guard duty before the attack began. The smoke evaporated, and the first pale yellow rays of morning sunlight streamed over the treetops. Birds warbled throatily, celebrating the new day. A monkey chattered noisily. The three men who had gone with Burke after the Thugs returned. Burke was not with them.

"Where—where is Burke?" I asked Captain Palin.

"I'm afraid I don't know, Miss," Palin replied. "We got separated in the jungle."

"Did you get the rest of them?" Reggie asked.

Captain Chapman nodded. "There were seven. Private Stanton here shot three of them. Palin and I finished off the other four."

"Good work," Reggie said.

Reggie came over to where we were standing. The others followed until all of us stood in a small group in front of the hut. Sergeant Norman put his arms around Sally, and Dollie slipped her arm around my waist, hugging me tightly. I fought back my tears. I had grown fond of the grim and rugged young corporal. I hadn't realized how much until this moment.

"Thank God you women are safe," Reggie said. "That was good shooting, Lauren. I could hardly believe my eyes."

"I—I did what I had to do," I replied. My voice trembled.

"They planned to murder us all in our beds. They crept up on Bates and Herlihy while they were on guard, murdered them quickly and silently. I was awake—most of us were. I thought I heard a noise, and then you shot that devil trying to climb through your window. That shot alerted the rest of us. If you hadn't acted when you did—"

Reggie cut himself short, shaking his head. There were dark shadows under his eyes. All of the men looked battered and exhausted, their uniforms dusty. Captain Chapman had a cut on his chin. Captain Palin's jacket was torn. Private Stanton's neck was bruised where the Thug had tightened the rumal around it. Eight of us remained: the two junior officers, Reggie, Norman, Stanton and we three women.

All of us looked up as we heard footsteps approaching. Corporal Burke sauntered into camp, entering by way of the path leading to the rajah's encampment. I felt a wave of relief sweep over me, and I wanted to throw my arms around him. Burke's face was streaked with dirt, and his gray eyes were full of worried concern. Deeply bothered, ill at ease, he came over to us and looked at Reggie, clearly reluctant to speak.

"I—I have something to report, sir," he began. "I—well, I was wondering why the rajah and his men didn't come to our aid. They couldn't help but hear the gunfire. While the other men were finishing off those Thugs we chased into the jungle, I went to the rajah's camp...." He hesitated.

"Yes? Yes? What is it, Burke?"

"I'm afraid they're gone, sir."

"Gone?"

"The clearing was empty. At first I thought they might have been attacked, the bodies buried, the goods carted away, and then I realized there wouldn't have been time—and if they had been attacked we would have heard it. I'm afraid they packed up and left in the middle of the night, deliberately."

"The horses?"

"They took them all," Burke said. "I reckon they figured we wouldn't need 'em. It looks like we were set up, sir. The rajah must have known we were going to be attacked. He has to be in league with the Thugs. There's no other explanation."

"You're saying we're stranded, then?"

"I'm afraid so, sir."

A silence fell as all of us contemplated the gravity of our situation. Dollie let go of me and stepped over to stand beside her husband. She took his hand and held it very tightly, and Reggie looked down at her with tenderness and pride that was poignant to behold. He patted the hand holding his. That simple gesture spoke volumes. I realized that they must have been in situations like this before, perhaps a number of them, and they had faced them together, their strength and their love for each other sustaining them as it did now.

"It looks bad, doesn't it?" Dollie said, almost chattily.

"Bad indeed," Reggie replied. "There are bound to be more of them back at their camp somewhere in the jungle. They'll assume we were wiped out, but when the others fail to return—" He shook his head, his expression grim. "When the men they sent to kill us fail to show up, they'll come to investigate. They're going to be a mite upset when they find all their men dead. They're going to have one thing in mind—"

"Vengeance," Captain Chapman said. "How long do you figure we have before they come to investigate?"

"Depends on a lot of things," Reggie replied. "If they'd murdered us all like they'd planned to do, they'd have probably looted the camp, would probably have buried us and erased all signs of the attack. That would have taken awhile. Offhand, I'd say we have three or four hours before those back in their camp begin to grow concerned about their colleagues."

"Well then," Dollie said, "that gives us a nice head start, doesn't it? We can't just stand around here waiting for them. It's a nice long hike back to the garrison, but I fancy we can do it. I for one could certainly use the exercise."

She sounded almost cheerful, a plump, improbable figure in her vivid red velvet gown, her girlish black ringlets still perfectly curled, bouncing on either side of her face. Dollie wasn't even going to contemplate defeat, and her bright determination immediately affected the rest of us. There was no time to be dispirited and pessimistic. Thanks to Dollie's jovial manner all of us began to feel better.

"Right!" Reggie said sharply. "We'll not be able to carry anything with us besides our weapons and ammunition. Anything else would only slow us down."

"I *told* you I had a feeling I'd never wear that dress again," Sally informed me. "Oh well, now that I've trapped Bill I don't guess it really *mat*ters."

"What's this?" Norman inquired. "What do you mean, 'trapped Bill'?"

"Never mind," Sally retorted.

"We can't just go off and leave our dead here for the Thugs to find," Reggie said. "We'll have to take time to bury them—the graves needn't be deep, we'll bring the poor chaps to the garrison and see they have a proper burial later on. Burke, you and Stanton see to it. Drag the bodies into the jungle, see that the graves are well hidden. You'll find a pick in my hut."

Burke and Stanton hopped to their grisly task. Dollie had fetched her first-aid kit and was doctoring the cut on Captain Chapman's chin. The captain winced. Dollie scolded him for being such a baby. Captain Palin had begun to gather up the weapons of our men who had been killed. Norman went to help Burke and Stanton, as did Captain Chapman when Dollie had finished bandaging his cut. It seemed to take the men a terribly long time to complete their task, particularly when every minute was precious, but they eventually returned, fetched weapons and ammunition, and we set out through the jungle.

"I deliberately didn't change last night," Dollie confessed. "I was busy packing, for one thing—naturally I had to pack for Reggie, too, he couldn't pack a bag if his life depended on it—and besides, I figured if my time was going to come, I'd go out in style!"

"I wish *I*'d thought of that," Sally complained. "I could be wearing my emerald silk now instead of leaving it to rot in the jungle."

"I must say, though, this velvet is rather warm. Dear me, it *is* going to be a scorcher today."

"We want to keep a good steady pace," Reggie said sternly. "There'll be no lagging behind."

"Don't look at *me* when you say that," his wife retorted. "I may be a trifle overweight—well, more than a trifle—but I can match any pace you set, McAllister, any day of the week. I used to walk quite a lot when I was a girl," she confided to the rest of us. "Of course, it wasn't through a steaming jungle, but what are a few vines and trees?"

"It's snakes I'm worried about," Sally remarked. "I've been in India all this time and I've yet to see a cobra that wasn't kept in a basket by a flute player. I *know* they're all over the place and no one need try to tell me any different. After all, Burke killed one in his hut just two nights ago."

"A huge, writhing specimen it was, too," Burke added, teasing her with a perfectly straight face.

Although Reggie frankly admitted it might be unwise, we followed the trail that had already been blazed by the rajah's caravan when we were on our way to the campsites. At this point, speed was much more important than anything else, and we could move much faster without having to hack away at vines and branches. We were in grave danger. All of us realized that. The Thugs might be on their way after us at any moment. Nevertheless, an almost festive spirit prevailed, primarily because of Dollie's encouragement and lighthearted comments. She trudged along in her gown, stumbling occasionally, already beginning to pant just a little, but she displayed a devil-may-care heroism that was an inspriation to all of us.

"I have to confess, it was *much* more fun when we were riding in those lovely sedan chairs," she told me, "although I'm sure those poor bearers didn't think so. They had an easy enough task with you and Sally, but I'll vow they rued the day I saw my first French pastry."

"Are—are you all right?" I asked.

"Fit as a fiddle, dear. This must seem a lark after what you and Sally went through. At least we have six strapping men to protect us. Poor Private Stanton still looks a bit wobbly. Being half-strangled this morning hasn't helped him a bit. I'll wager he'll hold up, though."

"I'm sure all of us will."

"I saw the way you were shooting this morning, dear. It was nothing less than amazing. I owe you my life, I should think. If you hadn't shot that Thug leaping off the roof...."

"Let's not talk about it, Dollie."

"Hold on, let me get to my point. What I want to say is this: I was dead set against your going out riding with Robert Gordon—I made a regular nuisance of myself over it, I'll admit—but I was wrong. He taught you to shoot like that, so, indirectly, I owe my life to him, too. I've complained about him since the day he arrived on post, but if I were to see him right now, I'd throw my arms around him and give him the biggest hug he ever had. I misjudged him. I think we all did. He may be *different*, but I'm convinced now he knows what he's doing."

"I think he does, Dollie. I—I have great confidence in him."

"Oh dear, I *do* wish those parrots weren't so loud! I wonder when we're going to take another rest stop. I'm not com*plain*ing, mind you, but my wretched feet are beginning to rebel."

Corporal Burke had had the foresight to fasten three canteens onto his belt. After we had been traveling for two or three hours, he left the group to go scouting for water. He was gone for almost an hour, and I was beginning to worry about him when he finally joined us with all three canteens filled to the brim. He announced that he had found a crystal-clear stream, that the water was delicious. Reggie said that we should stop for lunch. I lifted an eyebrow at that, and grinning, he began to pull chocolate bars out of his pocket.

"Thought they might come in handy," he told us. "I always carry a few with me. They're five here. We'll divide 'em up. If I'm not mistaken, that's a mango tree over there, and it's loaded with fruit. If one of you gentlemen'll climb up and shake the limbs a bit—"

Sergeant Norman leaped to the task, swinging up into the branches with great agility, swaggering a bit for Sally's benefit. The mangoes refused to fall when he shook the branches, so he had to pluck them loose one by one and toss them down to us. It was almost like a merry game, the sergeant yelling "Catch!" and taunting us when one of us missed. A small gray monkey suddenly leaped onto the limb beside him, and Norman let out a yell, so startled that he almost lost his perch. All of us laughed, Sally the loudest of all. Norman scowled and shooed the monkey away, but not before the audacious creature had grabbed a mango right out of his hand.

"I thought you were supposed to be *brave*," Sally said when he dropped down from the tree. "You looked like you were scared out of your wits, and by a perfectly adorable little monkey like that. I don't *know* about you, Norman."

Norman made no reply, sulking in a manner I found particularly endearing. He was robust and manly, yet that boyish charm was very much in evidence. Sally told him to act his age and reached up to smooth back locks of bronze hair plastered to his damp forehead. Norman grinned, plopped down under the shade of a tree and tugged her arm roughly. Sally came tumbling down beside him, voicing her outrage at such treatment but actually adoring it. Dollie perched on a rock beside Private Stanton, chatting amiably in an attempt to draw him out. I sat between Burke and Reggie, and Captains Palin and Chapman sprawled out on the ground. We were all dusty and exhausted and perspiring freely, but none of us complained.

We ate the chocolate bars and the juicy, yellow-orange mangoes, and Burke passed the canteens around. The jungle was steamy hot, noisy, an ominous rustling green-brown world festooned with flowered vines. Dollie fell silent, and, the food eaten, we rested, and even though none of us mentioned it, each of us knew that the Thugs had probably gone to investigate by this time, had probably discovered the bodies littering the campsite. Fleet, furious, they were probably rushing down the trail after us. How long would it take them to catch us? Two hours? Three?

Reggie stood up, brushing a twig from his trousers.

"I think we'd best be moving along now," he remarked casually. "We don't want to tarry."

"I should think not," Dollie replied, struggling to her feet as Private Stanton assisted her. "I don't know about the *rest* of you, but I feel utterly refreshed. Amazing what a good meal in pleasant company can do for one, isn't it? Are we ready?"

"Ready," Reggie said. "Let's—uh—try to move a mite faster, see if we can make a little better time."

"You lead, McAllister, we'll follow," Dollie told him. "After that lovely meal I feel I could run a relay race."

We moved down the trail, quickly, not really running, not sauntering. Dollie puffed and panted, and her springy black ringlets were beginning to wilt, but she still managed to make her lighthearted comments and call encouragement to the rest of us. I was bone weary, and it seemed my lungs were about to burst, that I would stumble and fall in an exhausted heap at any moment, so I knew how hard it must be on Dollie, older, heavier, yet forging ahead with considerable brio. We paused to rest every half hour or so, stopping for no more than five minutes at a time, and then we moved on, striving to keep up the pace Reggie set.

Two hours passed, three, four, and soon it was midafternoon, the sun pouring down in scorching rays, the jungle steaming. I felt sure the Thugs were right behind us, would fall upon us at any moment, but another hour passed, another, and the sun was going down and long shadows spread across the path and it grew cooler. Still they didn't come. Twilight was beginning to fall, the air taking on a hazy purple-blue tint, the shadows deepening, green gradually fading to black, and we were hungry and tired, and it was then that we heard the noises ahead: voices, shuffling footsteps, the clatter of tin, the stiff rustle of canvas, the unmistakable whinny of horses.

The voices were English. There was laughter, too, hearty, boisterous, carrying through the jungle like the sweetest of music. Five minutes later we stumbled into the English camp: canvas tents pitched in a clearing near the river, almost a hundred men milling about, camp fires glowing like yellow-gold flowers in the deepening haze. Major Albertson, Reggie's second in command, was in charge of the detachment, and he was both startled and relieved to see us.

"Thank God you're alive!" he exclaimed.

"Just barely," Dollie told him. "Am I imagining things, or is that beef I smell cooking?"

"It is indeed, ma'am. We didn't know whether you were dead or alive. When Gordon discovered that the rajah was involved with the—"

Dollie held out her arm, stopping him before he really began. "You're here, Major—it's a miracle, but you're here. We're eager to know *why*, naturally, but first I wonder if we could sit *down* a spell and have something to *eat*?"

Reggie frowned, not at all pleased with his wife's summary manner, but he was too exhausted himself to reprimand her. Major Albertson had his officers double up, providing tents for us, and then he saw that we were fed. Night had fallen by the time we finished eating, the jungle shrouded in a dense black darkness, the camp fires burning dark orange now. The nine of us sat around one of the fires with Major Albertson and two other officers. Dozens of stalwart men prowled about the camp around us, affording a glorious sense of security, and a scouting party had just returned to report that there were no signs of Thugs anywhere near the area. Reggie gave the major an account of all that had happened, and then Major Albertson told us what had transpired from his end.

"Gordon's responsible for our being here," he said. "The man might have unorthodox methods, but he certainly knows how to get the job done—I have to admit it. Somehow or other, it seems he got hold of one of those yellow scarves—rumals, they call 'em, the scarves the Thugs use to strangle their victims—"

"I gave it to him," Sally interrupted. "It must have been the scarf *I* gave to him."

"Anyway, he sent it off to have it analyzed, thinking he could learn something about the scarf—where it was made, what kind of dye was used. He was growing impatient, waiting for the report to come, so he went to Delhi himself, and, sure enough, the report was ready, just hadn't been sent. It seems the dye was a very special yellow. . . ."

The major hesitated just a moment, and I suddenly thought about those gorgeous yellow silk drapes I had seen in the palace, drapes like spun air tinted with color, and I knew what he was going to say.

"That particular yellow dye was created especially for the rajah. No one else is allowed to use it. Gordon rode back to Dahlkari, nonstop, arriving in the middle of the night. He went directly to the palace. There were a number of questions he wanted answered, and he figured the rajah's chamberlain could answer them for him. He—uh—he was in no mood to bother with protocol. He figured the chap might be uncooperative, so he slipped into the palace and kidnapped him."

"*Kid*napped him?" Reggie exclaimed.

"It was the middle of the night, like I said. The

chamberlain was in his room, fast asleep. Gordon pounced on him, tied a gag around his mouth, slung him over his shoulder and carried him out of the palace—I might add that the chamberlain weighs a good two hundred and fifty pounds." The major paused, grinning, clearly relishing every detail. "Gordon took him out into the woods, lashed his wrists together and strung him up to a tree, had him hanging there like a pig ready for slaughter. Then he took out his riding crop and tore the robe off the chap's back and told him that he intended to beat him to death if he didn't answer some questions."

"The man's insane!" Reggie blustered, and then he grinned, too. "Just the same, I'd like to have been there. Never could abide that bloody chamberlain. Fellow's a fat, pompous ass."

"Gordon got his answers," the major continued. "He tied the gag back around the chamberlain's mouth and left him hanging there—rather inconsiderate, I'll admit, but he was in a bit of a hurry. He roused the garrison, caused quite a stir, snapping orders left and right. He ordered me to bring a detachment to come after the rajah, and he took another detachment himself to head for the Thugs' camp. The chamberlain gave him specific directions. We were on our way by dawn."

"The rajah and his men left their campsite last night," Reggie said. "They crept off in the middle of the night, leaving us to die at the hands of the assassins. Makes my blood boil every time I think of it! If they were heading back to the palace, seems like you'd have run into 'em."

"We did," the major replied. "I haven't finished yet. The caravan was heading down the trail, and they ran into us in the middle of the morning—around ten o'clock, I'd say. The rajah was as cool as could be, pretended nothing was wrong. I asked him where you folks were. He said you'd stayed behind for another day's hunting on your own. Then I told him that we'd found out he was in league with the Thugs and would have to place him under arrest." He paused, savoring the dramatic effect.

"Well, get *on* with it, man!" Dollie snapped. "What *hap*pened?"

"Damndest thing I ever saw—begging your pardon, ladies. He ordered those chaps in silver and blue to attack us. There couldn't have been over twenty of them, and us with over a hundred. They just stood there, grumbling among themselves, looking dismayed at what they'd heard, and suddenly one of them let out a wild shriek and seized his dagger out of his sash. Before any of us could stop him he rushed over to the rajah and plunged the dagger into his breast—killing him instantly. Turns out the fellow's family had been killed by the Thugs a number of years ago. His men might be the vilest lot of ruffians you'd care to encounter, but evidently none of them had any idea he was involved with the Thugs."

The rajah was dead, murdered by one of his own men. It was hard to believe. Only last night he had been lolling there on the blue velvet cushions, clad all in silver, diamonds and sapphires flashing, a coarse, brutal male animal with a silken voice and smoldering dark eyes that devoured me. He was dead, like Michael, like all the others. I folded my arms across my waist, gazing into the fire, feeling nothing.

"The men will have to be questioned, of course," Major Albertson continued. "I realize that. There was nothing I could do but arrest the fellow who stabbed the rajah. I figured the important thing at the moment was finding you folks, so I sent the caravan on back to Dahlkari with an escort and the rest of us traveled hard all day, not knowing whether you were dead or alive, like I said. I knew we couldn't do any good at night, so I gave orders to make camp soon as the light began to go so we could be on our way first thing in the morning. Then you came staggering into camp."

"I guess it's almost over now," Dollie remarked.

The major nodded. "Gordon and his men should reach the Thuggee camp sometime tomorrow. He has a hundred and fifty men with him. They'll bring the whole lot of 'em in. They're the last, I understand. After tomorrow the society of Thuggee will no longer exist."

"I owe Gordon an apology," Reggie said quietly.

"I think we all do," Major Albertson agreed. "I disliked him the first time I ever saw him. Fellow rubbed me the wrong way right off. We were all prejudiced against him."

"He's done a superb job," Captain Palin said. "There's no denying he knew exactly what he was doing every step of the way."

Burke and I exchanged glances, both of us silent. He sat on the ground with his arms folded across his chest, his rugged face expressionless. The dancing flames cast flickering shadows over all of us. Sergeant Norman sat very close to Sally, his arm wrapped around her shoulders. Seeing them like that caused a curious ache, their closeness and contentment emphasizing the emptiness and desolation I felt inside.

"Well, I for one could use some *sleep*," Dollie announced. "I suggest we all retire to our tents. I assume we'll be heading straight back to Dahlkari in the morning?" Reggie was in command now, and the question was addressed to him.

"Right," he said. "I'll send some of the men to—to gather up our dead, the four killed this morning and Michael and those poor lads who were murdered in their camp the night before. The rest of us will return to the garrison."

"If the Thugs didn't loot our huts, it'd be nice if we could have our *bags* brought back," Dollie said.

"If they're still there, the men will bring them," Reggie said crisply. "There are a few more points I want to go over with Major Albertson before I retire. The rest of you might as well go on to your tents."

Two of the captains had vacated their tent for Sally and me, and each of us had a cot. She lingered outside to talk with Sergeant Norman. I was certain I wouldn't be able to sleep, knowing the moment I closed my eyes I would see the horror reenact itself: the shouts, the streaking orange fire, the smoke, the bodies, the blood. One of the captains had forgotten his boots, and the tent smelled of leather and shoe polish. I stretched out on the cot and listened to the quiet, muted sounds of the camp: low voices, footsteps shuffling over the ground, horses neighing. The wind caused the canvas to flap with a soft crackle, a soothing, monotonous noise. I sighed and closed my eyes, and I was asleep almost immediately, long before Sally came in.

I awoke several hours later to find Sally snugly curled up on her cot in her dusty-rose dress, one arm cradled under her head. Her tarnished gold curls spilled about her face, and her lips curved in a faint smile as she slept. I wondered what time it was. The camp was silent, but through the flaps of the tent I could see a vague suggestion of light. Wide awake and feeling amazingly refreshed, I knew I wouldn't be able to sleep anymore, so I got up quietly and stepped outside. Everything was a hazy blue-gray as night receded and the first flush of sunlight began to stain the sky. Although I couldn't see him, I could hear the guard pacing on the other side of the camp. I could hear the river, too, the rushing, gurgling sound of water quite near. My face and hands felt as though they were coated with grime, and I decided to stroll down to the river and wash up a bit before the others got up.

I should have told the guard where I was going, but I was afraid he would either forbid it or insist on accompanying me. I slipped out of the camp like a thief, moving slowly through the relatively thin stretch of jungle separating it from the river. The haze seemed to melt as I walked, pale pinkish-orange light streaming through the trees. I pushed aside a curtain of vines covered with white flowers. The ground was soft and spongy underfoot. A bird warbled sleepily. Everything was peaceful and lovely as dawn broke over the jungle. The river sparkled, and when I cupped the water in my hands it was icy cold. I bathed my face and hands, drying them on my skirt, and then I ran my fingers through my hair, smoothing out some of the tangles.

I started back for camp, and I had only gone a short way from the river when I heard voices to my right. It seemed I wasn't the only early riser. I turned, prepared to smile and call a greeting. I could feel my cheeks turn pale. They were standing in a tiny clearing not twenty feet away. The English soldier was tall and blond and well built, his back to me. He was talking to a native youth in white trousers and a jade green tunic. It was Ahmed. There could be no mistaking that handsome, arrogant face this time. The two of them were immersed in their conversation, and for some reason they hadn't seen me yet. I was stunned, so stunned I couldn't move or think coherently. My pulses leaped. My throat went dry. The Indian youth looked up casually, and when he saw me his eyes filled with alarm. He motioned quickly to the soldier. The soldier turned around.

It was Michael.

I stared, unable to believe my eyes. I tried to cry out. No sound would come. They rushed over to me, covering the distance between us in a matter of seconds. Ahmed seized my arm, gave it a brutal twist and shoved it up between my shoulder blades, clamping a hand over my mouth before I could cry out. When I tried to struggle he gave my arm a savage thrust. The pain was so shattering I almost lost consciousness.

"What are we going to do with her?" His voice was hard, vicious.

"We'll take her back to the camp," Michael replied calmly. "You're hurting her. Loosen your grip a little."

Instead, Ahmed gave my arm another thrust, driving it up even higher between my shoulder blades, forcing my head back against his shoulder, his palm crushing my lips against my teeth with brutal strength. He was breathing heavily, enjoying himself, enjoying inflicting pain. I thought I was going to lose consciousness. Michael frowned, displeased with his young colleague's disobedience.

"We'll abduct the other one this afternoon," he said wearily. "You can do anything you want with her. This one is mine."

"White bitch!" Ahmed hissed.

"We've located their camp," Michael said, "and that's what we came for. We'd best return to the horses now before anyone else comes sauntering by. Bring her along. Gently."

Michael moved on ahead with brisk, confident strides, pushing vines and branches out of the way. Ahmed held me firmly, forcing me to walk ahead of him, wrenching my arm whenever I hesitated or stumbled. Black clouds seemed to close in over me, only the sharp, searing pain keeping me from passing out entirely. We moved through the jungle, further and further away from the camp, and finally, an eternity later, we came upon two horses tethered to a tree. The morning sunshine was brilliant now, pouring down in dazzling rays.

"You can let go of her now, Ahmed. She won't scream. Even if she did, no one back there could hear her."

Ahmed let go of me and stepped back. I staggered, and I would have fallen if Michael hadn't seized my arm. He looked at me with gentle blue eyes, a sad smile on that wide, beautifully shaped mouth.

"It's a long ride back to our camp, Lauren. We must do it as quickly as possible. I'm afraid you might struggle, might slow us down. I'm going to have to put you out for a while. I'm sorry."

Still gripping my arm with his left hand, he drew back his right arm, balling up his hand into a tight fist, and then he slammed it against my jaw with stunning force. There was a blinding explosion of light inside of my head, burning, flashing. I felt myself falling, spinning into a void of blackness. I was dimly aware of strong arms catching me before I hit the ground, and then there was nothing but impenetrable darkness that not even the pain could break through.

I groaned, struggling against the thick blackness enveloping me, and one by one the heavy black shrouds lifted, ever so slowly, giving way to light veils of ashy gray through which I was dimly aware of sound and smell. My jaw ached painfully, as did my arm, and I groaned again. An arm wrapped itself around my shoulders, lifting me up gently, and then I felt a delicious cool wetness against my lips and Michael was telling me to drink, his voice soothing and tender. I drank. I opened my eyes. Michael set the glass aside and looked down at me.

"Are you all right now?"

I nodded, unable to speak. I was on a cot, cushions piled behind me, and Michael was sitting on the edge, leaning over me, that handsome face inches from my own. We were in a tent. A gorgeous carpet was spread over the ground, and there was also a small table desk and a chair. The tent was of heavy yellow silk, that special yellow that only the rajah was allowed to use. Michael brushed wisps of hair from my face, then touched my jaw with gentle fingers.

"I'm sorry I had to do that, Lauren. It was necessary. You understand that, don't you?"

"Where—where are we?"

"We're in the Thuggee camp—the camp Gordon sent me to find. I knew where it was all along, of course, and my main objective was to keep any of my men from locating it. Unfortunately one of the scouts happened to discover it and returned to announce its location in front of all the men. There was nothing I could do but order a massacre."

"You—you had your own men murdered," I whispered.

"I had to, Lauren."

"You sent them to kill *us*. Yesterday morning they—"

"Not you," he said. "I never intended for you to be killed. They were to abduct you and your friend Sally, bring you safely back to camp. That was why the tiger hunt was set up to begin with, so that you could be abducted. The rajah wanted you. He planned to keep you hidden away in the palace, forcing you to become one of his concubines. I had other plans for you, but I didn't tell him."

Michael got up and stepped over to the front of the tent, lifting the flap to peer out. The camp was noisy, and I could tell that there must be at least a hundred men. Michael let the flap drop and turned back around, looking at me with a solemn expression.

"You and the girl were to be abducted from your hut, the others to be killed quickly, with silent efficiency. Unfortunately, you were awake, alert. You shot the man climbing in through the window, and that caused the rest of your party to come out firing. From then on it was sheer disaster."

"How—how could you know what happened? All the Thugs were killed."

"Ahmed was with them. He was standing in the jungle, watching the man climb into your window. He saw you shoot him, saw you rush out with a pistol in your hand. While the others were swarming over your camp he hurried back to report. That's why he was so

265

vicious back there—he blames you for the deaths of all his comrades. He's been begging me to let him kill you. Ahmed's a hot-blooded youth, impulsive, too."

"He—he followed me in the bazaar one afternoon, spying."

Michael grinned. "The young fool actually thought he might have an opportunity to abduct you then, take you to the rajah and get in his good graces. He thought maybe he could lure you behind the stalls and knock you unconscious, somehow or other smuggle you to the palace. It was a foolish idea, but as I said he's hot-blooded, not always bright. The plan might actually have worked if that corporal hadn't been with you. As it turned out, the young idiot almost got himself caught."

"Those men who crowded around Burke—"

"Our men, of course. If they hadn't been on hand Ahmed would have been in quite a mess." Michael shook his head, the grin still playing on his lips. "His throat was sore for a week. When your corporal puts a stranglehold on someone he intends to hold him. Serves the young rascal right. He's a good lad, though, one of the best. That's why I've promised him a reward. I intend to let him have the girl—Sally."

I sat up, gripping the side of the cot with my hands. I stared at him, unable to believe what I was hearing. Michael still wore the high black boots, the clinging white trousers and scarlet jacket. The uniform was dusty and worn, but it was a *British* uniform. It was inconceivable that any Englishman could be so treacherous, could speak of such heinous deeds in a casual, chatty voice. It was almost beyond belief. He shoved a heavy blond wave from his forehead and sighed.

"You don't understand, do you?"

"How could I? You—you're British."

Michael shook his head, smiling a curious smile. "No, Lauren. My father was Indian. He went to England to attend Oxford. He met a woman there, an engaging blonde who worked in a pub, serving ale to rowdy students. She became his mistress, and ultimately she gave birth to me."

"The rajah. You're his—"

"His son," Michael said. "I know it seems incredible. Through some peculiar twist of nature I inherited none of his features, none of his coloring. I took after my mother, and no one ever suspected I wasn't one hundred percent English. It's not all that unusual, actually. I understand there are any number of Negro bastards in Africa who can pass for white. In America, too. Sometimes it happens that way."

"I—I can't believe it."

"It's true, I assure you. When I was in my teens my father decided to send for me. When I arrived in India he was startled to find a fair, blue-eyed lad with perfect English features. He had originally intended to find a place for me at the palace, but after he saw me he decided I could ultimately be of far greater use if I continued to pass as white."

Michael paused, his mouth lifting at one corner in a half smile. "He sent me back to England. I received the finest education his money could provide. Eventually I graduated from Sandhurst and received my commission and shipped out for India. By that time Sleeman had already begun persecuting the Thugs, trying to eliminate them. Those that escaped his purge began to congregate in this area. I spent two years in Delhi, passing information about special caravans to my

267

father, and finally I came to Dahlkari to be your guardian's aide. I managed to persuade him to let me head most of the expeditions against the Thugs."

"So—so you could cover up for them," I said.

"Precisely. I did a rather good job of it. Then Gordon came along. He will die this afternoon along with all the rest of the English besides your friend Sally."

"You plan to—to attack the camp?"

"That's why Ahmed and I were in the jungle this morning—getting the exact location. My father is dead. I know all about that. The English are responsible. This afternoon all the men here will join together in mass attack. Robert Gordon will die—they all will. Perhaps that'll serve as a warning to Sleeman."

Michael gave a grim nod, his mouth tight, his blue eyes filled with savage hatred. He knew that a large detachment of English soldiers had left the garrison, and he had located them this morning, but he obviously had no idea that there had been *two* detachments, that at this very moment Gordon was leading a hundred and fifty men to the Thuggee camp. That knowledge gave me great strength. My jaw still ached, as did my arm, yet I managed to stand up, managed to retain a calm composure.

"And what about me?" I asked quietly.

"I'm going to take care of you for the rest of your life," he said. "I love you, Lauren. I meant everything I said back at the garrison. I'm a very wealthy man now. My father saw to it that I received a five percent cut of everything throughout these past three years. The loot was converted into money, English money, and it's waiting for me in Australia, in a bank in Sydney. Now that my father's dead I have no desire to remain in

India. As soon as I've avenged him we'll go to Australia. We'll start a new life there, together."

He paused as a loud keening sound filled the air. It seemed to issue from a soul in torment, rising higher and higher. He frowned. "That's the wife of one of the men killed yesterday morning," he informed me. "She was staying here at the camp with us. We brought our dead back yesterday, her husband among them. She's insisted on suttee, and there's nothing we can do but oblige her. The pyre's already been laid. It'll be lighted in half an hour. The widow's in the next tent, waiting to join her husband."

The keening became a shrill, piercing shriek that shattered into a series of broken sobs. Eventually it subsided, replaced by occasional groans that were even more disturbing. Michael scowled, irritated by the interruption, and then he heaved a sigh, forcing himself to ignore those anguished groans.

"We'll be married," he continued. "You'll have everything you could possibly desire."

"You—you're insane."

"Don't talk like that, Lauren." His voice was hard. "You're going to be my wife."

"I'd rather die!"

He looked incredulous, as though he were unable to comprehend what I had said. I realized then that he was indeed demented. I knew that there were people who simply had no conception of right and wrong, totally amoral individuals who could commit the most heinous crimes without the slightest remorse. Michael was one of them. He had been part of a horrible conspiracy of mass murder for gain, yet he saw no reason why I should hesitate to fall into his arms. He planned to turn Sally over to Ahmed, planned to

269

murder Dollie and Reggie and all the others, and he actually couldn't see why that should make the least difference to me.

"You love me," he said gruffly.

"No, Michael, I don't. I never have."

He stepped quickly over to me and seized my arms, gripping them tightly. I winced, trying to pull away. He shook me viciously.

"You're lying!" he exclaimed.

"No—" I whispered.

"I don't believe you! You've *got* to love me."

"I—I'm in love with Robert Gordon."

Michael stared at me, shocked, profoundly shocked, and then, slowly, his expression changed. The corners of his mouth tightened, his nostrils flared, his lids lowered until his eyes were narrow slits. I saw his father in him then, saw the rajah's coarse savagery, surfacing now for the first time in his son. It had been there all along, of course. I had sensed a hard, ruthless quality from the first, but the mask had always been carefully maintained—until now. Hatred glowed in his eyes, hatred and brutal determination. He released me. He stepped back. A cruel smile twisted on his lips.

"Very well, Lauren," he said quietly.

He stepped to the front of the tent. "Ahmed!" he called, and a moment later the Indian youth stepped inside. He glanced at me with loathing, then gave his full attention to Michael. They spoke quietly, their voices barely audible. Although I couldn't make out any of the words I knew they were discussing me, making some sort of arrangements. Ahmed nodded twice, and then he turned to look at me, smiling a smile that caused my blood to run cold. His fingers stroking the hilt of his knife, he laughed, his dark eyes burning with anticipation, and then he stepped back outside.

Michael folded his arms over his chest and glanced at me with complete indifference. The intense hatred was gone now. I might have been some inanimate object beneath his notice.

"You said you'd rather die," he remarked. "It's just been arranged."

"Ahmed—"

"Ahmed's going to murder the widow. She should stop moaning any minute now. He's going to strangle her, hide her body under the cushions—he'll bury it in the jungle later."

The moans had continued all the while, and now they stopped abruptly. There was a shrill, terrified shriek, then a horrible gurgling sound that seemed to go on forever. It ceased. There was a heavy thud and the sound of something being dragged.

"Why?" I whispered. "Why did you have him kill that poor—"

"You're going to take her place." His voice was a casual drawl. "The woman has always observed complete purdah, wearing an all-concealing white burka, only her eyes visible. Ahmed will return in a moment with the burka. It should fit you nicely. You'll be gagged, naturally, and when the funeral pyre is lighted, you'll be hurled into the flames."

He looked bored, and I knew that as far as he was concerned I was dead already. His cool, indifferent manner was far more terrifying than outright menace. I hadn't really been frightened before, for he was Michael, Michael, someone I knew, someone who couldn't possibly wish to hurt me, and I realized now that this cool blond savage was someone I had never known at all. He sat down at the table, opened a drawer

271

and took out some papers, ignoring me completely as he went through them. I had been stunned before, too stunned to feel any strong reaction, but now the impact of it all hit me full force. My whole body seemed to go limp, and it took great effort just to stand. There was a terrible hollow sensation in the pit of my stomach. My heart leaped wildly, pounding so loudly that I felt sure he must be able to hear it.

"You—you *are* insane," I said hoarsely.

He didn't bother to reply, didn't even look up. The front tent flap lifted. Ahmed stepped inside, the voluminous burka draped over his right arm. Michael didn't say a word. He merely nodded curtly in my direction and went back to his papers. Ahmed grinned and came toward me like a lithe young panther, his eyes glittering. He paused to drop the burka on the cot, and then he reached for me, wrapping strong, sinewy fingers around my arm. I struggled violently, kicking at his shin, clawing at his cheek with my free hand. His handsome young face turned into a mask of venomous fury. I saw him ball his hand into a fist, saw him swing back his arm, and as the pain exploded inside my head I hurtled back into the swirling blackness of oblivion.

The motion caused me to awaken, and I opened my eyes to see sad, dark faces all around. I was walking, stumbling, strong hands holding my arms and leading me across the camp. There was chanting, and I saw the huge pile of wood and the two men with lighted torches standing beside it. I tried to cry out, and I tasted the cloth tied across my mouth, brutally tight. The white robe enveloped me completely, with only a small slit in front to see through. Ahmed held my left arm, another man my right, and they forced me to move. I struggled. Ahmed wrenched my arm with sadistic glee, chuckling to himself. I fell to my knees. They pulled me back up, dragging me forward, nearer and nearer to that pile of wood.

Almost a hundred Thugs watched, their faces grim, respectful, for they thought I was the widow. They stepped aside as we passed. The chanting continued, a dreadful dirge, mournful, monotonous. I saw Michael standing several feet away from the pyre, his arms folded over his chest, his face expressionless. My terror was so great, so overwhelming that, finally, I was unable to feel anything at all. Trancelike, I moved, and Lauren was far, far removed, observing all this with total disbelief, for it wasn't real. It couldn't be happening.

We stopped in front of the pyre, both men holding me tightly. Michael gave the signal, and the men with the torches tossed them onto the pyre. I saw the wood catch, crackle, the flames shooting up in a blaze of sizzling orange, devouring wood, turning brown to black. I could feel the heat as they rose higher, higher, and I could feel Ahmed's muscles tense as he prepared to hurl me into that blazing inferno. I shook my head. I was screaming inside. The screams rose, growing louder and louder, and then they seemed to be all around me, filling the camp.

Ahmed whirled around to see what was happening, and then he let go of my arm and gave a loud shriek and fell to the ground, clutching his chest. Streams of scarlet flowed between his fingers. He arched his back, kicking his legs out, then he fell limp. The other man screamed and, still holding my arm, pitched forward into the flames. If strong arms hadn't seized me, tearing me free, pulling me back, I would have gone into that crackling orange hell along with him. Gordon tore the robe off of me, untied the gag and flung it aside, and then he held me very tightly while all around figures leaped and yelled and darted, shouting, firing pistols, tumbling to the ground. I paid no attention. None of it was real. The only reality was this man, his strength, his arms crushing me to him as though he feared I might somehow get away.

Twelve

I watched the groom leading the chestnut back inside the stables, and then I turned to the young corporal who had been my escort this morning, thanking him for his courtesy. The corporal smiled a shy smile and nodded, then moved briskly across the cobblestoned yard. It was a dazzling, sun-spangled morning with a sky of silver blue, and we had had an exhilarating ride over the plains. I should have felt exuberant and glowing, but the sadness that had been hanging over me these past three weeks colored everything, made it impossible for me to savor youth and health, sunshine and fresh air, made it impossible for me to truly enjoy anything.

Five weeks had gone by since that dreadful day when I had been rescued by Robert Gordon. He had left for Delhi immediately afterwards, without a word, without making any attempt to see me, and three weeks ago I had finally realized that he had no intention of returning to Dahlkari. His job had been completed. He had done it brilliantly, succeeding where all others had failed. There was no reason for him to return. If I had been taken in, if I had believed his absurd, outrageous promises, that was my own fault. It had been sheer moonshine, all of it. Five weeks had gone by, and I had finally resigned myself, giving up all hope, yet the sadness lingered on, coloring my days in pensive hues.

At first I had expected him to come back right away. I had been filled with elation, hardly able to contain myself, and then, when he failed to return, I expected a letter of explanation. None had come. Not from Gordon. Corporal Burke had returned to Delhi, too, and *he* had written. It was merely a short, awkward note, clumsily phrased, but it had meant a great deal. He informed me that he had been promoted to the rank of sergeant, that his new duties were rather a bore. He said he hoped that I had recovered from my "unpleasant experiences" and wished me the best of luck, signing the note Sergeant Theodore (Ted) Burke. I had cried then, because I had been so fond of Burke, because he had been thoughtful enough to write me, because Gordon hadn't.

Leaving the stables, I strolled slowly past the white-frame buildings, beneath the tall, leafy trees that threw dancing blue-gray shadows over the sun-washed walks. I could hear men marching in the distance, hear a sergeant calling the cadence. There was a strong breeze. The skirt of my tan- and bronze-striped dress billowed, petticoats fluttering, and my chestnut locks were tossed about. As I passed one of the small, rather shabby bungalows where the married enlisted men lived with their families, a handsome and robust young sergeant stepped out onto the porch. Seeing me, he stood back near the front door, in the shadows, waiting for me to pass. I moved on, pretending not to see him. It was the Simpson bungalow. Sergeant Major Simpson was obviously on duty this morning. His wife and her new lover had clearly been taking advantage of his absence.

Poor Valerie. I wondered what would happen to her when that rich, exotic beauty began to fade, when that voluptuous body was no longer so enticing to men. She would probably turn to drink, or perhaps even drugs. She was a pathetic figure, actually, desperately searching for a fulfillment she would never find. I knew now why Gordon had been seeing her. The first time he had encountered her she had been wearing a lovely amethyst bracelet that he had recognized as a piece of property stolen by the Thugs. He knew that Sergeant Major Simpson spent a great deal of time in the village, consuming liquor in one of the native establishments, and he strongly suspected that Simpson was the man he was after. He had courted Valerie, pumping her for information about her husband, assuming he had given her the bracelet. He had built up quite a case against the sergeant major, and it was not until it was all over that he learned that the bracelet had been a gift from Michael.

Michael. I tried not to think of him, but it was unavoidable. He was dead now. When Gordon and his men had poured into the Thuggee camp, Michael had gone berserk, firing his pistol wildly, killing three English soldiers before he was himself shot down. I still found it hard to believe that he had been the rajah's illegitimate son. His fierce native blood and savage heritage had been carefully concealed beneath a cool English façade, but he had let the façade drop that last day. I had seen the real Michael, and I would never be able to forget the chilling terror he had instilled. He had been insane, quite insane, yet I knew that he had genuinely loved me, had sincerely planned to take me away with him until my horrified rejection had turned him into a merciless, unfeeling savage.

I tried not to think about Michael, and I tried not to think about what would have happened if Gordon and his men hadn't reached the camp when they did, if Gordon hadn't seen my tan kidskin boots showing beneath the burka and fired immediately. I remembered the way he had held me, so very tightly, so protectively, while chaos reigned all around and the Thugs were rounded up, their hands tied behind their backs. I had been in a daze as we made our march to the English camp, prisoners in tow, and Gordon had stayed close beside me. Reggie and Major Albertson had sent out three different search parties after I had disappeared, and Dollie was frantic. She had clasped me to her, and then the medical officer had given me something that put me to sleep immediately.

When I awakened I was in my own room back at the house, Sally and Dollie both sitting beside the bed with worried expressions. I had slept for over twenty-four hours. Gordon had already left for Delhi with a detachment of men and the Thuggee prisoners. That had been five weeks ago, five weeks without a word from him. Dramatic, tempestuous, larger than life, Robert Gordon had entered my life with shattering force, changing it completely, and now he was gone. I would never be the same again, and I knew I would never be able to love another man, for he would always be there in memory, taunting me, making any other seem pale in comparison. I bitterly resented what he had done to me. I wished it were possible to hate him. If I could hate him life without him might somehow be endurable.

I couldn't remain in India. That much was certain. In exactly one week Sally and Sergeant Norman were leaving for England. They were to be married day after tomorrow. It was to be a festive, formal military ceremony with crossed swords and all the trimmings.

Dollie was having the time of her life making all the arrangements, snapping orders, bossing people about, carrying on as though it were *her* wedding. Sergeant Norman would be demobilized at the end of the week, and the newlyweds would begin the journey that would take them to the charming little house in Chelsea. I was going to make the trip with them. I had sufficient funds to live on my own until I could find some kind of teaching position. It would be a dull brown life, true, but I would welcome it. The very dullness would be a sedative, would help me forget what might have been.

I was walking along beside the parade ground now, tall trees concealing it from view. Leaves rustled. Sunlight and shadow danced at my feet. The sound of men marching was much closer, the sergeant's husky voice bellowing commands. Seeing the gazebo where the military band played, I felt a sharp stab of pain, remembering that day when the storm had broken. It was flooded with sunlight now, shadows making moving patterns over the dazzling white floor. Unable to help myself, I moved up the wooden steps and stood there in the center of the gazebo, remembering. A bird warbled nearby. Through the limbs I could see the men marching on the other side of the parade ground, looking in the distance like toy soldiers in white breeches and vivid scarlet jackets.

My skirts fluttered. A lock of hair blew across my cheek. The sun was warm. I remembered the dark, dashing gypsy in his tight black trousers and white shirt, the red scarf tied around his neck, unruly raven locks tumbling over his forehead. I remembered that harsh face, lips twisting in a sardonic smile, the glowing, hypnotic eyes half concealed by drooping lids. Moving over to the railing, I gripped it tightly and

279

closed my eyes, trying to exorcise the images, but his presence was so strong that I could actually feel it in the air. He might have been standing right behind me. I was torturing myself, I knew, but I couldn't tear myself away. There would be time enough for forgetting in years to come. Now I remembered.

"I thought I might find you here," he remarked.

I turned around, and at first I actually believed he was an apparition. He was dressed exactly as he had been the day of the garden party, the same shiny black boots and creamy white linen suit, the emerald green tie loosely knotted. The thick black locks were tousled in the wind, the deeply tanned face as cruel and ruthless and fascinating as ever. Sunlight flickered. I expected the image to disappear. It didn't. Robert Gordon arched one dark brow and smiled, the black-brown eyes filled with that familiar wry amusement.

"I stopped by the house first thing," he said casually. "Dollie said you'd gone riding. I went to the stables. The groom said you'd come back quite a while ago. Then I remembered the gazebo—thought you might be lingering about here."

"You're back," I said. My voice was flat.

"I'm back. I'm a free agent now, no longer affiliated with Her Majesty's Army. We're going to be married first thing—I've already arranged it with Dollie. There'll be two ceremonies day after tomorrow. It'll take some *do*ing, she confessed, but she's more than up to the challenge."

"It seems to me you're taking an awful lot for granted!"

"We'll leave for England immediately afterwards," he continued, ignoring my comment. "I have to finish my book, but as soon as it's done we're going to Africa.

The Royal Geographical Society is providing funds for the expedition. We're going to locate the lost city of Azulah. We may encounter a few cannibals and a python or two, but—"

"I will *not* be taken for granted!"

"You angry about something?" he inquired.

"All—all these weeks! How dare you leave without—without a word. How dare you not write! If you think you can just—"

"I've been busy," he interrupted. "There were any number of loose ends to tie up—Thugs to be tried, reports to be completed, forms to be signed, all sorts of things to do. I didn't have time to write, didn't feel it was necessary. I knew you'd be waiting."

"For your information, Mr. Gordon, I—"

"You look magnificent like that—cheeks flushed, eyes flashing angrily. It's going to be a joy fighting with you—an even greater joy making love to you. I'm going to make love to you, you know. I'm going to teach you what it's all about. Unfortunately, your head is stuffed full of romantic nonsense, foolishness you've acquired from silly novels."

"You think all you have to do is snap your fingers. You think—"

"You're not going to need novels any longer," he continued, ever so smoothly. "You're going to have something far more exciting, far more satisfying. From this day forward you're not going to have time for novels. You're going to be too busy to read about rogues and highwaymen."

"Am I?"

Robert Gordon nodded and pulled me into his arms.

"Much too busy," he assured me.

BERKLEY BOOKS YOU'LL WANT
TO READ NOW

THE CHINESE BANDIT   (03403-8—$1.95)
  by Stephen Becker

THRALL OF LOVE   (03405-4—$1.75)
  by Riva Carles

THE MADONNA COMPLEX   (03528-X—$1.95)
  by Norman Bogner

THE OTHERWISE GIRL   (03386-4—$1.25)
  by Keith Claire

THE PALLISERS   (03521-2—$1.95)
  by Anthony Trollope

THE VAMPIRE TAPES   (03508-5—$1.75)
  by Arabella Randolphe

LORD ORLANDO'S PROTEGEE   (03408-9—$1.75)
  by Margaret SeBastian

LORD COURTNEY'S LADY   (03349-X—$1.50)
  by Jane Morgan

Send for a *free* list of all our books in print

These books are available at your local bookstore, or send
price indicated plus 30¢ per copy to cover mailing costs to
Berkley Publishing Corporation
390 Murray Hill Parkway
East Rutherford, New Jersey 07073